MEANT for you

BOOK ONE IN THE KINKY MATCHMAKER SERIES

By G.L. Tomas

Meant For You (Book One in the Kinky Matchmaker Series) by G.L. Tomas

Copyright © 2019 by G.L. Tomas

Published by Rebellious Valkyrie Press

All rights reserved

For permission requests, address publisher by email addressed "Attention: Permissions Coordinator, at the email address provided below:

rebelliousvalkyriepress@gmail.com

Publisher's Note:

This is a work of fiction. Names, characters, places, brands, media, and incidents are either the product of the author's imagination or are used fictitiously. The author acknowledges the trademarked status and trademark owners of various products, bands, and/or restaurants referenced in this work of fiction, which have been used without permission. The publication/use of these trademarks is not authorized, associated with, or sponsored by the trademark owners.

Licensing Notes:

Released and Printed in the United States of America

First edition e-book August 2019

First edition paperback August 2019

Developmental Editing by: Little Pear Editing

Cover Design by: Steamy Book Designs

Formatting created by: Vellum

ISBN 13: 978-1-943773-48-0 (e-book)

ISBN 13: 978-1-943773-49-7 (paperback)

ASIN: B07S1GY12G

TRIGGER WARNING:

Since we want this to be a pleasant reading experience for the audience, it goes without saying this title might not be for all romance readers. There is material meant for mature audiences and since BDSM is heavily apart of the main character's romantic and kink life, it may not be the read for you if you don't prefer those themes.

Their play may be tame to more experienced participants in kink or lovers of BDSM in romance, but the main characters exhibit the traditional power dynamics of a D/s relationship. If calling someone out of one's name one, rough play, spanking, anal play, confinement/bondage, light consensual-nonconsensual and impact play bother you, feel free to hard pass until the next read.

Thank you for taking the time to read.

-G.L. Tomas

Want to see how we pictured these characters? Check out our <u>Pinterest board</u> for the series planned so far!

<u>Kinky Matchmaker Series Pinterest Fantasy board</u>

MEANT FOR YOU

Summary:

Finnish investor Olli Tuominen was supposed to be marrying the woman of his dreams—but the day of the wedding, he's hit with the hard reality. In the eyes of the law, and on paper, he's still married to his first wife Benny. Walking away from a love like hers had always been difficult, but serving her divorce papers proved even more obstacle. Still the enchanting beauty he remembered her to be, his first love might still harbor a fire that can't be extinguished.

Bendicíon Obiang thought she'd never see Olli again. She certainly didn't plan after an eight-year estrangement that the reason he'd re-enter her life was to confirm her deepest fear. Her only true love was moving on. Could this happenstance reunion be the push she needs to finally reveal the truth after all this time? That they share a child?

Reuniting face to face should've been simple. Sign the divorce papers. Wish him happiness on his new life. Go back to California. Only a Nordic snowstorm has other plans for the past lovers; plans that include Benny on her knees succumbing to Olli's dominance.

It only takes one weekend to make two things perfectly clear. The former submissive was always his to claim, and the secret she's been keeping might just be the thing that breaks him.

This story is approximately 82,000 words and features a BWWM couple with no cheating and a HEA. This read is steamy and spicy featuring a dormant Dominant who reunites with his former submissive and despite what you take from the blurb features NO CHEATING! If Dominance and submission isn't your cup of tea, sit this one out but for those that enjoy it, this quiet, grumpy Alpha knows how to melt his way into your heart.

❧ I ❧

O^{lli}

HOW MANY TIMES WERE YOU GOING TO LOOK DOWN AT YOUR watch, you nervous wreck? As many times as it took to make sure I got down to the chapel on time, I told myself. It was too close to four to push it as it was, especially since Helsinki City Hall closed at five. Today was proving just how challenging I'd found it to efficiently manage my time, but I hoped it didn't show.

Even with Anna's incessant reminding, I still waited until the last possible window to pick up our marriage certificate. Two months of pushing it back were finally catching up to me. What would she say now, knowing I had waited mere hours before the ceremony? It would be fine, though. As long as I walked away with the certificate, nothing would get in the way of our wedding. I'm sure I'd never hear the end of it should anything go wrong.

After four years of ups and downs, my fiancée Anna and I were finally tying the knot. I hadn't done the best job of attending dress rehearsals, especially the one that mattered most, and I was praying I didn't screw anything up between now and my way to the church. *"You better not ruin my big day."* I could hear her scolding me in her native Swedish tongue. *"You waited until the very last minute? Why would you do such a thing?"*

Anna didn't understand that I'd been working on an investment deal for years that could change the course of both of our futures if it went through. Since moving back to Helsinki after a disappointing job search in the US, I'd been doing well for myself back home. I was on the path to being able to retire by the age of thirty-five, and since Anna enjoyed the finer things, I'm sure in time she'd be happy knowing she'd never have to work either.

But she was fixated on *this* day. Not the rest of our lives but the moment in time where we could pretend everything was perfect and capture it with the overpriced wedding photographer she just *had* to have. So, who was I to disappoint?

Anna and I loved each other, but we were far from perfect. Her feisty, extroverted nature was often a challenge to my reserved, calculated Finnish mannerisms. But over time, I'd taught myself to adjust to our differences. Today marked the day we'd be tied to those challenges forever, and if I didn't want to die before I reached the chapel, I had to have that marriage certificate, in hand, before I got there.

"Sir? Sir?"

The counter attendant attempted to flag me down. The waiting room was filled with individuals filling out forms, waiting in line to be called, or seeking assistance to other departments in the building if they'd stumbled on the wrong room. I assumed I was being called to pay for processing the certificate, so I made my way over to the counter and reached for the wallet in my pocket.

"Mr. Tuominem, how are you?" She spoke in Turum-accented Finnish, a sign that it wasn't her native language. I would've immediately known by her efforts at small talk. Native born Finns avoided conversation unless absolutely necessary.

"I am fine. How much will it—"

"I am sorry, but there is a small issue with the processing of your certificate."

My chest slightly tightened, but I fought the urge to let my nerves get the best of me. "An issue?" I questioned on the verge of panicking. "I'm getting married in less than three hours; I need that certificate today."

Her stormy blue eyes dilated, so she either had bad news to share or she feared what my response would be after she elaborated. Desperate not to show the hopelessness in my stance, I forced myself to stay calm. "The clerk I spoke to before you assured me and my fiancée that we would be able to obtain the certificate if we filled out all the required paperwork. We did that almost a month ago—"

"I understand that, Mr. Tuominem, and I apologize. Perhaps, I should have been clearer," she interrupted. "I tried to process it myself, but a red flag came up. I assumed it was in error, so I took it to the lead clerk. The problem wasn't with the paperwork itself. Since past marriages and separations are public record, our system shows that you're still legally married to a—" She paused, attempting to sound out the name that was foreign to her.

"Maria Bendición Tuominen?" The mere sound of that name threw me off. It was like, one moment I was present then the next, my mind was zooming through a time warp. I loosened my tie, all of a sudden, it felt tighter than before she dropped this bombshell on me, and I felt like I couldn't think with this noose around my neck.

"Could this be an error?" the clerk asked, genuine in her tone that I was not at fault.

"No." I blew out a hard but short breath, making a mess of my neatly coifed hair. "It's likely correct." Unable to even look the clerk in the eye at this point, I didn't have a solution to my problem. She wasn't likely to have one either.

"I'm sure there was something we could have done if there had been an annulment or divorce on file, but by law, you can't remarry. There is, however, a file for separation," She sounded unsure but tried to keep her pleasant tone and my hopes up despite my dilemma. "Perhaps, you could figure that out first, and then you can return at your soonest convenience?" She went on to explain that until I addressed the issue, she wouldn't be able to assist any further as the options available were limited.

I'm sure she had said more, but my ears had blocked out everything at that point. In fact, I'm surprised I heard past *that name*. I needed air. I needed vodka. I needed more than what was available to me.

The one thing I needed more than those things, I wouldn't be able to obtain, and I was finally coming to terms with that. But Anna? It would be hard explaining to her, at the eleventh hour of our wedding, that we would not be getting married today, or any other day, until I addressed the ghosts of my past.

❧

THE REALITY OF IT ALL HIT ME AS I SAT IN THE BACKSEAT OF MY driver's car. Jaako didn't immediately ask for my instruction, but he could tell by my throwing my head close to my lap that I hadn't heard good news. An overwhelming stream of memories took over my thoughts, haunting me ever since I heard *that name* spoken back to me.

Maria Bendición.

Bendición.

Benny.

My Benny.

An African beauty with a Spanish sensuality and an American boldness. Everything about her should have been completely wrong for me, but it had been the opposite. Benny was perfect. So perfect, that in the span of a few passionate months we'd eloped unexpectedly and lived like no other relationship I'd ever had. She was a woman who proved it was impossible to categorize her. In fact, she was the kind of woman you dismantled the whole system for and created new categories to fit her mold.

Sassy yet obedient. Patient and emotional. Firm yet willing. Explorative and intelligent enough to learn more about the world than she already knew. To put it boldly, she was more than I deserved in a woman.

She'd tried relentlessly, adjusting to the Finnish culture and way of life when we'd lived in my home country, but I'd found it difficult to adjust to her naturalized country—the United States. For her, I'd tried to make our love work, but the job market had made things difficult, and it wasn't before long that my unhappiness affected our marriage. Unintentionally, I projected my misery onto her, and our marriage suffered to the point where we mutually agreed to give each other space.

That time apart lead to filing for legal separation, nearly eight years ago, and a part of me—the weakest part—thought that if I never signed the divorce papers, there might one day be a chance for us.

As life went on, it appeared there would never be a chance for us, as I'd assumed we both moved on. I put myself back together in stages, praying one day I might get over the fact I still loved Benny. I dated and fell in love again until eventually I met Anna and put the past behind me. But now, I wonder. If neither of us had made the effort to reach out to confirm a divorce, could there be a way she might...

No. Benny had been the one to file for separation. She'd been the one who initially brought up giving each other space. She couldn't possibly still love me after all this time? Could she?

It didn't matter now. I was marrying Anna. Anna deserved the wedding of her dreams, and a sliver of disappoint shot through me as I asked my driver to start up the car. The day she wanted, I wouldn't be able to give to her. The fact that I was still married to someone else could only mean one thing: When I got to that church, there would be hell to pay.

❧

COUNTLESS EFFORTS WERE MADE TRYING TO CONTACT MY attorney, via mobile, in hopes of catching him before I reached the ceremony. I was grateful; my driver was forced to scurry through midday traffic, so it gave me the head start I needed. Was it bizarre that in the moments that I phoned him unsuccessfully, it gave me time to reflect on the past?

I'd spent years trying to forget her. That stubborn American. My stubborn American. My Bendición. My god, what was I saying? I was marrying Anna. The Benny of the past was no longer mine. But we'd shared something so phenomenal. Should all that be discarded just because I started over?

I bear the burden of rushing to that church only to ruin a day that meant the world to Anna. But the more I thought about it, the more I remembered how much I'd lost. I never admitted it to myself, so why would I to another that I'd never stopped feeling things for my first wife. Anna knew vaguely of my past, and what she had known, she hadn't liked.

If Anna was one thing, it was a spitfire in heels. If I had to explain to her, not only the truth, but to unlock the past as well, she would waste no time making me regret the day we met. She cared about me, but she cared about herself more. Bringing up Benny now? She would not be pleased.

"You dialed my mobile?" James' voice came through the speaker, after a bout of unsuccessful tries to his office. "You never dial my mobile. Please tell me you didn't kill anyone." James was well aware of the seriousness of my call by now. I rarely ever phoned him on his personal number but now was one of those times where a call to his office wouldn't suffice.

James was a British expat who'd settled in Helsinki after meeting a Finnish woman he'd met on holiday and decided Finland was where he needed to be. Strangely enough, that woman was my first cousin, and since they'd gotten married a few years back, he was literally family. His Finnish could still use some work, but he was conversational enough to speak until he displayed his sense of humor. Only then was his Welsh-English background prominently displayed. I wondered if it was a common occurrence to joke about killing someone in the UK, as it was a strange thing to ask in a crisis. But he was a damn good attorney, a valuable friend, and a colleague I could trust. A horrible sense of humor was the least of my problems right now.

"No, I haven't killed anyone. But while we're on the subject, in the next few hours, be sure to check the local hospitals and morgues just in case someone kills me." It was a bad attempt at trying to match his humor, but since I wasn't equipped for this type of exchange, it was no surprise he took it serious.

"Are we on a secure line?"

"Listen to me, James, and I will explain everything to you." I was losing my patience and with so little time between making it through traffic and reaching Anna, I needed solutions quickly. In time, I managed to piece all the details together for him and all the things that made it challenging. I could hear the spiel from him playing in my head:

"You didn't think to mention any of this shit as I drew up your prenuptials?" He asked, like clockwork, as I admitted I wasn't sure it would matter based on the circumstance. We'd filed for separation; we lived in opposite hemispheres. We had virtually no contact. How was I to know a pitfall like this would follow me well into the day I was scheduled to wed my current girlfriend?

"I'm about to sound more like your lawyer than your friend right now, but please tell me you signed a prenup." Silence on my end of the line answered all he'd needed to know about the question. "Hopefully, now, I sound more like your mate than your attorney. How could you forget to sign a prenup, you wank?!"

"It was close to a decade ago," I defended. "I was broke; what could she have possibly taken?" Against her better judgment, Benny had married me when I was a mere grad student. Loosely translated, the broker part of me I'd like to forget. I'd managed okay in my native Finland, but the move to the US was the worst financial and career move I'd ever made. In the six months I'd stayed there, the trouble it took to secure a work visa I could barely find internships, let alone paid work. Benny had taken it upon herself to support me in ways she could as I tried and failed to find reputable work with a living wage.

With all Benny had done in our relationship, it had been a goal of mine to one day have the earning potential to give her options and alternatives, should she prefer to work from home. I hadn't considered our relationship would reach an end, so now that I stood in that place again with another woman, I'd chosen to protect myself and get a prenup.

I hadn't expected Anna to bankrupt me should our marriage meet the same fate, but I'd be lying if I said I trusted her the same way I did Benny.

"Are you two on speaking terms?"

I hesitated answering, not because I didn't know what to say, but that I'd been embarrassed to admit the truth. "We haven't spoken since I moved back to Finland eight years ago. The last form of communication we had was through the separation papers I'd gotten through the post."

"Good, good. That might work to our benefit. What did you say her name was again?" he jutted off faster than I could process.

"I didn't. But her maiden name was Maria Bendición Obiang." Before I could ask him why he needed to know that, James began calling out random information from whatever resource he had, as if I'd instructed him to do so.

"Maria Bendición Obiang Tuominen. Born in Madrid, Spain on June 10, 1986 to Equatorial Guinean parents. Migrated to the US at age five, where she later became naturalized—"

"You're looking her up?" I asked in pained confusion.

"I'm covering my bases. I should know everything there is to know about her if I plan to fight for you should things get ugly."

I hadn't realized I still carried this torch, but the compulsion to defend Benny was more potent than I even thought possible after so many years of estrangement. "No, no. Benny is not like that. I can try and contact her myself. I don't expect her number to have stayed the same over the years, but if it hasn't, I can get in contact with her and fly her out here if she's willing. But just...let me do it my way. If it doesn't work then we can do it your way."

Benny and I had made a promise, though it'd been more verbal than any other form of agreement. If our marriage ever came to an end and we ever required an official divorce, we'd respect each other enough to do it face-to-face and not through some fax, email, or text message to avoid the other person. Even though I'd gotten separation papers via postal route, I'd never really considered divorce.

James didn't know Benny. She'd been so much more to me than my wife. She'd been my best friend. My beacon of self-worth. But most of all, Benny had also been my submissive. And that was enough to honor our commitment with the respect and dignity we'd asked for all those years ago.

Our relationship had been like no other experience and because it'd been so difficult to replicate, I never took on another submissive. When Benny and I loved—and most of all, played—it was as if the world stopped every time. It would be a surprise to most to learn we had met through a matchmaker.

Most people looking for soulmates might stick their nose up at the idea of being set up. But the stakes were different when you were into kink, lived in a foreign place, and didn't know where to find others who shared your affinity for dominance and submission. Which was why when Mistress Alice, a female Dominant who'd spent thirty years mentoring and teaching and providing public health, sex therapy, and human sexuality at universities all around the world had started her own matchmaker service, I'd been the first to inquire about her services.

She wasn't an official romantic love matchmaker, but it wasn't uncommon of her to offer her expertise to those she knew might match well based on their level of experience in the lifestyle. She offered her services at undisclosed fees, but for friends and people she'd saw potential in, she provided advice to them at no cost. Which, for me, at the time had been convenient as I hadn't earned even an eighth of my present income.

I'd gone through a few failed matches before she insisted on Benny, since we weren't far from the other as I'd been studying for my Masters in Spain at the time. I'd been reluctant, but after meeting, we hit it off. It felt like I blinked and all of a sudden we were married.

For a while, Benny and I had been happy. But our impenetrable bubble couldn't last forever. In time, the cracks in our beauty began to show due to my insecurities and failures as a provider. No man likes to admit when he feels inadequate as a partner, but if I had been more honest with myself, I could've saved us.

"Do you think she'd be hard to convince to sign the divorce documents without any pushback?"

"By pushback, you mean..."

"Without compensation."

I straightened my tie and considered how angry I'd sound to my driver if I didn't choose my words carefully.

"James, I'm about to say this as both a friend and a client, so hopefully you do not take my words out of context. But don't ever insult me by suggesting that my first wife deserves nothing from me after she nearly carried me on the back of her shoulders to get me where I am today."

"I wasn't trying to suggest—"

"When I'm done talking, you can say what you want. I never said I was done. Eight years ago, I was nothing. I had nothing. Benny gave me everything. This is not some stranger or woman I met on some street corner. I told you what you needed to know and what I expect of you."

James gave a short pause before asking, "Do you think Anna would be okay with that?"

"I think you're my attorney and not Anna's."

"Fine. I'll head into my office, come up with a respectable draft then you can look it over tonight."

"You do that."

James sounded like he was about to say something else but wisely thought against it. He settled on a simple answer, one that gave us both food for thought. "I hope you know what you're doing, my friend."

The call dropped as I hung up the phone. I honestly didn't know what I was doing, but there'd be consequences either way, so I might as well do the right thing. If I managed to get in contact with Benny, even if the divorce ran smoothly, even if we expedited every step, we were still looking at a two-week minimum delay in the wedding.

I had a feeling I'd be paying for this mistake for the rest of my life, whether or not Anna still wanted to go through with the whole thing. Our relationship worked, but it was not without hardship. Marrying Anna today was supposed to be the final ultimatum I was supposed to follow through with if I'd wanted to restore our cracking relationship, and I was moments away from telling everyone it wasn't happening.

If they asked me why, I'd have to tell them and just the thought of that terrified me. I was ashamed. Ashamed at the fact that despite actually loving Anna and wanting to spend a lifetime with her, I was riddled with relief that the show wouldn't go on today.

Was that horrible? Did that mean I wasn't as ready for this as I invested convincing myself I was? Had I thought what might have happened if everything had gone as planned? If I had thought this through as much as I thought I had, why did the thought of even a chance that I might see Benny again fill me with a level of joy I couldn't explain?

❦   2   ❦

Benny

THE THING I LOVED MOST ABOUT BEING A SKI INSTRUCTOR WAS that it didn't feel like work. I had so much fun doing it. Kids were always my favorite to instruct. Their laughs, their falls, their excitement when they learned something new on top of their fearlessness made them so much easier to teach. It helped that every once in a while I used my seven-year-old daughter, Olivia, as a guide when demonstrating a new move. For that reason, Olivia loved the snow, and while the resort I worked for was a bit of a drive from where we lived in West Covina, it was great that I got to expose my daughter to something different and beautiful every once in a while.

The first-time skiers, ranging in age from six to twelve, gathered around me on the beginner slopes, waiting for my final lesson for the day, but I only had one: just have a crap load of fun. They spent the last few minutes racing teacher down the hill, and I, of course, let them win as a boost to their skiing confidence. The kids squealed about how they couldn't wait until their next lesson and quite personally it made my heart sing; I was grateful to have this job.

It wasn't the career I could have had, utilizing my degree in History, but it paid well and the hours were flexible. It also made enough time for the demands of being a single mom to an ambitious second grader, who required most, if not all, of my free time. I would have done anything for that little girl. Olivia was, is, my pride and joy. The crunch of boots through the snow behind me prompted me to turn around.

It was my co-worker, Imelda. If it hadn't been for her similar American mannerisms and little knowledge of the Spanish language, she could've passed for that gorgeous indigenous actress from Mexico who'd gotten so well known off that Netflix movie. Sometimes we taught together when one of us had a group too large to provide adequate attention to each student, and other times, she was just my happy hour buddy when I'd actually had enough time in my day to have a quick drink after work. I got along with everyone at the resort, but Mellie, as I had called her, was my go-to work friend.

"The weather is becoming ideal for a good ski. Have you gotten a chance to check out the summit?" With last night's snowfall, it did make everyone's jobs on the slopes that much easier. Plus, I loved a fresh coat of snow on the mountain. It always reminded me of a time I spent in a place I didn't give myself nearly enough time to appreciate, given the person I had attached to all my memories of it.

"I know. We're supposed to be getting even more later on, I think." I was receiving winter weather warnings on my phone about a possible blizzard that I'd crossed my fingers, hoping for. I promised Olivia I'd take her to the resort this weekend to take on some snowboarding lessons. I wasn't much of a snowboarder, but my baby loved the snow and had felt like she'd surpassed everyone her age with her mother-instructed, Olympic-level skills, as she put it. It was fun when we could do those mother/daughter types of things. I knew that in as little as eight years from now she would probably choose hanging out with her friends over spending time with her mom. So, I cherished those moments I'd have with her while she was young. I only wished I was able to do more.

"Hey, I'm about to head to the lodge," I announced, hoping she'd join me but turns out she was on her way to a lesson. So, I took a lift back myself to make sure I didn't have any more lessons in my schedule today. Best case scenario was that I could surprise my daughter with picking her up early from school instead of her taking the bus to my mom's house, which was almost an hour's drive but a ninety-minute bus ride. When I arrived at the lodge, it was virtually empty. There were peak times for the resort and this time was usually our slowest. But still, we got enough visitors to meet the season's sales projections. There were rumors that they were laying people off, but at the moment it was just that—rumors. I had a lot of loyal, pocket-emptying students, so while the gossip had worried others, it hadn't crossed my mind enough to concern me. As far as I knew, my job was secure.

The mounted TV's hung high along the walls, displaying a multitude of programming, one confirming the upcoming blizzard. I was in pursuit of making my way toward the mountain eateries to grab myself a cup of coffee before making my way out when I was stopped by my boss, who'd claimed to have been looking for me since the completion of my last class.

"Do you mind if we talk in my office for a minute, Bendición?" he asked with a stern look on his face that was somewhat hard to read, but with what I'd learned from him over the years meant that he wasn't the warmest person to begin with. Silently, I followed him to his office, shutting the door behind me at his request, after which he offered me a seat on the opposite side of his desk. Folders and papers laid across his desk in messy, unkempt piles, but the photos of his family more than made up for his organizational skills. He had a beautiful wife and kids.

"I'm afraid the reason I asked you in here isn't exactly good news." At this moment, my palms were such a sweaty mess that I had to wipe them down on my jeans as I prepared for what bad news he had to tell me. My thoughts flew back to the rumor

that there could be layoffs soon, but I kept reminding myself that I was valuable. I'd been here a long time and there was no way my boss would ever fire me without good reasoning and sufficient time to search for something else.

"As you know this season hasn't been all that profitable as past quarters. While this is usually our slower season, this was been the worst season regarding projections we've had in years. Re-examining the company's budget, we've been forced to let go a third of our full-time staff. Your name, Bendición, I regret to say was on that list."

A wave of shock coursed through me. How could that have been? I'd been on staff the longest, and visitors who came here loved me. Requested me. It didn't make any sense as to why I was being let go over less tenured, qualified staff. My whole existence at the time being *depended* on this job. My daughter depended on my *having* this job.

"Unfortunately, you're one of our most expensive employees to keep on. The truth is we can't afford to keep every single seasoned instructor. We just don't have the money. Eventually I'm going to have to move everyone to part-time."

My heart sank into the pit of my stomach. I was being fired. I was being fired from the only source of income I had at the moment. I had rent, a car note, my daughter's private school tuition to pay for. How in the hell could they just fire me? What was I supposed to do on such short notice? There had to be something. *Anything*, even if the schedule I had dwindled down to half the hours I had now. I couldn't just be without a job. Not without the required time it took to find another while still being able to meet all my financial responsibilities.

"Ron, is there any way you could keep me on? What if you kept me on part-time just until I find something else?" I asked in one last act of desperation. He shrugged, finally giving me the sympathy I deserved with a regretful look whiskering into his expression.

"Unfortunately, Bendición, there isn't anything I can do."

There wasn't anything he could do, he told me. And now I bore the burden of informing my hopeful seven-year-old daughter that the plan to visit Mami's job over the weekend would be permanently canceled. Until I figured something else out, the only things on my to-do list was to find a job before all my savings ran out. This, of all things, couldn't have happened at a worse time.

❧ 3 ❧

O^{lli}

I'M RIGHT OUTSIDE THE CHURCH. BE HERE AS QUICK AS YOU CAN. Make sure you come with information I can use.

It was the last message I left on James's voicemail to make sure he was on his way. He sent a text assuring me he was "on it", and since I paid him enough to deliver on time, I expected him not to show up empty-handed.

It didn't matter what he walked in that chapel with; either way, I was walking into two possible situations. One, in the perfect world I knew didn't exist, I'd encounter an understanding Anna. An Anna who, while I'd expect there to be some pushback, wouldn't fault me for the mistake I hadn't meant to make. She'd understand we still planned to marry; it just wouldn't be today.

But I had a strong inkling the Anna I was about to confront wouldn't mirror that fantasy Anna in any way. The reality Anna wouldn't be talked down, no matter what excuse or plan of action

I had to offer to remedy the delay. I didn't expect her not to be upset, as she had every right to be. I was just at a loss of what it would mean if things didn't go as planned, which was bound to happen.

I had seconds to contemplate that I was about to walk through those church doors and inform all our friends and family that the wedding was still going to happen, but it just wouldn't be until a later date. Having spent tens of thousands on securing the venue for the reception and church Anna wanted, employing the best wedding planner in Finland, making arrangements for an exotic honeymoon, top tier catering, and designer wedding gown, I knew postponing this event would hardly go over smoothly without pushback, but what could I do?

I didn't even care about mercy at this point. I just wanted to marry someone I loved. It mattered not whether it was a lavish wedding or one that only required a Justice of the Peace. I was only interested in the starting my life over with my wife, or rather, my soon-to-be-wife.

By law, I was still married to my first love, Benny. She'd held all my dreams, all my fears, and helped me face some emotional drawbacks that I can't believe I hadn't reached out to her, even as just a friend. I shouldn't even be thinking about her in the manner I am, and surely not on the day I was meant to marry someone else, but as I made my way through the chapel doors, I was riddled by memories of what once was.Lavish flower arrangements were countered by the simplistic beauty of a single flower in Benny's hair and a modest bouquet of flowers she held to feel like a real bride. Neither of us had come from wealth, so the only option we'd had was to wed in our fanciest clothes, a far cry from the dream wedding most women fantasized about as young girls.

I'd never spoken the words out loud, but I promised myself that if I had ever gotten the chance, I would have renewed my vows to Benny, reimagined as the wedding she'd always wanted.

Or at the very least, the one she'd been too modest to admit to wanting.

We'd never gotten that far, so the most we had left of those times were memories. I'm sure that deep down it was why I never questioned the expense of what I'd meant to give Anna. I was about to give her the worst memory of her life, and worst of all, it would be tied to her big day. I mean, *our* big day.

I sent a text to my parents asking if they would meet me near the bathroom of the lower level, so I could at least provide a proper explanation, a privilege I wouldn't have with Anna. I don't think it surprised me to learn they weren't upset. If anything, they understood my fears, despite wondering how I'd forgotten something so crucial as already being married.

"Your challenge now will be explaining that to the Swede," my mother softly replied, her bad attempt at hiding that she wasn't disappointed. It's not as if my mother had ever disliked Anna; she just hadn't understood how she fit into my life once they learned about my past in the "life".

Since I'd been a kinkster since the age of twenty-two, I found that it would be difficult to hide for the times I didn't have a girlfriend but wanted to invite my submissive up for a family dinner. It was a coincidence that Benny had not only been my submissive but my girlfriend, and eventually, my wife as well. My parents were conservative, so they weren't well-versed in the lifestyle etiquette, but they were convinced Benny had been so polite because I'd trained her to be, which made me laugh at their stereotypes of being a Dom. Benny had been polite because that was her personality. Anna, not so much...

In fact, most of my ex flings, girlfriends, and even submissives, my mom had tolerated before Anna. I never knew what turned my mother off to her, but in safe spaces, she hardly ever referred to her by her Christian name. Oftentimes, "The Swede" had been so engrained coming from her lips, I'd programmed my mind to simply hear Anna instead.

My father was the complete opposite. He minded his business like a typical Finn, only injecting advice at the most vulnerable moments. "I'm sure she'll understand. She has to." He pat me on the shoulder, comforting me in the only way a traditional Finnish man knew how to for his son.

"And if she doesn't, you always have another wife." Even though it had been intended as a joke, Mother hadn't even cracked a smile, changed her tone, or offered any other subtle changes in expression. But she'd offered to find Anna and separate her from her bridezilla-like mother, who seemed just as, if not more, eager to see today go through without any hitches.

That would've been convenient, but the courage rising forced me to turn down the offer. If I was going to face this, I was going to do it as a man, not as a person who couldn't even tell his bride he'd made a mistake on the wrong yet most important day of her life. If I couldn't own up to my mistakes, why did I think we could even start a life together?

❧

ANNA WOULD BE IN THE BACK OF THE CHURCH, PREPARING HER hair and makeup before the ceremony. We booked this church based on the space Anna wanted to prepare herself. I, on the other hand, hadn't planned more than getting ready on the way. It wasn't the most romantic, but the wedding was far beyond what I would have planned if I had had any say in it. Today was just an event I wanted over with so we could move on to more important things like starting a family together. I never thought I'd get well into my thirties without ever becoming a father.

"Stop messing with my hair, Mother. It's already perfect." Anna's voice wasn't far beyond my reach.

"We could always use a bit more effort on a day like this," her mother offered.

Anna and her mother's comments ricocheted back and forth

until the conversation went into a unique direction that I'm glad I heard but deep down would have rather stayed ignorant to. "I swear, Mother, you always get this way when you become desperate." It was a good thing I spoke fluent Swedish; otherwise, I'd have no idea that the conversation took a turn for the worst.

"I wouldn't be so desperate if you'd just asked him for the money earlier, like I asked you to."

Anna's voice grew quiet, but with my luck, I could still hear despite the sudden quietness. She'd definitely only intended on her mother hearing what she had to say. "Mother, I love you. But I can't afford to have you ruin my big day. This is *my* day. Let me have one day where I'm allowed to think about myself. When we are married, I'll give you all the money that you need. Until then, please be patient with me. I do not have time to worry about Father's gambling problems."

There wasn't a time better than now to burst the idea around today falling apart. I could wait, or I could do it now, but either way wouldn't bring a better outcome. "Anna, I need to speak to you. Right now." I stormed in, pretending I hadn't heard pieces of their conversation. Anna screamed, almost smudging her intricate eye makeup in efforts to conceal her face and dress from me.

"Olli, what are you doing here?!" Her voice cracked under the weight of her current state. "You're not supposed to see me until the ceremony." She made sure to remind me how much bad luck we'd get for having seen her before I was supposed to. If only she knew that should be the least of her worries.

"What I have to tell you holds more importance. I'm sure nothing else will matter once you hear what I have to say." Anna looked over to her mother as she reluctantly left the room to allow Anna and me to talk.

For a day, I'd just wanted to get over with. It still went without saying how beautiful Anna had looked. She looked like a princess in a fairytale, with her overtly tight bun gathered over her head and make-up that made her appear both blemish-free and older than her twenty-six years. But the dress was what really made her appear like a fantasy. An hourglass corset to accentuate her modest hips, she may as well have been Cinderella.

It was a strange shift in memories, but my wedding day with Benny came to mind, and I couldn't help thinking I had never seen a woman more beautiful in a white dress. For as much effort as it took, they would've made equal impacts on me had I gone through with this the way we'd planned.

"What is it, Olli? What was so damn important that it was worth giving me bad luck before we get to the ceremony?" I didn't believe in luck, but I had believed in fate. It just wasn't as friendly as it'd used to be when it came to me and Anna.

"Before I go on, you must know it wasn't my intention for this to happen—"

"Get on with it!" Anna screamed.

"Obtaining our marriage certificate. I ran into a minute yet unavoidable problem."

Anna narrowed her elven eyes, testing me with dagger-like stares. "Like?"

There was no better way to say it, and if I fluffed and dragged it out, I'd make it worse for myself. It was best to just start with the truth. "Legally, I can't marry you because I'm still married. To my first wife."

At first, I was sure she hadn't heard me clear enough. Her initial reaction wasn't nearly as loud or filled with the passion I'd grown accustom to defending with Anna. In her calmest tone possible, she held her bouquet close to her chest, faked a smile, and asked, "Olli, what exactly does that mean?"

"It means it is a temporary setback at best. It's not something that can be settled today, but if we play this right—" Though I hadn't gotten the chance to say much more before her crystal eyes widened, her pupils dilating to the point where most of the blue had left her eyes. I was halfway into explaining that today would be difficult not to postpone and that all I needed to do was finalize my divorce and we'd be right again. But somewhere between all of that, I must have triggered her. One moment she was listening to my explanation of where we went from here; the next she was striking me over the arm with her bouquet.

"I ask you to do *one thing*, Olli. Take care of the marriage certificate. I took care of everything else; that was all that I asked you to do. But you didn't do it when I asked. You wait until months of preparation had already been made. Family and friends are sitting out there waiting for us to become husband and wife. I didn't even make a big deal when you were too busy to show up for rehearsals.

Because all I expected of you was to show up. *With* the marriage certificate. Now, you walk back here and cause me emotional stress because I can't go back on you seeing my dress. And you have the nerve to tell me—*on my wedding day*—that you're still married to someone else?"

When Anna and I first met, I'd made her well aware that I'd been married nearly a decade ago, though I'd only mentioned our separation in passing. She'd held my separation as seriously as a divorce, implying I had to have taken care of it in the time we'd gotten serious, to the time we'd begun planning *our* wedding planning.

Having spent four long years with Anna, I didn't push back when she thought our relationship should naturally progress to marriage. It hadn't meant I'd actually thought about what it would take to finalize my divorce, and since Benny and I lived thousands of miles apart and hadn't been in contact for years, in the moment, it felt like a thing of the past.

"Do you know what would have happened if you had tried to obtain that certificate when I asked you to?" It was a rhetorical question, but there was a chance she'd wanted me to answer anyway, just so she could have the upper hand. "You would've known you were still fucking married, that's what. And prevented this whole shit situation from happening—"

"I know, Anna, and I'm sorry. I don't know how many times I can tell you from the bottom of my heart how I hadn't planned for any of this to happen." An apology was the last thing she'd wanted to hear, but it was all I had, at least until James drafted out those divorce papers to my preference. Before I could say anything else, he rushed through the doors, arriving in my weakest moment of need.

"Trust me, Anna; Olli has been making every effort to make things right about today; otherwise, I wouldn't be here." James assured us that he had a way to deal with the situation swiftly, but Anna wasn't convinced by mere words.

"Olli, what is he talking about?" she asked, pointing in James's direction.

"Your solution," James interjected, before reminding us this was why I paid him his worth in the services offered to me, "is if we can just get your soon-to-be ex-wife to sign the paperwork, we'll be likely to handle everything in as little as seventy-two hours," he said matter-of-factly as Anna snatched the draft of the divorce documents from his hand, unable to suppress her curiosity by flipping to the page with my favorable settlement.

"If she could hop on the next flight, you're looking at a push-back of a week, two weeks tops. It'll be like today never happened, and you'll two love birds will be hitched by the end of the month," James added, but there wasn't a solution that would've satisfied Anna at this point.

In justified anger, Anna threw down the copy of the draft and crossed the room with her arms held over her head, emitting a muffled scream of frustration. "That still doesn't remedy the fact that I still have a room full of people waiting for me to walk down that aisle and get married, and I have to tell that that I'm in fact *not* getting married."

"Anna, if this is about money, you know it's of little object to the situation."

"You bet your ass it won't be an object to our next wedding."

Anna interrupted. "Because there wouldn't be a need of a second one if you'd done what was required of you in the first place. I plan to have a brand new dress, all new catering, completely new arrangements... and you will see that I get all of it. I want the best wedding planner in the world, not just the best Helsinki can provide," She spoke with an arrogant confidence, mumbling something under her breath before either of us could decipher what she said.

She ripped the dress' detail in the torso, claiming it was no longer acceptable, considering everyone, including me, had already seen her in it already. "Now, I have to go back there and tell everyone the truth." She walked past James and stuck a hand in his face before spewing, "Fix this." Anna disappeared through the chamber doors, and that was the last we'd see of her until we sought her out.

"Thank you." I reached out for James's hand and was humbled when he took mine to shake on it. "You really saved my arse."

"I was only doing what you asked. And I assume that since you haven't mentioned it that Anna knows next to nothing about the investment deal?"

Not if I wanted her where her nose didn't belong.

"I've taken the necessary measures to keep this deal under wraps. Nothing else is going as planned, but at least I know that will." I took the additional paperwork James wanted me to review and buried that, along with the divorce draft, deep within my coat.

"It's probably time you call Bendición."

"You're probably right. I hate it when you are right." James pat me on the shoulder before wishing me luck about next to everything else. He said he'd make sure to call me to confirm that I'd reached out to contact Benny. Even though it was a necessary step, I wasn't sure I even wanted to put myself in that scenario. I wasn't scared to do a lot of things, but to imagine a life where

Benny was permanently not in it? I hadn't thought about it until now, and the idea of it made my stomach turn.

Even if she'd moved on after all this time, the churning in my gut convinced me everything was about to change once I made this call.

$$\maltese \quad 4 \quad \maltese$$

Benny

I wish this woman would get off her cell phone. God, did anyone have any regard to the safety of those around them on the road? It's bad enough traffic was as backed up as it was, but having to worry about the drivers who thought their phones were more important than keeping their eyes on the road made me even more irritated during the drive to Olivia's school.

"Hey! I'm trying to get over!"

"Asshole!"

The result of a heated exchange between two drivers, a lane away, yelling from car to car. There was a longwinded honk that accompanied the encounter that could raise the dead. My psyche focused on the combination of grinding brakes, wheel tires feeling the weight of the potholes that West Covina needed to fix, and the consistent beeping at my bumper that happened every time a car behind you didn't think you were driving fast enough.

Anything to get my mind off of losing my job. I was going to be a few minutes late, but at least I had called Olivia's school ahead of time. Money was going to be tight. I couldn't help but be grateful that I had at least received a severance that would get me through two solid months or until I found another job. Olivia's tuition was paid up for the semester, so for now, that was the least of my worries. But something told me I was not about to get any sleep tonight, fearing how I would provide for my daughter once my severance is depleted.

I could just hear my mother's voice now. *"Only fools test the depth of water with both feet."*

Whenever something went wrong in my life, you could be sure there'd be an Equatorial Guinean proverb to go with it. Mami was harsh, but even harder on me ever since I had Olivia without her father in the picture. Ma had only seen what she wanted to see: me following her footsteps as a single mother based on her bad choice in my father. Unbeknownst to her, Olivia's father wasn't in the picture due to his own accord. That was all me.

It had felt so long ago and deeply rooted in the past that it was hard explaining that while I hadn't been ready when *I* was pregnant with Olivia, I didn't trust Olivia's father would be ready even less. But I moved past it. I let the past stay there and took responsibility for my choices and have managed to make ends meet so far.

I knew if I just started looking soon that things could work out; I would just have to be diligent and have faith that I could find work in a decent window of time. If I thought positively, my outcome might end that way. I just needed a job for now; that way, none of my expenses for the month would suffer from the loss. Worst case scenario, I could move back in with my mom.

It wasn't ideal, but I wasn't too proud when it came to my daughter having a roof over her head. I would have to deal with the consequences of that situation when I crossed that road.

The soft hum of my rain-simulated ringtone went off and on *this* road, there was no way I was going to answer it. Hypocrite much?

But what if it were my daughter's school? What if they were calling to say they'd lost her or that there'd be no one to watch her because I was running late? My pessimism was definitely affecting me in a way I thought would go away if I maintained positive thoughts. This was my daughter. If the school officials were calling, I needed to pick up. I pulled onto an exit with a rest stop and pulled into the first one I saw. I placed my cell phone into the clip against the vent on the chance I'd have to put it on speaker.

+358905587887

What the hell kind of number was that? That couldn't be right. It was clearly an international number, but unless some foreign prince was calling me to deposit half a million dollars into my bank account, I didn't care who it was. I put my car into drive and thought it best to ignore it for now. I'd only lost a minute or two hopping onto the exit. It had just been a huge relief that it didn't have anything to do with Olivia.

I'D DROPPED OLIVIA OFF AT MY MOM'S PLACE AS I DIDN'T KNOW what else to do but drive around for a few hours. I should've been looking for work. I'd definitely told my mother and daughter that's what I'd planned to do after explaining the bad news. But I think I just needed some time to myself to figure out my next move. I didn't want either of them to see how scared I was. I was minutes away from having a mental breakdown.

That number started to call again. In fact, since I'd been on the road, it had been the fourth time that number showed up on my caller ID. I was a little annoyed; did a telemarketer want my business that bad? They'd be disappointed to hear not only did I have little money but that within the few hours I'd lost my sole source of income, too. A part of me wanted to pick it up and just admit that, just so I could be mad at someone who wasn't my former boss. Or at the very least force someone to listen to my problems right now.

The ringing hadn't stopped by the time I finally picked it up. "¡Buenos dias Benny! Cómo estás?"

My torso nearly felt like my insides were hardening and forcing the air from my lungs. It was as if my entire midsection felt like a delicate and fragile piece of ice, ready to break if I so much breathed the wrong way.

"Hello?" A voice in a heavy yet clear, thick Finnish accent flowed throw the speaker. Maybe it was because I was rendered mute that the person on the other end thought I'd hung up. My mind was lost between somewhere and nowhere for several seconds before I realized I never answered the voice back.

The foreign number? The attempt at Spanish? That Finnish accent? It was Olli. My...

"Hi," was all I could think to reply back. My heart nearly melted when he softly returned the greeting.

"Hi."

Now that I thought of it, Olli's voice wasn't one I'd heard—or heard from—in close to eight years. It was like one day we were two madly in love kids getting married on a whim, to a couple who couldn't figure out how to make our homesickness work to save our relationship.

Olli and I had met in Spain through a matchmaker who had, in her own time, created a non-formal BDSM matchmaking service to those she'd encountered from her travels all over Europe. Olli had been studying there to earn his master's in International Business, while I'd been traveling to my birth country in efforts to decide whether I planned on studying past my bachelors.

Mistress Alice had encountered so many people in her thirty years of being a Domme that she was convinced she could create a network of kinksters and match folks based on her knowledge of their needs and reading others' auras. It didn't always work out well when you were limited to an area with very few participants in BDSM, but she was always honest of what to expect should we decide to take her advice on if we wanted to meet potential kinksters in her network.

When Olli and I had been set up, it had been a blind date. I was reluctant to meet with a Dominant with less experience than me. I feared he wouldn't wow me like more experienced Doms I'd matched well with but clashed greatly in our vanilla lives. Mistress Alice assured me he'd met all the prerequisites I'd laid out for her before she suggested a match in my area: tall, European, if unable to speak Spanish, at least converse clearly in English, and most of all—single.

I was surprised upon meeting in a public place, the six foot four import was originally from Helsinki, and it just occurred to me that I'd never pursued or been pursued by a man from a Nordic country. His lips had been full and poetic, much like his virescent eyes that screamed man of nature. For all the pre-reqs he'd met physically, there was something interesting about his Finnish mannerism that I thought would eventually turn me off. All I could remember thinking the whole time we sat down for the first time was how a man could be so handsome yet so awkward at the same time.

But he was surprised to meet me as well, as he had his own reluctance meeting an American. He later admitted that he hadn't known I'd be black, but it wouldn't have mattered anyway because he never specifically asked to be matched with someone white; it just was more likely to happen considering the location. With just one date, we'd agreed to see each other again so that we could get to know each other better. As one thing lead to another, we were married.

For most of the two or three months of our marriage, we'd been happy. But when we'd gone back to his homeland of Finland, I grew homesick. We compromised on spending some time in the States, but he found it difficult to find work. It wasn't long before we mutually decided that maybe we'd been feeling so much intense emotion that we'd likely rushed into a situation that couldn't be solved with just passion, love, and Dominance and submission alone.

There'd been no hard feelings from our separation, as we promised to keep in touch. But days turned into weeks. Weeks turned into months, months converting into years. I wouldn't have even thought about him past the few nights I felt lonely in that way only a man's touch could shake me out of. We were a part of each other's reckless decisions in the past. There were reasons why I should have kept in contact, but as the years flew by, it became more difficult to.

Why would he be calling me now? What would warrant communication after years of barely acknowledging one another's existence?

I wouldn't have to wonder for long. Lucky for me, Olli wasn't one to dwell long on small talk. "It is good to hear from you, Benny. I know it has been a long time since we've spoken. I hope you are well." He went on to say that my voice sounded the same, even nearly eight years after our last encounter. Apparently it had taken him a moment to decide if he'd even wanted to ring me. Even though we had unintentionally become estranged, he hadn't wanted to disrupt my current life or remind me of what we were. When he did get to his reason for calling, I have to admit—I wasn't ready for it.

Granted, it had been my idea for him to go back to Finland. Deep down, I knew it disappointed him that I didn't want to leave with him, but seeing as how I had a challenging time in Helsinki in the same way he'd had in West Covina, it had been better *at that time* for the both of us to part ways.

Little did I know, the next time I might hear from Olli that he'd be in the process of living his best life. *Without* me. "I do not wish to burden you, Benny. I wouldn't even be calling if it weren't absolutely essential to my current circumstances."

Eight years. Eight years since I'd last heard his voice. That voice that once made every nerve in my body light up upon contact. The same voice that made me wet for just the chance to be with him at some point in my day. The voice of the only man I ever loved.

He was getting married. And our marriage had caused him grief in his new relationship that could only be resolved by contacting me. "It's so good to hear from you, Olli. I'm glad you finally found someone," I managed to say without crying. "I'm happy for you."

I'm happy for you. I really meant it because even though I'd never had to say it to myself until now, I still loved him. Liked him. Loved him. Still *in love* with him. I wanted the best for him even if I wished the best was me. I learned the most about myself in my relationship with him. I learned how to be in love and submit at the same time. I'd learned how to be a supportive wife, which to a Finnish man held a different meaning to a man of a similar culture to my own. I'd learned my core values, and along the way, learned I could orgasm fourteen times in twenty-four-hour span.

I wish I were hearing from him under better circumstances. Hell, maybe I wouldn't even be in this place if I'd fought for us, or at the very least made him aware of things he deserved to know about after he'd left for Finland. But that wasn't our situation. Our situation featured the love of my life getting on with another woman. Another woman he wanted to make his wife, another woman he made love to. I wanted it to be me, but it wasn't. And I wasn't about to stand in the way just because I'd made the mistake of not fighting for us in the past.

"My lawyer has drawn up the paperwork. I could've faxed them to you, but given our history, I would prefer to fly you out and do things in person." Olli had taken care of a round trip flight, not to mention, he'd also taken care of my accommodations.

"I don't know what your financial situation has been over the years, but I've been comfortable. I am more than happy to provide a settlement to make sure you have what you—"

"No. I couldn't take your money," I interrupted.

"Benny, I insist. It's taken a while, but over the years, investments have worked greatly in my favor. All my initial fears about the financial risk my career would give I have been able to overcome with the encouragement you gave me so long ago," Olli admitted. While Olli had always had his mind focused in finance, which he later admitted to pursuing, he'd always wanted to get to a point where he wasn't working his entire life. He had wanted to retire younger than the traditional age of sixty-five, and from his perspective, he could only do that with investing.

I wondered how close he'd gotten to meeting his goal, but any money he'd earned over the years didn't feel right in my hands. It would definitely help my current situation, though. I had to wonder if that was fate's way of telling me I'd be taken care of in my time of need, but hearing Olli's voice made me remember him in ways I cared not to. I could take his money, but it would never replace *him*. If I took money from him, it would feel like a type of payoff or an invitation to never cross paths again. The selfishness in me wasn't sure I wanted that.

"Olli, whatever life you've made for yourself was all you. You've earned what you have and have every right to keep it. You're about to get married! You're rearing up for a future that will likely need it." Indirectly, I was speaking to the lavish wedding I'm sure he was going to have.

He'd never wanted one personally but mentioned wanting to give something like that to me one day. Guess I shouldn't count on that promise to come true any time soon. I agreed to take the trip to Helsinki if it would expedite the process, deciding I would figure out the details with my mother later about Olivia's care. It wouldn't be as big a deal as she'd make it, but I knew I wouldn't be able to make the trip without another lecture.

Olli took down my travel information, surprised that I still lived in the same place since our estrangement. I'd saved the two letters that he'd written me from his part of the world, but considering our situation, I wouldn't have known what to write back. He wanted me in the air within the next few days as he confirmed that my ticket he purchased remained open when I was ready, as the next few minutes were filled with nervous chatter and lasting farewells until next time.

We said our goodbyes and waited for the other person to hang up the phone. I was hoping he'd hang up first. I stood for just a second, thinking of all the information I had to take in from our fifteen minute exchange. I heard him breathe on his end and say "Hello?" almost as if a question, as I finally decided it was time to part with the line. Olli's new life would start the minute I signed the divorce papers and left.

Hot, burning tears streamed down my eyes, and I broke down into an uncontrollable crying fit. As if my day couldn't get any worse, I had to go back to face the only person I'd ever wanted a future with create a future with someone else. My heart felt so heavy, that I don't think I could ever love like that again.

O^{lli}

Then

THE ARRANGED SKYPE SESSIONS REQUIRED FOR THIS PARTICULAR matchmaker service was coming to its final session before I'd be matched with someone Mistress Alice felt might suit me. It wasn't a public service; therefore, you had to be referred by someone in the community before any interviews occurred. Luckily for me, I'd known her partner through the Dominant that mentored me, so that made the screening process a breeze. I wasn't sure if they'd find me a match, as I was a very selective person and required a woman of a certain skill set to fully understand my quirks as well as my conventionally positive traits. I'd already been set up a few times and neither had panned out exactly as I planned, either from a lack of communication or a misunderstanding between cultures.

I found that I didn't mesh well with American women. They tended to talk about superficial things that didn't matter to me, and despite being in search of a submissive for play time, I was also equally interested in dating her, and that made a difference in whether or not we were compatible. Even if we had little in common, I wanted to feel a connection within the first moments of meeting her. For the most part, I'd found American women alarmingly attractive, but thus far, not one had been a good fit for me.

Studying abroad in a foreign country gave me the opportunity to meet other women in the community that I didn't already know. Who didn't have the desire to alter their usual dating preferences while having the chance to date so many women of different cultures? In my native Finland, I did have a few instances to date a Russian woman, but that had been the extent of my mingling with other people. As long as she spoke English, it didn't matter what she looked like. As long as we got along well before we auditioned each other to become play partners, I was open to almost anyone who was open to me.

"*Bonjour*, my Finnish friend. How are you today?" I could hear her on my laptop before the image buffered clear. She was a mature woman, at the youngest sixty from what I'd known about her, and enchantingly breathtaking. It was hard to compare her looks to someone who was half her age. While she didn't have youth on her side, there had been no race to stop the clock with supplements or surgery. She possessed the face and figure of someone who'd clearly taken care of themselves when it mattered most, and it showed how intimately she carried herself. Sharp blue eyes with soft, wispy moonlight white hair and lips that were always adorned with a rosy shade of pink that perhaps matched her natural, full pout. She was the epitome of French womanhood.

"*Bonsoir*, Mistress Alice. *Comment ca va?*" I asked in her native French, which ashamedly, I wasn't particularly good at. She always appreciated the effort, but we'd mutually come to the conclusion that English was just easier for us to communicate.

I had to admit, at first, I was a bit reluctant with a modern day matchmaker service for people in the kink lifestyle, but what I'd learned from the experience was that it was the person, not algorithms and matches based on percentages, that helped you find the perfect fit. It meant getting to know her clients inside and out, something your standard dating app wasn't able to provide. She learned early on that crowded play parties, group outings, and dungeons weren't my ideal place to meet a potential submissive, and despite attending and even enjoying those particular experiences, I'd always found them daunting and overwhelming. The intimacy of being set up with one person when I wouldn't have to fight for anyone for their attentions was initially what attracted me to the service and what I preferred.

"So, I have some good news for you. I have a new prospect for you. If you have time this weekend, I've arranged for you and my match to meet locally."

"She lives in Madrid?" She nodded, aware that while I was studying for my Master's in International Business at the Universidad Carlos III de Madrid, I'd been interested in meeting women where I was staying. The less traveling, the better. She knew me well enough to know what I liked and disliked, but because the matches often never saw each other until their first in-person date, I never had a chance to screen them and do a quick profile search on social media. For the most part, I was always attracted to the women she matched for me, but when I got into a conversation about preferences, she let it be known that while she usually honored "types", this time, she made an exception because of our past interviews about expanding my horizons.

"I must confess. She is not your usual type, but I have a feeling you'll like this one. She has this indescribable love for the world and is such a beautiful soul. I've actually known her for a few years. I met her at a play party in Las Vegas in 2016—"

"Is she *American*?" I cut her off, unintentionally sounding ruder than I intended . She grimaced, trying hard not to let on too much while having a chance to fully explain herself.

"Technically, yes, but"

"No Americans. We've already discussed this." I felt my nose flair at having to repeat myself after the last failed attempts but also acknowledging that she was essentially my superior. She'd been a Dominant probably longer than I'd been alive and despite my frustration, she deserved my respect. She tucked in her pouty lips and adjusted herself on the other side of the screen. When she took a deep breathe, I acknowledged that I needed to take a step back and listen to what it was she was planning to tell me before I rudely interrupted her. Her eyes, blue and steady like waves brushing lazily along a coast, had a calming effect on my mood. I'd choose my words more sensibly before I questioned her wisdom over my often selfish partialities.

"Olli, *mon chéri*. What is it you are looking for? Tell Alice because if you don't, then I won't know." For me, the answer was simple: I wanted a woman who was a good communicator and who'd help me to become a better one, not just to address or satisfy my needs but hers as well. I wanted openness and honesty from the very first encounter, and the many women I had encountered were terrible at providing that. It wasn't their faults, really. Even women in my own culture didn't always focus on what they wanted and needed from a partner. And what I was coming to realize was that many just didn't know what they wanted or rather how to communicate what they wanted from a relationship for them to flourish. They were always so focused on what society told them men wanted that they weren't quite certain what they wanted for themselves.

I wanted a woman who was confident in her needs and wasn't afraid to tell me what that was. If sharing resources with her was how she felt valued, I needed to know that. If emotional stability was a prerequisite, knowing in advance would better help me not load all my underlying issues on my mate when I could just see a therapist. Love letters, grand gestures, making time to spend time with one another to let one know they are appreciated were all things I longed to hear by the second date. But I was beginning to feel like that woman didn't exist, or at least not in the scope of my matches.

"I want to meet a woman who is sure of herself, a woman who won't settle for any Dominant but the right *Dominant*. Someone who makes getting to know her just as exciting as dominating her. A girl who challenges me in ways that I didn't know was possible. Does that make sense to you?"

She leaned on the desk where she sat and rested her chin in her manicured hand.

"Olli, the woman you just described is Benny, my match for you. Why do you think I'd go out my way to set you up with someone that isn't your usual type? She was born in Spain if that helps, but even if she hadn't been, I'd still think the two of you were a good fit. You don't have to trust my judgment, but so far, I've always delivered in giving you what you've requested. I wouldn't steer you on the wrong path."

I took a moment to consider her words. Perhaps, she was right. I most certainly was being stubborn about this. What did I really have to lose by just showing up and meeting someone new? It wasn't as if I were obligated to stay if it didn't go well; after all, it wasn't a marriage proposal but a date, screening a potential playmate that could lead to something more. Mistress Alice's process was arduous, so chances were if I didn't go on this date, it'd be another few weeks before she started her extensive process all over again. Maybe I'd regret this, but after a few more exchanges, I promised I'd follow through with her choice.

A warm smile spread across her face, pleased with my decision as she demanded an update as soon as the day after the date to know how the two of us worked out. All I realized was that if I didn't, I'd do nothing but consume myself in my studies and sacrifice my personal life. A inkling of doubt felt the pessimism brewing, thinking this girl would just be another failed attempt in finding my ideal relationship. Although for the sake of my trust and faith in Mistress Alice's methods, I really hoped my pessimism could be replaced with me stumbling along just an inkling of what I was in search of.

Now

EVEN AS SHE ENDED THE CALL, I CONTINUED TO HOLD THE phone close to my ear. It had been so long since I'd heard that voice, her voice, I'd forgotten how sweet and melodic it sounded to me. Every word that left her mouth had the ability to both bring me to a place of peace and unlock the darkness I needed to become the dominance that both scared and exhilarated her. Because of her, I'd developed a love for American intonations; or rather, it had been *her* accent that had driven me senseless. Even as my wife, she'd remained my submissive and my most intense relationship to date. Perhaps it was better this way. Moving on hadn't always felt like the easiest thing to do, but it had been long enough between us to where if we had plans to reconcile, we would've done so by now. I suppose a small part of me always wished we would have. But now, I was marrying Anna and soon if we managed to fix this current mess I put us in.

Reentering the house, Adam, my butler, assisted me with my jacket as he tucked it away in the guest closet. He was helpful in more ways than one, often sensing when I was going to have a good day or a rough one. Judging by the way he'd described Anna's recent behavior earlier in the day, I predicted that it was going to be the latter.

Ever since I'd made a mockery of her at our wedding, it was like walking across blazing coals in an attempt to avoid any confrontation. Unfortunately, that was Anna's middle name. Any time she could throw a colossal tantrum about something, she proudly did so. This time, I couldn't exactly blame her. It had been *my* responsibility to see to it that things ran smoothly. It would be *my* responsibility to make sure by the end of the week, we could finally get married. I couldn't wait to get it over with— almost. I was so fucking tired of hearing about it.

I found Anna in the bedroom we shared, doing what she did best: being her overdramatic self as she threw a handful of her clothes in an empty duffle bag. I exhaled a deep sigh, knowing just how to diffuse the situation but also realizing that no matter what I told her, she'd still find an excuse to yell and be angry. She was always so emotional without ever being *emotional.*

"Good news." I leaned on the post of our sleigh bed as she adjusted her icy gaze toward me. "I just got off the phone with my ex. She can be on the soonest plane this week to finalize our divorce. That means we can be married as early as next Saturday, according to the venue's first availability," I explained, hoping it would make her happy, not that I was counting on it. Anna always chose a way to be negative in any situation as long as it meant getting her way.

"Did you make your ex sign a prenup?" she asked, which made me think she'd been talking to my lawyer behind my back. I rolled my eyes. "No, I didn't." Choosing honesty always meant transparency.

"So, why did you make me sign one?" Her eyes blazed as she tossed one of her blouses angrily in my direction.

"Anna, we've spoken about this. When I met Benny, I was young and living in the moment. The last thing I considered was prenuptials when I was still a struggling student. A prenuptial agreement just protects the both of us." What I didn't tell her was that while I was what I'd call "in deep infatuation" with her, I didn't know her well enough to trust that if things didn't work between us that she wouldn't drain me dry of all my assets. She was already an expensive habit to maintain and believe it or not, I enjoyed spoiling her. Getting her things she asked for was easy and maybe the only thing that made her happy. But that didn't mean I wanted to support her if she changed her mind that being married to me wasn't what she wanted for the rest of her life. That was something I never worried about with Benny. She was humble and gracious and even declined the settlement I'd offered her. She didn't even know how much it was for; she just didn't want it.

In the time we'd been together, I learned what Benny truly desired in life was stability and happiness, something money could help with but certainly couldn't buy. I trusted Benny. I'd gotten to know her in intimate ways I'd never let myself experience with another woman. And that was why I had planned to help her financially despite her refusal. Without her encouragement and guidance, I wasn't sure I would have become the success I was today. She'd loved me when to most the world, I was a nobody.

"Something tells me I shouldn't wait around until I get new paperwork to sign. If you and I are really forever, we shouldn't even need a prenup," she argued with an empty threat. She was going to marry me no matter what, but if she could throw one last tantrum about it, she'd do it to test me. This subject, however, I was quite firm on. It was a waste of both our times for her to keep rehashing it.

"Anna, don't be so dramatic." And at that, she swung her long, blond locks to face me. The aggression in her eyes, a pent-up collection of reasons I'd angered her, turned her pretty face into something horrific.

"Dramatic?!" I'm being dramatic?! Olli, you embarrassed me on my wedding day. My entire family came from Gothenburg to be here and witness what was to be the happiest day of my life. Most of my friends don't have the luxury of taking another weekend trip to attend a second ceremony. Do you know how bad this made me look? Not to mention your irresponsibility. As much as you've managed to bring up your ex in past conversations, you never once made me question that your relationship was anything but over."

"It is over," I assured her. I wasn't easily frustrated, but the topic of my marriage began to prove that this was becoming a sensitive subject for me. "It wasn't over enough to stop her from coming back in your life to sign the documents. Why does she need to come all this way anyway? Why couldn't you have just faxed them? It makes me feel like you don't even want to get married to me. All this trouble you're going through to pull out the red carpet for your ex."

At this stage, there was just no getting through to her, so instead, I let her vent as she packed a few of her other things, planning to go home with her family until everything was finalized. How dare she accuse me of not wanting to marry her? Would I be going through all of this trouble and her dramatics to expedite everything if that hadn't been my plan?

It was definitely her fire I'd always been attracted to, but even she took it to the point where I felt like shutting her down and drowning her out. I didn't know how to talk to her when she was like this. Truthfully, she wouldn't take the time to listen even if I tried, so when she walked out, duffle bag in hand, I let her go. It would be easier to talk to her once all this mess was resolved, and with no reason to whine, she'd conform to being the trophy who just wanted to be the rich Finn's wife. I personally couldn't wait to fly her friends and family back to Sweden. While we got along on the surface, I wasn't their biggest fan, and I'm certain they weren't mine. Her family had a tendency to burn through assets, and I was sure what I'd overheard her and her mother talking about at the church was more or less her family being in need of the only thing they called her for. Money.

I wasn't angry about it but I'd make damn sure that once the two of us were married, all the unnecessary loans would come to an end. If I made Anna chose herself over her family, she was predictable in always choosing herself. Perhaps a few days of peace was what I needed while this all brushed over.

With Anna out of the way, I decided to ring Benny again when I received a second text from my assistant about the details of her trip. I wasn't sure why I was nervous to call her again, but her voice always did something to me. When she picked up on the second ring, this time, I assumed she was expecting my call, which was good. My assistant Sanni wanted to finalize her itinerary as soon as possible.

"Hello, Olli." My stomach was in knots at the sound of my name leaving her sweet lips.

"Hi," I replied in a slightly delayed reaction. I was still recovering from what it was like just to hear her smooth as honey voice again. To think I'd almost forgotten it. I wished I didn't have to forget it ever again. The calm, soothing influence it had on my recent mood was becoming evident that it was good for my soul.

"I mean, Hello, Benny. It's me again. I hope I'm not calling too much but given the time-sensitive matter, the plan is to get you on a flight at your earliest convenience. Does tomorrow work for you? The last-minute, first-class flights are quickly booking up, so knowing sooner is better than later."

"Wow, tomorrow?" she started. "That's so sudden. I knew the ticket was open, but I didn't know you wanted me to fly as soon as tomorrow. Would it be too much trouble to fly out on Friday instead? I'd really like the extra day to sort my stuff out and make sure I don't forget anything. I haven't traveled in a while, so I just want to make sure I don't run into any problems."

It was growing harder to hear her over what sounded like her entering a public place where more voices could be heard in the background. A child's excitement, an announcement being made over an intercom. It sounded like she was inside a department store. She was probably shopping. What else explained all the noise on her end? Sanni texted me the detailed confirmation of an early am flight on Friday, which I passed on to Benny while I still had her on the line.

"So we've booked your flight. Would you like for me to email or fax you the confirmation so you can print out the boarding passes, or would it be easier for you to pick them up at the airport?"

"It might save me some time to print out the tickets. If that's not a problem."

"Of course, it isn't," I reassured her. "Would there be an issue with you flying out on Sunday? I didn't see the point of you coming all the way to Helsinki for just one night of signing divorce papers. Besides, it'll give you a chance to meet my fiancé and if we have time, we could all have a nice dinner." The silence from Benny made me think that the line went dead, but then she responded with a genuine "I'd love to". That made me feel a bit better about what I was getting myself into.

Perhaps it was selfish but it meant a lot to me what Benny thought. If she liked Anna that would be reason enough to not have any doubts about the current woman of my life. She had always been a great judge of character. I only hoped she saw and experienced the Anna that was on her best behavior.

"Hey, remember that time our flight got canceled when we spent the weekend in London?" she said, snapping me back to reality and easing me into what could have possibly been one of my fondest memories with her. After making a huge deal out of the inconvenience the airline caused us, they'd put us up in one of the few rooms they'd had available at the nearby hotel, which happened to be a very romantic, very expensive honeymoon suite that at the time, neither one of us would have ever been able to afford. I'd lost how many times we'd made love in a single night after a spontaneous round of play time. But the way she made me feel that night had confirmed that I wanted to marry her. So strong yet so delicate. I've yet to meet a woman who made me want to fight by her side but at the same time take care of her. How could I ever forget a weekend like that?

"I do," I said finally. She let out a low, sweet laugh. "Well, that was my last real memory of flying. Since we returned to the States, my traveling has been minimal." She released an anxious sigh. "Ugh, I'm nervous."

"Don't be nervous." The thought brought a slight smile to my face. "But be sure to dress warmly. We are in our dark winter season. It won't be a walk in the park for someone who lives in sunny California," I teased. During her time in my native Finland, she was always in denial of how cold it was until we stepped outside. She'd always seemed to find her way into my arms to shield herself from the cold. She'd never not managed to feel good in my arms, I recalled, as I cleared my throat at the discomfort I felt for hoping I'd get one last chance to experience that. Even if we could find a way to become friends at this current stage of our lives, Benny's presence would continue to have lasting effects on me. Was it egotistical of me that I didn't want to lose that?

"Well. Olli, I don't want to take up too much of your time. I know you have a wedding to plan. If all goes well, I'll see you this weekend, okay?"

"Very well," I replied before we ended the call. This weekend couldn't get here soon enough.

❧ 6 ❧

Benny

I don't know how she always managed to do it. Be it witchcraft or voodoo or just plain guilt of being apart from the snap pea that grew inside me, but Olivia always seemed to break my heart any time I had to be away from her for more than a day. It wasn't often I made the choice to do so, but even three days would feel like forever when your only reason for living was going to be thousands of miles, an ocean, and dozens of countries away. She loved spending time with my mom, her abuelita, but she was at that age where she rarely wanted to leave my side. When I could, I took her everywhere but unfortunately, this was one of those times I couldn't, and the sadness on her face as we drove to my mom's made me consider canceling the trip altogether.

But I knew I couldn't. I needed to go. Not for just him but for me. I needed this closure to fully move on from the fantasy of reuniting with my first love. I often daydreamed there was going to be this point in our relationship where we would just pick up where we left off. A small part of me held onto that idea for so long I was afraid to admit it was what made dating again a lot harder. I suppose I'd let being Olivia's mother become my number-one priority.

Becoming a mother had shaped my identity. I loved my daughter and I felt like children deserved most of your time because they needed that secure feeling of being loved and cared for. Unfortunately, underneath that identity, I was still a woman with her own needs. I still carried the fantasy of being held and protected. Coming home to a bed filled with a man who cherished my body and filled the void in my heart that even motherhood may never offer me. Ending my marriage with Olli could help bring me one step closer to moving on in my love life, just as it appeared he had, and perhaps when Olivia got older, I'd be able to find someone who would be all the things I asked for. I couldn't do that chasing the dream of reuniting with the first man who made me feel truly alive. Yes, I *needed* to sign those papers—like yesterday, but that didn't make leaving my daughter to do so any easier.

"Preciosa, I promise. I won't be having any fun without you. If I could bring you, I would, but it's not that sort of trip. I won't be doing any sightseeing. All I'll have record of, maybe, is seeing the inside of a hotel. If that." I shrugged as I pulled into my mom's apartment driveway. She didn't have to know the exact details of my trip, but if all went well, perhaps Olli could soon know of Olivia's existence. I'd planned to tell him if the time was ever right. For a long time, Olivia had always been curious about her father, but I was so relieved when she stopped asking about him. If his fiancé was as understanding as I knew him to be, telling him would be simple. But if she wasn't, I never had to worry about him randomly popping in and out of my life. Sure, she had the right to know her father, but people changed over the years, and I wanted to be sure it was safe to introduce her to people, even the man who helped create her, into her life. She didn't understand things quite like an adult did, but she was bright and perceptive; she at least knew how to detect toxic behavior.

"Aren't you looking forward to spending time with tu abuelita? You always used to like going over there before you got a phone." With doe eyes, she peered at me.

"I still liking going over Abuelita's house; it's just she always takes my phone and makes me read all those old Spanish classics with words I don't know. She says the reason I don't speak Spanish well is because I don't try, but I don't want to speak Spanish. Literally, everyone at my school wants to learn Korean."

I rolled my eyes, feigning sympathy. My daughter hadn't known the mother I'd been privileged to grow up with. The woman who longed to be educated. The woman who left her life in Central Africa in a time where her homeland's government was so corrupt that to give her only daughter a better life, she relocated to Spain to clean houses, only to start all over again when I was five when we moved to make our permanent home in the US.

My mother didn't have the pleasure of knowing how to read and write, so when she learned, she consumed anything, devoured everything in her native Spanish she could get her hands on. In addition to working multiple jobs in the span of my lifetime, she exhausted all her efforts to come up with ways for me to be able to go to college without the burden of me having to take up a part-time job to help pay for it. African mothers were selfless in that way. Always trying to shield their children from the problems in their own lives. I knew in a way I'd inherited that burden. The last thing I ever wanted was to worry my child with the news of me being laid off. The less she knew, the happier she was. It was her laughter and joy that made me feel like if I worked hard enough, everything would just work out without her ever knowing there was a problem to begin with.

"Nena. It's good to read sometimes and get your attention away from that phone. All you do is play games on it anyway. It makes tu abuelita happy to see you take interest in something she wasn't afforded when she was your age. Can you imagine what it would be like if you couldn't go to school every day, mi amor?"

Her wide eyes grew the size of silver dollars at the idea of thinking not going to school meant you stayed home all day and did whatever you wanted. I was sure the mischievous grin forming on her face would falter knowing that in Equatorial Guinea, where both of my parents were originally from, it only meant you started working earlier. Grew up sooner. Experienced life harder. This little girl had a hard enough time understanding the importance of making her bed every morning. Sometimes it was hard explaining to her that the sacrifices women made for you in the past, made things easier for you in the future.

It was hard teaching the younger generation that what your elders taught you were lessons you wouldn't learn any place else. It was something I didn't even appreciate until my grandparents passed. I wished I'd gotten more time to spend with them, and I know that was my mother's greatest regret in not sending me back home enough. When the money was there, we tried to visit both Spain and Equatorial Guinea, but with my mother's health worsening each day, I limited the travel I did to just me and my daughter. Besides a few distant relatives in Equatorial Guinea, we didn't have much family there anyway, but it didn't mean I wasn't interested in showing Olivia where we'd both come from. My daughter and I were all my mom had at this point.

"You'll understand when you're older but spending time with Abuelita is something you'll look back on and appreciate that you did. Swear to me that you'll mind her," I pleaded. My mom had the spirit to be around children but not always the energy.

"Plus, I'm sure if you ask nicely, she'll make you her famous Nkate cake." At the suggestion, her toothy grin took up half of her face knowing her favorite snack of all time could be within reach. The thing with Olivia was that she had no problem getting what she wanted from adults. All she had to do was flash that adorable smile of hers and like that, she could convince the Queen of England to adopt her.

When we got out of the car, I was greeted with my smaller-framed, spitting image at the hilt of her door, waiting for us. We shared the same deep, dark skin and I was fortunate to be blessed with her striking cat-shaped eyes and model-like cheekbones. I used to hate the full lips I'd inherited from her but it was those same lips that garnered me my first compliment ever from the first boy I had my heart set on. From then on, I learned to love the skin I was in; in hindsight my mother was my first example of beauty. If she hadn't been five inches shorter than me, we could've passed for sisters.

She lived in Baldwin Park, a place she decided would be easier for her to navigate since her Spanish was that of a native, making it easier for her to find a job and blend in. Many of the Mexican and Central Americans assumed that we were from The Dominican Republic, only to find out we weren't Caribbean at all but instead African. I loved the history lesson all our neighbors received on how my mom's little speck on the map became the first and only Spanish-speaking country on the African continent. It was a loud neighborhood, sketchy and definitely a place where I couldn't see raising my daughter in a permanent setting. But for me, it was home.

"Mama, como está usted?" I asked which she then followed by asking me the same question in her Equatoguinean Spanish. Olivia proceeded to greet my mom in the same manner, but with the limited phrases she knew how to say. I'd wanted to get around to teaching her conversational Spanish, but where we lived and where she went to school, she had no desire to learn. No one spoke it to her but me and although she was only seven I still had faith that she was attentive enough to learn when I was ready to school her. For now, it served as a way for my mom and me to communicate without her worrying about adult problems.

"María Bendición, estoy bien, mi hija. Especially now that my favorite person is here." She kneeled down to Olivia as she flew into her arms. Sure, my mom wasn't as young as she used to be, but in the presence of my daughter, I often forgot. Upon entering her home, I was reminded of both Catholic and Central African traditions that made up the mélange of my identities. As Olivia rushed to the kitchen, our conversation in Spanish ensured we could speak privately without the little one asking us any questions.

"So does the Finn know or are you still going to keep him in the dark? You of all people should know what it's like to grow up fatherless. You would think he'd want to know his own child."

I rolled my eyes at her comparing my situation to Olivia's, which wasn't the same at all. My father knew about me and just didn't want to give up his freedom of being responsible for someone other than himself. He had no desire to travel the world or was even curious to know me. Olivia was different. I'd gotten pregnant with him at a time I'd thought Olli and I were over. His discovering I was with child would have only forced him to stay in the US where he was miserable. I wasn't trying to keep Olli any more than he was trying to be kept. In the short time we were married, he didn't talk about wanting kids right away, nor did we discuss what would change if we decided to family plan. No, we rushed into things so fast that we'd both discovered that first love didn't always mean last love.

We were both trying to move on. A baby would have only forced him to stay in an unhappy situation. I loved him but I loved my unborn baby more. Olivia was my choice, even knowing I'd end up being a single mom due to my decision not to tell him.

"Ma, you know that my dilemma is much different than my daughter's. I'll tell him if the moment presents itself, but if it doesn't, Olivia can seek him out when she's older. I'm not going to force fatherhood on a man who's about fly me out to divorce me just so he can marry another woman. My child doesn't need that sort of rejection."

My mom gestured for me to bend down on the sofa. There were often times when I appreciated her advice, but sometimes I just wanted her to take me in her arms and comfort me without chastising the decisions I made for my life.

"M'ija, I know you see yourself as strong, but there's nothing stronger than the effect a man's promise could have over you. Even if you don't tell him about Olivia, just don't go over there falling in love again. I guarantee you, the second time you won't recover from it. To fall in love at this stage of your life, you have the tendency to think of everything with finality. I remember for months, he was all you talked about because you were so happy. I don't want him to be the reason why, for months, you talk about how heartbroken he's made you. Sign the papers. Let him marry this other girl but don't let him be the one to break you again. Men like that tend to bulldoze whatever they have to get their way and don't care who they end up tearing down in the process."

As much as I hated to admit it, my mother was right. I was headed to Finland for one simple task with an even tougher truth to carry. He had the power to still captivate me, but I had to stay strong and not give in to the words or the promises from the past we shared together. The man was getting married for goodness sake. What more reason did I need not to fall victim to the feelings we had for each other for what seemed like a lifetime ago?

Then(Eight Years Ago)

Sweat lined my perfectly powdered forehead as I entered the restaurant where I was set to meet my potential partner. In the two years I've frequented my birth country of Spain, I'd used the service twice and was pleased with the screening process provided to seek out a kinky playmate as I lived out my fantasies before I returned home to the real world. The usual lifestyle sites were a mess to keep up with while you were living in another country, and the free ones were just full of horny dudes who often weren't true, what I liked to call "lifestyle junkies". All they wanted was rough sex without the ins and outs of providing a true sub like me what she needed to flourish in a relationship. I longed for order and discipline but I also loved Doms who were thoughtful and romantic.Which was why it was good to make friends in the community; otherwise, this kinky matchmaker service would have completely gone over my head.

Mistress Alice, an insanely beautiful and ageless French woman, had been a Dominant for over forty-five years, and I'd met her at a gathering over three years ago in Las Vegas. After an enlightening exchange, she learned of my plans to travel once I graduated from school and told me to link up with her if I ever came back to Europe. Time passed and things got hectic to the point where I'd almost forgot about my dear friend Mistress Alice until I was in search of something that helped keep my mind off of the loneliness I felt from being away from home. I learned that she along with another good friend in the European community, had started a matchmaking service with the promise to match the right kinks to the right people.

My first ever Dominant in Europe was from Barcelona and while we fit on a kink level, he didn't mention having more than one sub, which I expressed early on that I wasn't okay with. My second, a native of Madrid, like me, was my perfect Dom in a kink sense but he was unemotionally available to me. That was something I needed being so far away from my only family. I needed to feel loved and secure or at least for the rest of my time here. Long distance relationships rarely ever worked out, so I was prepared to rev up for an intense relationship only to have to break up at the end of my last few months here, a time that was quickly approaching. What I wasn't primed for was the six-foot-four Finnish import Olli Pekka Touminen, who unknowingly planned to rock my world and have me altering my entire life plan.

He sat there, drink to his lips, waiting for me. We hadn't been given much about each other's descriptions outside of the distinguishing red roses we'd been asked by Mistress Alice to wear. I chose to wear mine in my thick mass of curls, feeling it would take away from my winter white wrap dress that highlighted the best parts of my womanly body. My small waist, feminine hips, and what I considered my long legs until the moment Olli became aware of me approaching our table, stood and towered over me with his overpowering Nordic frame.

A moss green button-down layered over a white tee shirt hugged his naturally built form; the red rose clipped to his front pocket making him easier to spot in a crowded restaurant. But it was his eyes that made me feel like a poor, little bunny getting its leg caught in a bear claw. He had these wide, arctic green eyes that anyone could get lost in, and although he didn't greet me with a smile, he came around to pull out my chair after confirming I was his date for the night. His eyes studied me in an almost hawkish manner before I finally broke the first thirty seconds of silence with my first question.

"Do I have something on my face? You're just staring at me," I added with a breathy laugh. Not that I minded. The way he looked at me, a girl could get used to it. His face was charming and undeniably masculine. Sharp lines made up his cheeks and jawline; however, his lips were pouty and unusually full. At first glance, he could have been described as odd-looking, but to me, I'd found that to be the most striking thing about him.

"My apologies, it's just...you're much prettier than Mistress described you." At that, I didn't know whether to laugh or take offense. Just how did Mistress Alice describe me? Maybe I wasn't the standard of European beauty, but I set my own standard of what I thought to be beautiful. I didn't compare myself to other women because the only competition I had at this point was me and only me. "Okay, I'm curious as to how she described me," I asked, attempting to lighten the mood.

He took another sip of his nearly devoured drink. "She told me that you weren't my usual type of girl," he started in heavily accented English, "but that I would like you anyway. I thought that it would mean that I wouldn't find you attractive."

"And do you? Find me attractive?" I asked with a coy smile curving at the right side of my lips.

"Yes. Overwhelmingly so. In fact, when you first walked in, I silently prayed that you weren't Benny. In my experience with American women, I'm rarely ever their type. I'm not loud or flashy, and those seem to be the most common traits that women from the US like the most. If I'm offending you, please, don't be afraid to let me know." Mistress Alice was right about one thing. He wasn't the best with words, but I adored his honesty and sincerity. Plus, I liked the strong, silent type, just as long as he was able to communicate his wants and needs to me.

"Did she tell you that I was Black?" He scooted in closer to the table when the waiter came to ask if we were ready to order. In my mother's native flair, I placed our orders. That seemed to ease Olli's anxiety with his limited knowledge of the language.

"She didn't but it wouldn't have made much of a difference to me if I'd known. I told her that I was interested in meeting women in the kink scene of different cultures, being that I'm not in my home country. All I wanted was someone who spoke English as well as I did since my Spanish could use some practice. She informed me of a girl she knew was born in Madrid but who was naturalized in the States and spoke perfect English. As long as she thought we'd be a good fit for each other, I trusted her opinion." Well, that was a relief. Periodically you had your fetish-obsessed white guy who had a thing for black pussy, especially in Spain where the average Spaniard mistook a Black woman for a prostitute. It calmed my concerns that he didn't have a "thing" for darker skinned women but rather openness to diversifying his attraction.

"She mentioned you studying business?"

He nodded. "Yes, at UC3M in their master's program."

"Interesting."

He shrugged. "Ehh, maybe," he dismissed, sounding not too impressed with himself. At this point, I assumed he was just being bashful so I took took the opportunity to call him out on it.

"Listen, Olli, you don't have to be shy with me. I don't bite, but I do expect *you* to," I said with a flirty wink that finally got a smile out of him for the first time since I sat down. He had a beautiful smile, actually. Two rows of the straightest, whitest teeth I'd seen on a European. They weren't as mouth obsessed as Americans, but you would have never known it seeing Olli's smile.

"Benny, I apologize. I promise I'm never this nervous. It's just being in a foreign country and one of my first experiences being set up by a matchmaker looking for..." he hesitated, "what it is I'm looking for. Getting to know you as a person is just as important to me as getting to know you in a kinky sense. I feel I am doing a poor job at the former," he admitted as he went to scratch his nose.

"You're doing fine, and it is okay to ask me personal questions."

"Are you married?" At twenty-four, the last thing I was thinking about was being someone's wife, but it didn't mean I wasn't open to it. I learned that he was also completely single and had no children from any previous relationships. A plus for me.

"What kind of relationship are you looking for? A playmate? A friend with benefits? Something more serious?" The waitress dropped off our plates as I cut into my chicken and popped a piece into my mouth before I answered his question.

"I guess I'm open to all that you've mentioned, but the truth is I'd love a relationship that was headed into something more serious."

"Why?" he asked as the simplicity of the question took me by surprise. "Why am I looking for something more serious?" I felt my eyebrows cinch.

"Yes." His pale, sage eyes studied my reaction.

"Well, because I like playtime, sex, trust, and comfort to come from one source. My last relationship remained pretty vanilla as he wasn't interested in exploring that side with me, and in my most recent D/s relationship, there was just a lot of dishonesty that made me wished I'd asked more questions upfront. Monogamy isn't for everyone, but even in a kinky relationship, it's what a woman like me prefers. I require a lot of attention. I'm not sure if that turns you off or not."

Again, he rewarded me with another barely there smile. "No. It's more or less the answer that helped me decide that I'd like to go out a second time with you if that's okay? Perhaps dinner at my flat? I'm not the best cook, but you can learn a lot from someone from the way their food comes out. With patience, even the worst cook can make a decent meal.

We can talk more of our specific relationship preferences then, but for now, I'd settle for your favorite musical genre."

Now

I think I'm going to be sick. The flight into Helsinki landed six minutes ago and despite being in first class, I'd let nearly every person in coach stalk by me until there wasn't a single person left on this damn airplane. Had I been this bad on my stop in NYC? Maybe, but I definitely wasn't hyperventilating like I was now since I landed in Finland. Now that I was here, I didn't think I could handle seeing him. If I was even *ready* to see him. But when the second flight attendant in a five-minute span approached me, asking if I was alright, I knew I couldn't stay on this plane forever.

"Would you like for me call someone for you ma'am? The plane landed and has been emptied minutes ago. I'm afraid you can't stay as we need to prepare everything for the next flight. I however don't want to overlook that something may be of concern," she soothed in her heavily accented Finnish accent. The Finnish weren't what I considered to be a particularly friendly people, but they did have a lot of love in their hearts, which she demonstrated so thoughtfully just now.

"Can I ring up friends or family you might be staying with during your stay here?"

At the suggestion, I stood up and thanked her for her concern as I grabbed my small luggage from the overheard compartment, where she then directed me toward the station's terminal. I'd been to this airport twice before, the first time in the spring just after Olli and I eloped; the second, only a few months after when the weather was reminiscent of what it was now; dark, wet, and wintry. I heeded Olli's advice and packed a warm, thick jacket and long Janes to wear underneath my clothes in case shit got real. I'd only brought two changes of clothes, three if I counted what I had on, along with another pair of boots that I should have been wearing in place of the trendy, thigh-high ones I was wearing right now.

Could I fight the urge to want to look cute? It wasn't like we were getting back together or anything, but that didn't mean I couldn't look my best knowing for sure he's probably looking his. First class flights didn't come cheap, so I prepared myself to say goodbye to the Olli I'd remembered. I followed the destination signs around the airport as it led me to the area of newly landed passengers meeting up with their families. I half-expected Olli would send his lawyer or some other person in his place to pick me up to avoid what could have been a painfully awkward reunion. But that's when I saw him.

Leaning against a wall, he lowered his fingers from his mouth and stood to his full height, and in that moment, I was sure he saw me, too. From his slicked back, perfectly trimmed hair to his sleek charcoal grey, tailored suit, the proof was there. My soon-to-be ex-husband had changed.

The young, hopeless boy I'd fallen in love with had managed to transition into the man I'd always known he was destined to become. He was mythical; he was magical, and there was no secret that he was different now. The way his light green eyes regarded me the closer I approached him was breaking down the last few shields I'd spent convincing myself to put up during my connecting flight here. But it was his next gesture, his signature, barely there smile, that had demolished my final wall. I would be breaking that promise I made to my mother.

Whether I liked it or not, I was going to fall in love with him.

All over...again.

❦ 7 ❦

Olli

"Did you have a pleasant flight?" was all I could manage to muster while I took in the full effect of her otherworldly beauty. If it hadn't been for the extra weight she carried in her legs and rear end, I would have said she looked exactly the same after not seeing her for nearly a decade. Her skin, to this day, had always been my favorite shade of brown, a warm, deep espresso that calmed me on even my bleakest of days.

"Honestly, it was long. If I never get on a plane again, it would be too soon." She smiled that sweet smile that used to give me butterflies—that still gave me butterflies. She'd taken my advice to dress warm. These winter months were some of the worst it could get, and being the California girl that she was, Finnish weather had never been kind to her.

"You look good, Benny. Although, I'm not sure about your hair," I teased, remembering a time when she'd chosen to wear it in the large mass of coils and curls that I'd immediately fallen in love with. Her hair now hung across her shoulders in thick, dark, long waves that made her blend into a crowd of naturally straight-haired people. It was sexy in its own unique way, but her hair in its natural state had always played a large role in my instant attraction to her. Despite that, she still was the remarkably beautiful girl I'd found myself smitten with and now, I couldn't help but wonder if it wasn't just her hair that had changed. What else about her was different?

"It's not permanent. Nothing a little water and conditioner can't fix. Do you really not like it, though?" She stroked her hair with newfound insecurity. "I figured it might be easier for me since my last visit this time of year. I could barely manage to find a hat to fit over it."

"It's fine, Benny. I only tease. It's just new to me, that's all. Are hugs not in order after over eight years apart?" She smiled, laying her only bag on the terminal's floor as I took her medium frame into my arms. The rich scent of her perfume, a hint of freshly bloomed hyacinths with a dash of the sweet stickiness of honey, engulfed me, causing me to pull her in even closer. This feeling. I wasn't sure anything else would ever come close to this feeling. The comfort of having a soul so strong yet so vulnerable, trust me with the honor of being her Dominant. Her protector. Her lover. If there was anything I was ashamed to admit, it was that she still had this uncontrollable effect on my temperament. I only wished we were reuniting under less challenging circumstances. That was just the way fate worked, I suppose.

"It's good to see you," I honestly admitted, placing a light kiss on her forehead. The slight whimper that escaped her lips sent a tinge to my cock that strained painfully against the constraints of my tailored slacks. To the outside world, we looked like a pair of lovebirds reuniting after a short stint of business trips. If only the case wasn't that we were coming together for the sake of severing our ties to one another, so that I could marry the current woman in my life. I hoped in my heart that she'd at least found someone worthy of her and that she was leaving here to return to a promising, healthy relationship back home. After all, Benny had deserved the best the universe could offer.

"Here, let me get your bag." We detached ourselves from the embrace as I tried not to appear apprehensive in letting her go. Her bag was light in my hand, and even though she insisted she could carry it, the suggestion was lost on my stubborn ears. She may be my future ex-wife, but that didn't mean I had to suddenly stop taking care of her.

"So, the documents are back at my place. It's also where you'll be staying while you're here. I suppose I should have made sure that was alright with you first."

"It's alright, Olli. You know I don't know much about the geography here, so I really appreciate you letting me stay with you instead of a hotel," she stated warmly. It was one of the things that had drawn me to her in the first place. She was humble and gracious. Instead of complaining of the things she didn't like or couldn't control, she chose to make the best of a less-than-desirable situation. That was more than I could say for myself and definitely more than I could say for Anna. I really did hope the two women got along. Perhaps it didn't make much of a difference if I ever got Benny's blessing to marry another, but her opinion was something I valued more than my own business partners. She was the one to convince me to follow my passion and learn more about investing. It's not difficult to surmise how well that decision panned out for me.

My driver will meet us at the departures exit. Will you come with me?" With a kind smile, she nodded as I walked with carefully shorter strides so she could keep up in her sky-high boots. Did I mention how stimulating it was to see her boots sensually hugging her lower thighs? It was a wonder how she'd managed to find boots that were comfortable and flattering to her curvier limbs. In a better time, I would've had the pleasure of ordering her to my flat in nothing but a long coat and those seductive boots highlighting her gorgeous, deeply toned legs, but now, I was only left to my imagination, which wasn't the ideal situation given the now fully erect member locked away in my trousers. It was rare when I ever fantasized about another woman; why am I starting now?

Together, we navigated through the anxious families and exhausted airline workers to the departures gate to meet my waiting driver. Thankfully my town car was parked close to the arrivals entrance, so the walk outside was no more than a few steps. My driver Jaako signaled if I needed any help, but with only one bag, it didn't make much sense for him to get out, so I insisted I could handle it. The loud crunching of snow mixed with ice followed us with every step as I instinctively took her hand to ensure she didn't slip. Her winter layers have garnered an "A" for effort, but the heels were perhaps *not* the smartest choice for someone not equipped like a native to handle the hurried gusts the wind carried.

Taking my time, I helped her inside, assuring her that her bag wouldn't be far as I rounded the car to secure it and its contents in the trunk of the car. Upon doing so a small, beaded bracelet spilled out of one of the extended zipper compartments. Dark blue and white beads adorned a retractable string, the letters O-l-i written across in small accented lettering. It had been so long, I had to ask myself if I remembered her buying it for me at one of those flea market bazaars we regularly visited ever during our unplanned trips to Barcelona. It was sweet but if I couldn't remember it, I wouldn't have wanted to disappoint her should she ask me about it. I also didn't want to be accused of going through her things. When she questioned if everything was alright from upfront, I took my phone out pretending to be immersed in an important text message exchange as the bracelet went back into its compartment.

"Is everything good?" she asked again, her perfectly sculpted eyebrows etching in concern as I climbed in next to her on the left side. "Everything's fine. It was just my lawyer texting me to let me know the rest of the agreements I asked him to draw up are on my fax machine at home." At that confession, I sensed a bit of tension form at the pit of my stomach. Wherever this car led, and whenever it arrived there, we were becoming one step closer to being Olli and Bendición, man and ex-wife. Out of each other's lives for another decade, maybe even forever if we were unlucky.

I didn't like this discomfort between us, this distance. If there was something I could suggest to prolong seeing her smile again, I would've given anything.

"Ugh, where are my manners? It's obvious you just engaged in a series of long flights to be here; would you like to accompany me for a late lunch or early dinner? I'm sure you must be starving."

She flipped her long hair over her shoulders, directing her mysterious, deep brown eyes hidden behind thick beautiful lashes at me. "Now that you ask, do you know if they still serve that hot chocolate I was addicted to at that cute little café you used to take me to?"

It had been the only place I could afford to faithfully take her while we were on a strict budget in midst of my job searching. Personally, I was just grateful that she loved that little hole in the wall eatery. It was lovely but surely wasn't anything special besides their steamed drinks and pastries. Here I was, fully prepared to splurge on a five-star restaurant, and all her heart desired was a cup of hot cocoa. She never failed to surprise me with her humility.

"Yes, I believe they do. Are you sure that's all you want? If you remember, places out here don't deliver food just anywhere like they do in the States. Once we make it back to my place, you'll be subject to whatever's availably stocked."

"That's okay," she replied with an adorable squeal. "I just really want that chocolate, and I ate a few sandwiches that I packed before I got here. I'm more thirsty than I am hungry." Her expression was dripping in happiness. I admit it also brought a small smile to my face. Very few could disarm me like Benny could. The muscles in my face were even beginning to hurt.

"Fine. Then cocoa it is." In Finnish, I directed my driver to make a brief stop at the café. Hell, now even I was thirsty for a cup. I wasn't in a rush to sign the papers just yet. I ached for just one more memory we could share together as husband and wife, for old time's sake.

❧ 8 ❧

Benny
Tantalizing hints of cocoa soothed my olfactory senses, yet also sent my taste buds on edge. The candied aroma of bittersweet chocolate cooled to where it was finally safe to drink, and I was surprised that for not having it for years that it was just as good as I remembered it. It was one of the first things I didn't have to *train* myself to like.

One of the best things about exploring other cultures, at times, was also the hardest things about them, too. Different cultures uniquely interpreted cuisine like desserts, staple foods, and many other things that weren't necessarily wrong; it just took a while getting used to their gateway to it. For a country as cold as Finland in its winter days, I figured it wouldn't be too difficult to find a good cup of hot chocolate.

Helsinki was known for many good things, but I learned quickly that many of the offerings in coffee shops proved that hot chocolate wasn't their specialty. Past attempts at finding the perfect cup found the liquid to cream ratio unbalanced, as if it'd just been pure chocolate syrup poured into warm milk.

The place was small, and their prices were reasonable, and the hot chocolate was just as sweet as it was hot, and creamy enough to satisfy my expectations of it.

There had even been a spooned version of the aromatic treat that I wish I had tried in the past but hadn't even worked the courage eight years after. The traditional cup was so good, how could I try something else?

Melted memories and ghosts from the past that were brought on by the warming drink made sitting across from Olli difficult. I could recall us walking there when our beginnings were humble, sharing kisses between sips, something he claimed to never do in public before me. Wanting to appeal to my cultural norms, he stripped himself of his inhibitions. While he'd been as stern and as stoic as a Finnish man could be, I provoked a different side to him he didn't know he possessed.

Oftentimes, I'd forget just how much he appeased to the submissive side of me, just to be the type of Dominant I needed, let alone boyfriend then later, husband. Despite being a struggling grad student, he'd managed to make most of my dreams come true, and I couldn't stand that a sip of hot cocoa was forcing these memories to resurface.

❦

THE RIDE TO OLLI'S LUXURY HOME HAD BEEN QUIET AND peaceful. I think I would've liked if we had talked more, but I definitely appreciated observing the ambience created by the light snowfall that couldn't be matched by any winter back home in the States. Living in California, I can't say I missed the harsh winters in Helsinki, but I always regretted Olivia never getting to see a diverse four-season change that wasn't manmade.

Olli's driver parked in the open driveway as a man came out to take the luggage out of the car. Olli must've been doing better for himself than he led on. It was strange to see he employed this many people for things he was capable of doing himself. His door opened, and he snaked out, allowing me a chance to gather my things without the fear of his eyes burning holes through me. The time spent alone had only been brief; it wasn't long before he opened my door and gestured me to exit the same way. "Adam will take your things. I will help you inside."

I almost didn't take it, but I'd understood why Olli had offered to walk me from the car to the steps of his home. When I was roughing it like any native Finn, I'd been prepared for a little snow. Or in Finland's case, *a lot* of snow. In my haste, I hadn't realized the boots I'd worn from the plane ride, nor would any of the sneakers I brought, be as safe or compatible during such a dramatic weather change.

Olli's help, step-by-step in the snow, was much appreciated. Without his assistance, I would have probably fallen. Once we reached the front door, he let me walk ahead of him but made sure I knew he was close behind. He'd come a long way from the studio apartment we shared in the past as evident by the clean yet opulent style of the house he silently led me through. It wasn't flashy or overt, but it managed to reflect his worth.

I was about to congratulate him on his perceived success when we reached a hallway in his home that made my heart skip. Framed sets of lockets, various trinkets or low-level antiques were built into the walls, but this didn't surprise me; since we started dating, Olli had shared his love of antique collecting. He didn't collect them for any sense of value but he'd always had a preference for specific diverse items with historical significance.

He loved to collect stamps, junk or any form of ornament from different countries in the same way some liked to collect coins or currency from all over the world. In his own little way, he'd found that all countries advertised their distinctiveness and history through their antiques. Admitting that interest, he was sure he would bore me, but I actually found it quite cultured to find your own way to connect to the world around you.

There were pieces from all over the world. Bhutan. Israel.

Singapore. Canada. Ghana. All proof of places he'd visited. I nearly stopped to look at one but didn't want to bring attention to myself. So, to say it caught me off guard would have been an understatement.

Even though I'd been born in Spain, with branches that stemmed from the U.S., my roots had been planted long before I was born in Equatorial Guinea. Olli had always found it interesting how intersectional my culture, its mother language, and all the places I'd called home were. But most of all, he held a personal interest in my mother's country of origin.

I'd managed to get my hands on a book of stamps my mother kept around as old keepsakes and had her send them to me, hoping that despite being tight on cash, he'd appreciate the belated birthday gift. Olli almost cried. That was huge for him, considering he wasn't one to show his emotions so openly. Later on, he admitted to feeling as if a gift catered to a personal interest he'd already had, in addition to it being a part of me, my culture, that it had been one of the best gifts I could have given him.

"Come to the kitchen. I'm sure they're waiting for you." Olli spoke with an air of confidence that definitely hadn't hinted at what he'd meant by it. He led me to a modern, sleek, minimalist kitchen, and it wasn't until then that it all made sense. "I know you want one. Do not pretend as if you don't," he teased with a soft smile.

It had taken me no less than one hundred failed attempts, but what stood before me on the table was no other than Omenalörtsy. I'd loved and devoured the stewed apple-filled pastry long before I could say the damn word. He remembered. It'd been so long ago, but Olli would prepare them every night so that I'd have what I referred to as the Finnish donut, even though it wasn't like any American—or African pastry for that matter— that I'd ever had.

"Well...if you insist," As I wasn't about to pretend I had the self-control to resist a single one. I went for the one with the most powdered sugar. Finnish desserts were modest in comparison, so I know if he'd had them prepared, he had me in mind when they were made. I took a bite and I swear I was seconds away from swallowing my tongue. The sweet taste brought back so many memories; it made me wonder why I'd left in the first place. It was enough to make my blood slightly warm. Why was everything trying to remind me to stay, knowing this trip was meant to be a one-time thing?

Olli eyed me with the same stoic-like enjoyment he displayed in the past; he was expressive but not as much as I was used to living in the States, so I could tell by his almost smile that he got just as much pleasure remembering how much I'd liked them as I did actually eating them. It was stares like the one he gave me that got us into a lot of trouble in the first place. The look in his eyes forced me to keep mine in the opposite direction to avoid getting lost in them.

The moment wouldn't have lasted long even if I had. A woman I'd never seen before stalked into the room. Deep down, I knew who she was—I could've asked, but I don't think I had to when the tall, leggy blond walked into the kitchen, without looking in my direction before she asked, "Is it done yet?"

❦ 9 ❦

Olli

"What is wrong with you?" I asked Anna disapprovingly in Swedish. Having spent most of my primary education learning the language, in addition to the time I've been forced to spend in Stockholm based on business, the conversational Swedish I had acquired was never judged among peers and especially not Anna, given that my Swedish was better than her Finnish.

"What's wrong with me?" Anna's tone tried but failed at hiding the venom behind each spoken and unspoken word to come. "What's wrong with me is that *she's* still here—"

"What's wrong with me is that *you're* still here." My response was a meager attempt at holding her accountable for her deplorable behavior. Benny was sitting *right* there. Surely Anna would have found it as equally rude if Benny decided to speak to me in the only mother tongue we both understand but respectfully wouldn't have done such a thing. It was as if Anna had wanted things to be cold and awkward. Benny dropped everything to be here for *our* benefit. The least Anna could do was give the same respect she required.

"I'm not going to let some foreigner make me feel like a burden in my own home." She chuckled unpleasantly, wearing a fake smile to hide behind her native language used to speak maliciously about our guest. "Pastries. Accommodations. Why not just make her feel right at home and fuck her? You already defend more than you—"

I'd held in my frustration until now, but Anna's demeanor forced me to put my foot down. I grabbed both of her shoulders, trying my damnedest not to show the full extent of my anger. "I defend her because she is my wife! While she is here, if your plan is to be my next one, you will show her respect or leave."

Anna's eyes narrowed resentfully, challenging my unwavering stance. Never in our four years together had I seen her be so spiteful and petty. I almost felt sorry for her. It would be a few hours before I realized how it must've sounded to say those things, but Benny was here. She'd agreed to sign the papers; what more did Anna want?

I could sense the tension Benny felt through her mannerisms. She ate her pastry in uncomfortable silence as Anna stormed off, and I secretly assumed she'd hoped that conversation hadn't been about her. I'm sure she was relieved she couldn't understand us; at least she could feign ignorance that we argued about pre-wedding jitters. If she did, she would be wrong.

The last thing I wanted to do was make Benny feel unwelcomed or regretful over her evanescent stay here, so I did all I could do is apologize for Anna's behavior. "I'm sure you have your suspicions about what we were—"

Benny wiped a smidge of powder from the corner of her heart-shaped lips. "It's none of my business either way," she interrupted. The moment was simple but made me see her warmth and kindness in the tiny gesture.

"It's just been...a rough couple of weeks," I admitted. "Anna has not been herself, and I'll own up to that. If it weren't for me, she wouldn't be treating your presence like an inconvenience. I can assure you she's angrier at me than this situation."

"You don't have to explain," Benny's attempted to smooth things over. "Her feelings are valid. Maybe I wouldn't go about it that way, but I'm sure I'd resent the person standing in her way of solidifying her future with you. You're a great catch. She has every right to hate me being here."

I hated how empathetic Benny was, even to her detriment. She could easily put herself in the headspace of another to justify their behavior. I was convinced she could see the best in the worst of humanity, so it shouldn't have surprised me she'd attempt to excuse Anna's anger.

Anna had a beautiful side, too. She wasn't all bad and I definitely wouldn't be marrying her if I hadn't seen that part of her. But it was hard not admiring Benny's heart in moments like this. She was probably making whoever she had back home extremely happy, and if she weren't attached, any man would be lucky to have her. I know I'd felt lucky when she choose me.

"Do you have them?" Benny stood, wearing a warm smile and fixed gaze. I almost didn't know what she was referring to before I realized she wasn't here on her own accord. The divorce papers had been in my study, but she was going to be here overnight, so I hadn't felt it necessary to throw them in her face as soon as we saw each other. She gave me time to retrieve them, choosing to keep them together in a manila folder.

I explained to her what she was signing as I directed her to each and every line she was required to sign. All twelve points in the legal document she signed without question, pushback, or a fight. Her main concerns only had to do with making my life easier, and I couldn't help but think that she deserved more than she'd asked for. At the very least, more than this.

Her having to drop everything to fly across the world, lose income, and then to have her turn down anything I'd offered to secure that her financial situation was as taken care of, just hadn't felt right. Not after the way Anna acted.

Benny slid the last of the documents across the table, toward me, refusing my gaze or direction as I placed them back in the rightful place.

"If you follow me, I can show you where you will be staying for the night so you can be well-rested before your flight tomorrow night."

❧ 10 ❧

Benny

With so many memories packed into one room, it was hard not to get a little nostalgic about the time I'd spent here when it was just a two-bedroom cottage. I was surprised I hadn't recognized it, but it had been close to ten years and my memory only stored the most important these days. I wouldn't have even known if Olli hadn't brought it to my attention this wasn't the first time I'd been at this location the new place stood.

Sure, the floor plan was different and the property had expanded but in ways, this room reminded me so much of the nursery I'd dreamed of turning it into when I discovered I was pregnant. The cream walls had a cozy if not calming effect on me, and the little decorations of our time spent at El Rastro, a popular flea market in Madrid, made our tiny house a home. The spring we'd spent here after we got married, I begged Olli to let me decorate when it was just a small cottage.

Now, he'd had the money to buy the land where our once tiny house stood, turning it into the manor it was today. But the colors, the furniture, and even the décor were still reminiscent of when this place was just ours.

My alarm went off, startling but reminding me of the time I set to check in on Olivia. Even though I'd only been gone for less than a day it felt like I was gone for a whole week. Yeah, yeah, yeah, I knew that my mom and Olivia were bonding, but I didn't want to risk the chance of calling at an inconvenient time because of the ten-hour time difference. Getting myself settled, I pulled up Olivia's cell phone number and hit dial. Maybe it was a little spoiled for a seven-year-old to have a mobile, but in this era, there were so many things that worried me in regards to her safety. Kids today had to worry about a dozen things we didn't worry about as children. I just liked being able to reach her at any time. Especially times like this when I was away.

Instead of the standard phone call, I opted for video because I missed the sight of my baby's face. Although we were reuniting in a day or two, I never got tired of seeing that adorable face.

"Hello?" She picked up on the fifth ring, easing my frustration but with laughter I wasn't quite expecting since the moment I left she went on about how she couldn't go one day without me. With how happy she looked, it hadn't even seemed like she missed me, which only made me miss the munchkin more. I had to say, though, I really loved the relationship she had with my mother. I only hoped that one day she could have that same closeness with her father.

"Hey, Mami. Look what Abuelita helped me make?" She held up a poorly constructed sock-like mitten that made me laugh out loud since clearly, some steps had been skipped due to its questionable construction. My mom had learned to knit in the States and was somewhat an expert at it. Whatever she'd taught to Olivia had clearly gone over her head.

"Well, isn't that *lovely*," I lied. "When are you going to make another one for your other hand?"

Her round face met me with furrowed brows and a loveable smirk. "It's not for me; it's for you. And it's not a glove. It's a hat. See!" Her angelic smile shined as she put it over her thick head of loose curls. Well, I be damned. It was a hat. And here I was thinking it was a glove with the extra compartment she crafted that seemed more fit for a thumb. When I got back, the first thing I'd help her work on was her stitching.

"Abuelita says you're freezing you butt off in...umm where did you call it, Abuelita?"

"Finlandia," I heard my mom say in her heavy Equatoguinean accent off-screen.

"Finlandia? Ohhh...Is that where The Little Mermaid lives?" she asked with an unmeasurable amount of joy. A vein of anger popped up out of nowhere, knowing that my mom had mentioned to Olivia the exact place I was traveling. It wasn't as if it was a secret, but I wanted to be the one to tell her myself, should I get the chance to tell my ex about the daughter he fathered. The girl was smart, probably too smart for her own good, so I knew she'd be able to put two and two together about why I was here if I had been more vocal about her father's Finnish background.

Yes, my mother and I would have a later, more *private,* talk when Olivia was tucked away in the bed, but for now, at least she was having an easy time without me while I was away.

"Te extrano, m'ija," I cooed, trying not to tear up like a baby.

"I miss you too, Mami. When are you coming back again?"

It had occurred to me while Olivia had inherited my eye color; her eyes looked nearly identical to Olli's. Whatever love I saw in his eyes, I saw in her eyes, and the thought of that made me hopeful that he would feel the same way about her if he only got a chance to know her.

"Mami, I have to go. Abuelita's making that caramel sauce I like to pour over ice cream. See you when you get back." The call disconnected as the screen went idle. If there were ever a time I got over emotional, it was when I couldn't tuck my daughter in at night. It wasn't a question to whether I'd get a good night's sleep in Olli and Anna's queen-sized, luxury guest room bed but with

Olivia fresh in my thoughts and considering that the time difference had totally thrown me off, I knew that a quick sleep was just not in the cards. It couldn't hurt to check the kitchen to see if the house had its collection of sleep-inducing teas. Chamomile was my first choice, but even in desperate times a decaf black with a splash of lemon was quick to calm nerves. I couldn't be picky; after all, I was a guest and not the lady of the house.

Changing out of my traveling attire, I slipped into a casual sweater and a dark wash of skin-tight jeggings that fit seamlessly under the thick knitted socks I pulled up to my lower calves. Although the heat was turned all the way up, the floors had a tendency to feel chilly and quickly spread to other body parts when you weren't wearing something on your feet. As I ventured the layout of this beautiful home, I couldn't help but feel a tad resentful that I couldn't give Olivia this sort of worriless life. Chances were, to be able to, I would have to find a job more catered to my degree and move us to an entirely new city.

Part of the reason I liked being a ski instructor was because the job was flexible and it gave me the time and freedom to both work and be there for Olivia when she needed me. If I took a job teaching at a private school, I knew most likely I'd have to schedule time to see my own daughter, and I couldn't see putting other kids above my own.

I believed that all would work out if I kept my head on straight and didn't give in to worrying, but I would likely have to take Olivia away from all her friends and transfer her to public school if I wanted a way to successfully fall back on my feet in the meantime.

From outside one of the kitchen windows, I could see the storm beginning to fall in heavy blankets of white snow, thankful that I could barely feel the weather worsening with the fine design of Finnish insulation and heating. Despite its inconvenience, there wasn't a winter more breathtaking to look at than a snowy Finnish background. It looked right out of a page of a

Christmas story. It almost had me tempted to break out my holiday playlist. I would have loved for Olivia to see a winter this grand. For a girl who loved the snow, she would have been completely taken by this scenery. I could already picture her taking it upon herself to build the world's biggest snowman or to show her father what a great skier she was.

I ran into some luck when I opened one of the kitchen's many cabinets and stumbled upon a wide collection worth of teas. Sleep would be within my or, at least, I thought it would be. The second I turned around to turn on the stove's burner, Olli's fiancé, Anna appeared from what seemed out of nowhere. I mean, it was possible to be friends with your ex-husband's new wife, right? For my sake, I hoped it was since when I finally found the courage to tell Olli about Olivia, Anna would be part of his packaged deal and for the sake of daughter, I hoped we would get along.

The moment she opened her mouth, though, it became pretty clear to me that was going to be more than just a wish on my behalf; it was going to be a challenge.

"I have my assumptions about you but please tell me. What game are you playing? Because Olli sees you as the patron saint of wives, and I don't see what's so special about you besides that you're clearly a pushover. He says you didn't ask for *anything*. What I want to know is *why not?*"

At this point, Olli's fiancée was just getting on my nerves. It was bad enough the moment I arrived she'd made it clear she wasn't happy with me being here but now, I couldn't even turn down his money without her feeling like it was some strategic plan to make Olli change essential aspects of his current life just because I was back in the picture. What about me leaving the picture was so hard to comprehend? What part of me being gone by Sunday did she not understand?

After the weekend, I'd no longer be her problem, and she could have the outlandish wedding and honeymoon Olli and I never had. I didn't even need for him to give me the wedding most women dreamed about. Every day, for months, he'd managed to make me feel like royalty and although he didn't have the money he appeared to have now, he never failed to support or take care of me in the ways I'd felt necessary at the time. She was getting everything she wanted, and me? Well, I was leaving with less than I came with in that. She, on the otherhand would have my former husband. Did she not see that the real winner was her in this scenario? She had the perfect looks, the perfect life, and the minute I signed those papers, she'd have the perfect man all to herself for the rest of her life. Comparing our situations, I had nothing except a broken heart from setting the love of my life free so that he could be happy.

"Let me get this straight?" You think I'm a pushover because I refused the money he offered me? I didn't take the money because I don't *need* for him to support me. Especially not after knowing if I had, it would have most likely caused more problems between the two of you."

"So, you did it for me?" she asked with an amused laugh, and I swear I wanted to knock that sneer right off her face.

"No, I didn't do it for you. I did it for Olli. Whether it pains you to acknowledge it or not, Olli had a past before you, and I was an important part of it. I knew the things that bothered him. Affected him. And I don't want to cause him any more pain by upsetting you. This wedge between the two of us is, for sure, stressing him out. Probably more than it's stressing you."

I couldn't explain the look she gave me just then, but one thing was clear. She didn't like me, and she had no problem letting me know it.

"How about you worry about yourself and that child you spoke with on the phone, and I'll worry about Olli. It's obvious you have other obligations in your life that serve a higher purpose than planning a reunion with a man you married when you were both children— "

And in that second, I had no idea what came over me, but I

just lost it. Bringing my child into this was just uncalled for and petty, not to mention intrusive for listening in on my phone calls. Here I was thinking we could be civil like adults and friendly toward each other. There was no competition between us; by default, she was the winner.

The last thing I was going to let her do was discuss my daughter as if she had any inkling of what my life was like outside of her narrow scope of me. Feelings for Olli or not, that wasn't going to fly.

"Okay, first off, keep your comments to yourself about my daughter." I closed in on her, not intimidated by her towering five inches over me. "I get that you don't care for me being here, but that's something you should have communicated with your fiancé. When he contacted me, I was under the impression there would be no animosity between us. If I was as petty as you are, I wouldn't have even signed the papers."

"So, why did you?"

I was beginning to realize this woman just wanted to see to it that she had the power to break me. That she had the access to influence Olli's very last thoughts of me. If I went off on her, she'd only paint me as bitter, angry and jealous. My love for Olli meant I didn't want him to remember me as someone who'd held him back from what he wanted for himself. I hadn't done it eight years ago, and I wasn't about to start today, but she had to know in this situation; there was no endgame with me. No hidden tricks. No plans to crash their wedding with declarations that I loved him. The reason why I'd signed the papers was really just that simple.

"Because my love for him runs deeper than my dislike of you. When you care about someone as much as I care about Olli, all you want for them is their happiness. If that's what you are to him, then who am I to stand in the way of that in this stage of his life?" The way she looked at me with such disdain and confusion in her eyes had clued me in on one major flaw. She just didn't get it. She didn't understand how you could love someone so sincerely that their needs were just as important as your own. Sacrifice. If this was the woman he'd deemed as his one true love, I loved him enough to fully support that.

"I knew you still loved him. I knew the second you laid eyes on him that the feeling had never left."

"And what if I do?" By now, I was screaming at the stop of my lungs, my arms spread out to my sides. "I only came here to finalize our divorce so that you could marry him. What more do you want from me?" I ran my fingers through my thick hair, hair I was afraid would become frizzy if I didn't wrap it soon. My fingers massaged my temples as I sensed an oncoming migraine.

"He's yours," I said in less than a whisper. "He's fucking yours."

Silenced by my declaration, Anna only stared at me, pity mixed with satisfaction in her cryptic blue eyes. If there was anything for her to say, she didn't even bother saying it. What was there left to say when the person you were running the race against conceded and acknowledged defeat. Only it wasn't really defeat but an acceptance of a harsh reality. I was ready to get this woman out my life, even if it meant Olivia never knowing her father. Someone who could be that spiteful and disgusting was not someone I wanted around my daughter. The decision was made. I wasn't going to tell him of the child we'd made together. At this point, all I wanted to do was go home and see my baby.

"I wish you and Olli the best," I said as I surrendered to my quarters, hanging my head down with no other plans other than to cry myself to sleep.

Olli

It wasn't until the weight of the mattress gave in that I realized Anna hadn't been in bed. I'd always been a heavy sleeper, but something told me in that moment, nothing good came from her restlessness. I was about to ignore her, but I didn't trust that she hadn't been up to something as the clock confirmed how late it was in the evening.

"Why are you still awake?" I rubbed the crust from the corners of one eye, noticing she hadn't looked the least bit tired, nor had she looked like she'd attempted to sleep at all. "It's after three in the morning."

In a hushed tone meant for no one else but me, she went off in Swedish, forcing me to pay attention. "Another woman is in my home. Do you expect me to be happy with this?" She shuffled around as if her goal was to make me as uncomfortable as Benny's presence appeared to have made her. She was supposed to be back home with her family but she couldn't leave with the thought of Benny being here. I knew that last outburst from her had been merely for show. "I can barely keep my eyes closed, let alone sleep."

I fought the sudden compulsion to defend myself about Benny one last time considering it'd likely make the situation worse if I brought up the fact this had been my home before it had ever been hers. It'd also be best not to mention that until our divorce was finalized, by law, this was just as much Benny's home than anyone's. Most of the interior design and layout of the custom-built home had been made with Benny in mind, despite never assuming we'd reconnect or that she'd actually live in it.

Anna didn't deserve to feel self-conscious about our relationship, so I decided to keep that information to myself. I had one job and that was to make her feel secure in our union and future. I'd have to diffuse the situation for now. "I'm sorry what I said to you earlier. It was not my intention to be so harsh. I'd just thought you were being unreasonable and unnecessarily unkind to Benny considering the situation."

"Thank you for the un-apology. I happen to think I handled the situation well considering she still loves you." She crossed her arms as if she hadn't been satisfied that I disagreed with her.

I unconsciously rolled my eyes as I finally gave her the attention she wanted. "Anna, what are you talking about?"

Anna was busy jumping to conclusions in her own head—talking out loud but not necessarily to me. "I knew there had to be a reason she wouldn't take your money. She all but admitted it when I walked right up to that foolish face and told her stay away from you—"

Now, I was upset, far past annoyed. "Do you ever stop to hear yourself?!" Anna tried to whisper over me, but I would not be deterred now that I was awake and forced to face her envy. "Benny has been nothing but sweet and kind since she got here. She didn't accept my settlement offer; she flew out on a moment's notice to sign the divorce documents. What more would you have her do? Grovel at your feet?"

Anna's eyes narrowed into those signature slits that let me know she's mentally conceded but wouldn't dare voice her defeat.

"You paint her out to be this saint." Her resentment seeped into the air, making the spot we lay in toxic. She was frustrated; I wanted to spend whatever time I had on this earth making her feel confident again, but before then I had to admit I'd been legally married to someone else. Until this was over, I had to deal with the side of Anna that was a bully and naturally intimidating. I didn't expect her to be dainty, feminine, and quiet all the time, but I certainly felt times like this made me question whether I could deal with this for the rest of my life.

"I do not paint her any special kind of way."

"You do, though. All while ignoring the fact she's been busy in the time you've known her. Do you know she has a kid?" Her mouth continued to move, but the words *kid* and *she* in the same sentence froze time and put me in a mind warp. She was talking, but I heard not a single word. Had Benny really become a mother in this time we hadn't seen each other?

Worlds apart, there was this entire life created without me, and still, Anna was threatened by her presence. For all we knew, she could've had her own life, seeking this divorce as much as Anna was. I meant, as much as *we* were. The last of her ramblings had encompassed wondering how a woman could leave her child 5000 miles from home just to make lovesick eyes at the man she'd used to be married to, and honestly I wouldn't have even heard that if the knock at our bedroom door didn't put me on alert.

It wasn't a common thing in our home to have strangers knock on our bedroom door, so it could either be my butler Adam or Benny. I only had staff in the home three to four times a week when I would host company for business venture dinners or well-planned family gatherings. Adam lived in his own quarters on the property, and Aida, the housekeeper who didn't live on the premises, wouldn't start her shift for another four hours. I got up to open the door to find Adam on the other end, appropriately dressed for slumber but alert nonetheless.

"Mr. Tuominen. You asked me to inform you if anything of

interest happened in the next few hours?" He almost asked as a question.

"Yes, what is it?"

Adam kept his calm, despite his voice cracking to reveal he was seemingly nervous about what he were about to say. "Your guest, Mr. Tuominen. She asks that she leave immediately. I'm afraid she will not take no for an answer."

I didn't dare turn my head in Anna's direction in fear she'd be wearing a wicked smirk that read how pleased she was how her plan to get rid of Benny was working out. She must've loved this.

"Give me one moment." I reached for my slippers and robe to make myself presentable. "I will try and talk to her.

❧ 12 ❧

Benny

I don't know what came over me. One minute, I was moments away from crying and the next, I was packing my bags with no real intention but to get the fuck out of here. What was I thinking, believing I could stay here the whole weekend without feeling some kind of resentment? Anna had made it clear that she thought I was on some game to keep in Olli's good graces, when in reality, she'd felt threatened by my presence. I couldn't stay another second in this house and subject myself to her mistreatment of me, so I decided that I would just do them both a favor by leaving immediately.

With the papers signed, there was no other reason for me to be here. As of this moment, I was ready to go back home and face the problems that awaited me head on. Anything was better than staying another night in this house with my now ex-husband and his soon-to-be wife. What peeved me the most about the situation was that she didn't realize just how good she had it. So focused on the negative, she didn't see that she was marrying a man who truly devoted himself to you and exhausted all efforts to take care of the woman he was with. She didn't see that he wasn't going to be some husband where everything you did for him went unnoticed or unrewarded.

With Olli, she would be his true equal, just as I'd been when he'd become my husband eight years ago. She was going to have the life with him that I never had, yet she still managed to treat me as if I were going to swoop in and steal her man. I was so done with this place, and I was especially done with her. If someone didn't get me to that airport soon, I was going to don a pair of skis and get there myself.

When the butler didn't return to the foyer after I informed him of my departure, I decided that if he wasn't going to make the man of the house aware of my sudden desire to leave, I was going to take it upon myself to arrange my own transportation to Helsinki Airport. There had to be transportation services that still operated in this weather; after all, snow like this wasn't exactly uncommon in this part of the country. People had to be prepared for it. Even if I had to pay a 100 EU surcharge, I was getting the hell out of this house.

App after app, I checked to see if there were any available driving services that were still taking clients, but with my luck, I got the same message with every single one that they weren't honoring service calls at this time because of the weather conditions. Just great.

A low, irritated sigh escaped my lips, the soft squeaking of my boots following me with every step I made on the reclaimed hardwood flooring. It wasn't until I saw the image of Olli's lanky, svelte frame making his way down the steps into the foyer that I actually began to calm down my raging emotions about being here.

His pale green eyes cast a hint of sleepiness with a brush of exhaustion from the obvious argument he had had not too long ago. I assumed it was bad since they chose Swedish and not Finnish to yell at each other, which in essence I was grateful for because I had no desire to understand them. In the time I'd spent in Finland, I'd taken the time to learn enough Finish to be conversational, but Swedish had no similarities to pick apart to understand. As far as their conversation went, it was between the two of them. If I could find any way out of here, I could leave them to handle their brand of dysfunction without any assistance from me.

"It has been brought to my attention that you'd like to leave," he stated as he leaned his wide spread arm against the wall closest to me.

"I didn't really want to bother you, but when Adam asked me why I had my bag packed, I figured it couldn't hurt to let you know that I've apparently worn out my welcome. I was actually trying to get in contact with transportation services. Are there any ones outside of Uber?"

"None that have licensed drivers on record. There are a lot of scammers who will take your money, especially if you are foreign and don't know any better. You're better off trusting the official ones only. Right now, I'm afraid that's not possible. People are not going to start plowing right away, so very rarely will someone risk their safety in a storm of this nature. Even if I could get you to the airport, there would no flights scheduled to go out at this time or in this weather." He crossed his arms, peering at me with genuine sympathy in his arctic green eyes. That made me feel a little better. It meant he didn't condone his fiancée's behavior, and I knew deep inside his heart he only wanted me to feel comfortable in his home. But I didn't feel comfortable, and while the airport wasn't an option for me tonight, it didn't mean that I wanted to stay here either.

"Bendición." The cadence of his Finnish accent said my Spanish name as if it were the sweetest song. "I apologize for Anna's behavior. Sometimes, she can be abrasive in a way that's uncharacteristic of her. If she made you feel unwelcome in any way, I want to remind you that you are *my* guest this weekend, not hers. You don't have to walk on eggshells and tiptoe around in fear of having an altercation. I wouldn't allow that. If you reconsider returning to your room, I'll see to it that Anna stays in her place for the remainder of your stay."

As nice as it was to hear those words leave his beautiful mouth, it wasn't exactly the news I wanted to hear. I rubbed my temples at the memory of her challenging me and in that moment, I decided the damage had already been done.

"Thanks, Olli; you don't know how much your words mean to me but even if there wasn't a chance I could get to an airport, staying someplace else tonight would really help me get a better night's rest. I'm homesick and being here knowing I'm adding unnecessary stress to you and your fiancée isn't making me feel any better about it."

"Is it because of your child?"

My eyebrows cinched, taken aback by his question. I'm sure his little fiancée told him about my daughter, but it wasn't really any of her business to mention anything about her to him. His doe eyes held my gaze, searching for something in mine that I wasn't entirely sure of. It was so intense that I had to look away, sensing if I'd given into him one more second, I would have been compelled to tell him the truth about Olivia. It was just better he didn't know. Our lives had been separate for so long, there was no need to make things more complicated now.

"Yes," I said finally. "I don't usually spend this much time away from her. This is the longest and furthest I've ever been away," I confessed. At my admission, he lifted my chin with the crook of his long, resilient finger, sending an ease down my spine at the feel of his intimate touch.

"I promise to get you back to your daughter as soon as time will allow. In the meantime, will you reconsider leaving? I want you here..." he hesitated, "with me," he murmured, barely audible. But it was for that very reason I didn't want to stay. Olli always had a way of making me feel like no other man could. Because he wasn't big on small talk, the seriousness of his words had a long-term effect on my thoughts and emotions. He never said things he didn't mean, so analyzing his last words were taking my mind to a labyrinth I wouldn't be able to find my way out of.

"I know you want me here. Believe me, I do, but I'm just not comfortable and the only way I'd be comfortable is if I were able to stay in a hotel or even a hostel for the rest of my stay here. Please, Olli." I resorted to begging. He loved/hated to see me beg, but it was the one thing that forced him to always give into my past demands. Running his fingers through his hair, his nostrils flared as he exhaled a deep, frustrated breathe.

"Would you consider staying in my parent's cabin? Maybe a hotel is closer, but I remember you loving it there. You'd have the place all to yourself, and I'd feel better you being there than a hotel. I'd even take you there myself." With a pitch like that, it was hard not to take him up on his offer. The thought occurred to me that going out his way to accommodate me was the exact reason his fiancée had been pissed in the first place. The last thing I needed was for her to think I was kidnapping the man. It was bad enough she knew I still had feelings for him.

"I don't want to cause any further issues between you and your fiancée. Despite what she believes, I respect her and her home."

"Just gather your things. Let me take care of Anna." He waved off my concern with a brush of his hand. And with that, he disappeared back onto the second floor, clearly annoyed and irritated with each step.

❧

OLLI

When I entered the bedroom, Anna sat on the bed, covers pulled up to her belly with a tablet and stylus pen cradled in her hand. She read a great deal at night, but the fact that she could behave as if she hadn't caused any trouble had internally infuriated me. She didn't look at me. In fact, she hardly even acknowledged me until she noticed the clothes in my hand that I'd grabbed from the walk-in closet. It was nothing incredibly fancy, but with a pair of heavy jeans and a thick, fitted thermal, I appeared to have gotten her attention as I stripped down to change into actual clothes.

"Olli, where are you going in this weather?" she asked, placing her reading glasses on the nightstand beside her, crawling closer to me when I sat on the bed to put my socks on.

"I plan to take Benny to my parents' cabin. For some *reason*, she feels unwelcome here. Care to elaborate why?" As I turned around to look at her, she gave me this spoiled little girl look, complete with an eye roll and a bratty cross of her arms.

"Can't you find someone else to take her? I'm not sure why she's pulling this little diva moment. I'm doing what you told me to do. I'm staying on this side of the house. Does she really insist on leaving?" I stood up, walking back to the closet to grab a pair of my favorite impenetrable winter boots, slipping them on one by one. Finally, I grabbed a hat and a wool scarf that would help keep the cold at bay. When I reentered the bedroom, her expression hardened as if she believed I'd back down. Foolish woman; by now she should've known I did what I wanted. A change in attitude wasn't going to change my mind.

"Anna, do not make a big deal of this, especially since you caused this to begin with. I wouldn't have to go anywhere if you hadn't done your usual meddling. She did us a favor by signing the divorce papers. All I asked of you was to be cordial to her, but even something as small as that proves to be difficult for you. So yes, I'm leaving to take her to a place where she can be by herself and not have to deal with all of our drama. You of all people have given her nothing but your ass to kiss. I thought you might actually be ecstatic to see her leave." She stood, walking over to me as her long, gentle fingers caressed the outline of my chest. She was trying to soften me up, and it usually worked but not tonight. She had to learn that her actions resulted in *consequences*.

"Can I at least come, baby?" A look of surprise cast across her expression when I took her wrist in my hand and jerked it away.

"No. You are to stay here. I'll be back as soon as I can." Without another word, I left the room and was thankful when she did as I instructed and didn't follow me.

IT HAD BEEN AGES SINCE I SHOVELED IN AN ACTUAL SNOW storm. I usually waited until the winds died down at a time like this. I didn't have to do an incredible job, just enough to unblock the garage door when I opened it. Once I got the driveway cleared, the one car I always took out in the snow was my reliable Nissan Qashqai. That car withstood any condition you threw at it, and it was the only vehicle I felt comfortable driving Benny all the way to my parent's cabin, where I knew the roads would be a lot worse. Although Adam had offered to help, I declined, wanting the solitude, fortunate for the time I had to myself to process what I was actually feeling these past few hours.

I'd gotten what I thought I wanted. For Benny to finalize our divorce so that I could make my life with Anna official as husband and wife. So, why was I secretly having regrets about taking Benny away from her life back in the States just to do this selfish thing for me while I caused her nothing but stress in return? Was it possible that being reunited with the first real woman I loved so intensely had me reevaluating my relationship with the current woman in my life?

Now, even thinking back to my proposal to Anna, it wasn't really a proposal at all. She picked out the ring. She made the announcement to all our family and friends. The only thing I did was show up and pay for everything. But with Benny, everything had unfolded organically. I'd cleaned out my savings to buy her a modest sized ring. Not because she didn't deserve more but because I promised myself when I could afford something grander, I would buy her the ring of her dreams.

Her last day in Spain, I'd come up with a dozen, maybe more, unusual ways to give her this unforgettable proposal, but we weren't even on speaking terms due to my insecurities. After all, she was honest with me on our first few dates that she hadn't planned to be in Europe forever, so I knew our epic love story would eventually come to an unfulfilling end. But it was at her apartment, seeing all her things cleared out, that an overpowering feeling came over me, knowing that if I didn't ask then, I was never going to know a love like hers. Her eyes welled with tears of never-ending joy when I'd dropped to one knee and asked her to be my wife. Little did I know that by her saying yes, she would leave an imprint on my life that would leave me forever altered.

Memories like that I didn't have with Anna. In the long run, it always had to be her way, even if it affected the thrill that went behind it. All I knew was that something died with me today when Benny made our divorce official. It meant that on the record, neither one of us belonged to each other. Free to align with others who fit our needs at the time. But what if who I needed had always and never stopped being Benny? The devastating truth was that from this day on, I may never know the answer to that question.

With one final shovel of snow, I tried the garage door, grateful that I was patient enough to wait to ease the snow fully off. Passing my two sedans, I pressed the automatic start key to my Nissan as moments later I was safe inside and pulling out to the front of the house. Thankfully, I didn't have to retrieve Benny as she was already walking towards the truck with her one bag. She helped herself inside before I could even get out and open the door for her. Shivering, she put on her seat belt as I offered to adjust the heat in her seat.

"Would you like for me to turn on the seat warmers?" She nodded with a soft "That would be great" as I gave her the option of choosing the ride's soundtrack from the vast selection satellite radio offered. I, for one, was a classic metal fan but when she settled on a mellow, old school rhythm and blues station, I didn't object, allowing the smooth sounds of a soulful singer transport me back to when times were simpler and she was my one and only. While a part of me was perfectly fine with sitting in silence, I predicted the ride to be a long one, given that I took the long roads for safety reasons. There wasn't a more perfect time to provide Benny with the apology I felt she deserved back at the house. Conversation hadn't always been my strongest suit but with her, the words had always been easy to flow as we'd established an effective form of communication that worked for the both of us. To this day, I haven't been able to open up to anyone with the same level of honesty as I had with my former love.

"Bendición, I want you to know that despite what's happened I truly appreciate what you've done for me. Now and even back then. I always hoped you and I would reunite under different circumstances, but I'm happy I got to see you again. Even if it doesn't mean the same for you, I'm grateful to have known you. You are and always will be Mi Bendición." My blessing. It only seemed fitting that her mother would give her a name that fully encompassed the role she'd take on in the world. Blessing everyone and everything she touched.

"Olli, I just want you to be happy. If you are, then I'm happy for you. You don't need to apologize for something we should've done years ago," she retorted. There was a possibility she didn't mean it the way it sounded, but it provoked a bout of silence from me the rest of the car ride. I didn't want to make things worse by making her feel any angrier than she felt. Perhaps, we'd be able to discuss things more in the morning should I get her to the airport on time, but until then I'd chosen to become mute, even as I reached the cabin and helped her bring her only bag inside.

I switched the lights on, relief coursing through me that the power was still up and running. Without hesitation, I turned up the heat, assuring her that it wouldn't be long for the space to warm up as I laid her bag on the couch with the promise that I'd start a fire before I left. Venturing the hallways for where I usually kept the wood and lighter fluid, I had come to a realization that I wholeheartedly missed this place. The coziness. The simplicity. Its quaint qualities all made me upset with myself that I didn't leave my city home often enough to enjoy this diamond in the rough I'd inherited from my parents. Given that the last real time I'd spent in this place was when Benny and I first moved back to Finland, I suppose it just brought back too many memories of the life I had before. I didn't think I wanted those memories back; turns out I did truthfully treasure the time we'd spent together in this little house.

When I returned to the living room, Benny had grabbed a few comforters from a nearby closet and cozied up inside them as she watched me pile all the logs necessary to keep a fire running long enough to hold her off until the morning. She always liked to watch me start a fire, especially since it was always something she saw on TV but didn't think people did in real life, being from an urban area. There were many upsides and new experiences to be had when your lover happened to be a Finn.

An abrupt shake of the ground caused us to lock each other's gazes at the revelation that an alarming event was happening outside. As I rushed to the door, my eyes darted to the snow-packed windows, telling me what I already knew before I tried the front door. I would not be going home to Anna anytime soon.

The snow had made a forceful fort around this—and what I assumed was every other door—that led to the outside of the house. We wouldn't be going anywhere. Not without the help of someone from the outside digging us out. We were officially snowed in.

$$\maltese \quad I3 \quad \maltese$$

Olli

Why did I believe it might be possible to avoid a Finnish snowstorm? Determination was one thing but possibility? I should've trusted my instincts and accepted that Anna wouldn't be satisfied no matter how or when Benny left. I was trying to be accommodating to both of them. Respectful of Anna's feelings while not making Benny feel like a burden. Our situation was far from a model one, but I hoped Anna—and I for that matter—could match just an eighth of an ounce of Benny's civility. I can see now that hope was naïve.

Now, all one could do was peer out the window and watch as my vehicle got nearly devoured by the snow. "This is a nightmare," Benny repeated to herself, wondering why neither of the events, of late, couldn't have waited until spring. This storm, my wedding; if I were being honest, Anna and I could've afforded to think things through more clearly.

I certainly loved her, and I was confident she wanted a life with me, but we were polar opposites. While I'd performed a healthy combination of ignoring/admiring all our subtle differences, there were things about her I didn't know, that she didn't know about me. We were compatible in the moment, but I had no idea how we'd fair sharing expenses, what we'd be like as parents. Hell—I didn't even know if she wanted to be a mother.

Was that a deal breaker for me? No. Not yet…Anna was still at that age where she could think about what she wanted to do with herself before cultural norms imposed what it thought she should be doing, unless she'd married well. Which is why she'd made it clear if I made no plans to marry her that I best not waste her time.

I wouldn't call it an ultimatum, more of a push to take her as seriously as she took our relationship. I couldn't think of many reasons why I shouldn't marry her. But were we the type of couple who fell maddeningly in love and couldn't bear to spend a second apart? No. We were both attractive people who benefitted more being together than being apart.

So what if I didn't long for her touch and she merely used moving in with me as a way to move out of her parents' home? Not every love had to be strictly romantic. We complimented each other in the ways that mattered, and well, turned a blind eye to the ways we weren't. Maybe, that's why she instantly hated Benny.

She could sense from the moment she witnessed Benny's presence around me that we'd once shared a bond like no other. Benny hadn't just been my lover; she'd been my submissive, too. It would've been difficult to recreate that if she weren't willing to learn about dominance and submission. It wasn't our intention to come off that way, but I was naturally protective of not just someone who'd been my best friend and companion, but also someone I'd nurtured and broken to build back up.

Even in normal settings, you didn't just forget that. I wasn't just born into existence the moment Anna and I had met. I'd been a fully recognized, whole and functioning human being. At times, it was almost as if Anna resented that I'd had a past before her, especially one so far than our relationship had taken us.

She'd made it clear the moment I brought it up that she'd under no circumstances do anything remotely close to submission. The truth was she didn't know anything about the delicious side about being someone's submissive. She just knew the stereotypes. I didn't push submission on her because she voiced that it didn't appeal to her much, and that turned me off more than the idea of her being a bad submissive. We had a service-level, *normal* relationship. We even communicated like most couples, meaning little to none at all.

I doubt I would even feel confident enough to voice issues that weren't overt. With Anna that's what she wanted, so that's what I gave her. I was exuding the version of masculinity she found acceptable. Emotionally withdrawn. Comfortably wealthy. Great in bed. So, why did I long for a time when I was more than just those things? Why did being confined within these walls make me feel truer to myself than I'd ever been?

Was it because *she* was here?

My first real love.

My Benny.

Then

"I've dealt with bratty submissives before. While we are on the subject, I'd like to bring up that bratty behavior brings out a natural aggression in me in a D/s scenario. I'd like to be upfront about that since we're addressing our personal tastes." The conversation naturally progressed into that subject as Benny and I were delving deeper into our courting stage of getting to know each other. We wanted to know each other's Dom/sub styles as well as what time of the day either of us were the most active.

We wanted to be on the same page with our schedules as the more time we had for each other, the more we could learn about each other's habits. No subject had been off limits, though the first two weeks of our courtship had been spent on the phone, nearly five times a week. I wanted to know everything about her, not just because I wanted to sound and look like her ideal Dominant—I wanted to *be* her ideal Dominant.

Being so would take compromise, something I resented people assuming Dominants weren't capable of. I was about combining our strengths and weaknesses, and negotiating the type of relationship that'd not only benefit both parties, but also naturally evolve as our romantic relationship did. "I can handle a little aggression most times, but I'd require more aftercare the more intense things get." She made sure to mention that before the subject had passed.

It had become a personal preference to play with a submissive who can, at times, take things a little rough. "If you have a threshold for certain impact activities, I'd prefer you use plain English communication. That way, everyone or everything is being communicated, even in a scene. I'm not against you breaking a scene to address a concern should you need to." I made sure to mention the time I'd played with a former submissive who didn't vocalize her concerns and agreed to only things I wanted to explore. Long story short, a sub who didn't communicate wasn't a submissive for me.

"So, when you mention impact, what toys do you use to play with?"

"I feel the most connected to my sub when I can use my hand to spank, but if the submissive requires more stimulation, a paddle or flogger is my impact toy of choice."

Exploring my deepest and darkest fantasies, I was far from a sadist. However, I did enjoy the behavior of a masochist. It felt like a gift that someone would take their punishment with grace.

Growing up in Finland had been vastly different than living in Spain or just dealing with American women in general.

I was taught to see women and men as equal to one another, so it'd been a difficult transition to navigate cultures that were the complete opposite and thrived off gender roles. Hypermasculinity was what most other countries celebrated, so while I wasn't that way in my vanilla life, it was a fantasy to explore it in my dominance.

"In the future, I'd enjoy the aspect of exploring consensual and non-consensual play. You would very much be in control but feel as though you're not. Would that be okay with you?"

"I would need examples."

Which meant she was open to the idea; she just wanted a short look into my head. I gave as many clear, concise examples of scenes I'd performed, had yet to perform, or had the most interest upon getting to perform with her. I'd only been a Dom for about three years, but I was already communicating with her better than I had with other subs.

"I don't want to spend all night on this subject, but just know I want to only take things as far as you allow while still receiving pleasure." I smiled. I wasn't the best at it, so I'm sure I looked dopey to a beautiful woman like Benny. She laughed, and I'm guessing was her shield against the awkward silence that followed my smile. "Shouldn't your pleasure be my pleasure?"

"Yes." My smile this time more confident. "But I intend to nurture you as much as I intend to punish you. You should know what I like, and if that works for you. But most of all, I want to know what you like, and what you respond positively to so I can make that work for me."

Now

"Anna, things are getting out of hand. Do you not trust me? Are you so devoid of faith in me that something as small as a snowstorm could tear us apart? How hard is it to see we're divorcing one another, so we can get married! What more can I do?"

"'What more can he do' he says," she replied as if she were saying it to anyone else but me. "You could've taken care of this weeks ago instead of waiting until the very last moment. If you were going to have me waiting for you, the least you could've done was take care of if through fax or email. But no. You didn't take any of those precautions because you knew deep down you wanted to see her. I suppose now you got your wish."

Anna continued in a heated rant about why I had no right lying to her about love when I couldn't admit my true feelings for Benny. Feelings for Benny? Of course, they were still there, but I hardly doubt they'd resurface in our relationship. Or at least they hadn't until now. "From the moment she stepped foot into this country, you've shown her nothing but concern you could never show for me. At least now I know fucking why."

I wasn't about to entertain the subject, but in my silence, she came to her own conclusion, the singular thought she'd been battling with since she'd known Benny was on her way here. "It's because you can't control me like you could her."

"So, that's what this is about—"

"Hasn't this always what it's always been about?" Her tone was defeated yet full of fire.

So, there we had it. The real reason fueling Anna's anger.

Would she believe me that it took great courage to even share that I'd had D/s courtships? Even in the vanilla relationships that followed Benny, I'd been able to admit my kink, even to an unwilling party. The more I dated vanilla women, the harder it became to be forthright about the lived experience as a Dom. I decided Anna would be the last woman I ever shared my past with unless I was willing to go through the courting process of finding another submissive.

Deep down, I knew I'd never look. I would never intentionally replace Benny and haven't until this day. I was loyal, vanilla or not. But in loving Anna, I was forced to endure her miseducation about the life, including the idea that a woman couldn't be independent, strong, and submissive as if all those terms were mutually exclusive.

I respected her choice to not be submissive, but I can't say the same about her feelings toward my need to dominate. Most my romantic life, post-Benny, was a little lacking because of it. Anna was the first woman I'd been in something tangible with for more than a few weeks. But she was still a woman confused at how her lovemaking skills hadn't cured me of my desires. She wanted to believe I'd never have something deeper than what we shared, but forcing me to consider what that was made me realize I'd never shared something as intensely as I shared with Benny.

"I don't know how many times you need me to say it, but I love you. Though times like this make me question it to begin with when you behave so childishly."

"You can't even say you love me without preconditions. You haven't been able to say a single disparaging thing about someone you claim is from the past but can't even just say you love me. My parents warned me that I was making a mistake falling for a Finn. But I didn't want to believe them."

"Now, I have to deal with them being right while you're stuck in the middle of nowhere, living out your wildest, most depraved sexual fantasies with that woman you married a million years ago. I don't think you could have planned it more perfectly."

Nothing I could have said would have convinced Anna, but I had to try. Not trying meant I had to admit there was truth to what she said. "Tell me what you want to do, Anna. What can I do to show you the kind of man I am?"

"You can't!" She said despite her fatigue. "If I'm being honest, I don't believe you want to. Why should I play second place while I have a field of men lining up to be with me? Consider what we have, what we had—finished. By the time you get back, every trace of me will be gone. As far as I'm concerned, that slut can have you." Without saying another word, she hung up on me.

I couldn't defend most of what she had had to say. I wasn't a perfect man, but I thought I had at least made her feel loved and cherished in the way she needed. But maybe I just hadn't known how to love her. I couldn't strip her down to her true self, so how could I really know her?

I was forced to self-reflect and figure out all the ways I'd gone wrong. Maybe I just didn't belong in a vanilla relationship. I hadn't wanted to be lonely, but I hadn't wanted to replace the bond I'd had with Benny. My fate as a lover, as a man, was doomed from the moment I'd tried to move on when I received separation papers.

Despite our distance, I'd had an unrealistic expectation that one day, maybe Benny and I might rekindle our flame. Having been her Dominant and she, my submissive, we'd fulfilled each other's needs in a way no other person could have understood, but a majority of our time spent together was quite vanilla. But she hadn't suppressed that side to me. It was free to come out whenever I needed it, and Benny welcomed it.

Knowing that, I couldn't help thinking Anna was right.

Then

"WHAT TYPE OF LANGUAGE HELPS GET YOU INTO SUB-SPACE?" A fair question to ask, so close to our planned scene. Benny's eyes danced, as I watched her eyes close, as her head tilted to the side to consider information. We were in our final stage. This was the last conversation we planned to have before our first scene, and while I didn't expect every single aspect to be covered until we'd exactly experienced the moment, we were sure to bring up every boundary we weren't meant to cross before our D/s relationship would occur.

"I know everyone is different." She blinked. "But some language makes it hard for me to let go. Context and trust are everything. There are some things I've let Doms call me that I'd never let another one refer to me. I prefer specific terms."

Plain English communication. Instead of asking her where I couldn't go, she wanted to know where I planned to. Sub-space was different for every submissive, but I knew for me, Dom-space was relatively easy to get into once I referenced certain terms of endearment, and whether my sub responded to them positively or not.

"How do you feel about being referred to as my little slut? Would that be an acceptable term of endearment?"

"How might you use it? The closest you could get without getting into Dom-space?" Her eyes were wide and curious and ever so soft and feminine.

"Rise to your feet." My voice stern and entitled. The intent wasn't to bark an order before we'd agreed to anything, but to showcase enough authority to give her context. "I'm not going to ask twice."

With that, she finally stood, and with a careful stagger, I closed in on her until I was an inch away from her face. "Do you really need that much direction? Am I going to have to teach you how to behave, until you're used and begging to be my little slut?" I gently stroked her neck, but even now I could tell she wanted more. The tone of the room had changed. I hadn't actually played with Benny yet, but the way her eyes glassed over, I was sure if she wasn't in her sub-space, she was at least close enough to where I could discover my own way of getting her there.

She exhaled a deep breath, biting her lower lip as I created a respectable distance between us. Benny was coming down from a high, and if I wasn't so respectful, I would've very well taken advantage. "How was that?"

Now

STARING OUT THE WINDOW WAS ABOUT THE ONLY THING I could do that didn't make me feel guilty about the recent turn of events. I not only struggled with how I'd made Anna feel, I regretted how I'd settled things in the past.

I should have fought for Benny. At least half as much as I had tried to fight for Anna to prove I wasn't still in love with my ex-wife. Current wife.

So much time had been lost. By now, our situation was broken. Where did we even go from here? The questions were easier to ask than the answers I would never get. Right now, I just wish I could forget.

"Care to indulge?"

Being stuck in my own head, I hadn't even realized Benny had wandered off. From the looks of it, her hands were full from my basement, as she'd found a home in my spirits collection and brought what could take the edge off. She didn't choose lightly either.

In Benny's hand, she held a bottle of Salmiakkikossu, a salty licorice commonly eaten in Finland, which we'd found a way to infuse in vodka and brandy. A decent choice that was sure to get me to a place of forgetting.

"Why not? We're stuck here," I said indifferently. "I'll go get the glasses—".

But she would have no such thing. Benny shook her head, insisting if I were really as tough as she remembered, I could handle it from the bottle instead. It was clear her memory of me was still sharp. Being a Finn in a foreign place, often the only way I could ever say more than a few words to someone I wasn't actively trying to Dom, always required a bit of liquid courage.

The more I grew confident in my relationship with Benny, the more I didn't need to down my weight in alcohol. But in times like this, I'd say it called for a change of heart. Benny took a gulp of the bottle she'd retrieved from the cellar, as she nearly choked on the fire the Finnish liqueur left in the back of her throat.

"Silly American. Salmiakki is for Finns," My attempt at dry humor. I took the bottle from her and did the same. It was harsh, but I could handle it in my broken state. The more I drank, the more comfortable I got with things that were on my mind. "I should probably slow down. I wouldn't want you to take advantage of me in my vulnerable state." Another attempt at a joke.

Benny just coughed through a laugh and asked, "What vulnerable state?"

I hadn't wanted to say things this soon, but with nothing else to talk about, I couldn't keep the news to myself long. Benny would find out anyway, right? Depending on how long it took to get help, surely she'd notice when Anna made no attempt to call me.

"I spoke with Anna earlier. From my understanding, our wedding is off."

Benny sensed I wasn't joking and tried to assure me it was all in my head. If only it were that simple.

"As far as she's concerned, our entire relationship is over. I really fucked up this time."

"I'm sure I had a lot to do with that—"

"Don't." I wasn't about to let her take the blame for our problems, no matter how convenient. "Anna and I had problems way before you came along. I didn't expect them to get better, but I wanted to make her happy. Every attempt was met with hostility —which I deserve. But calling off our wedding? Telling me our relationship was through. Call me a cynic, but a bigger part of me is just...relieved."

I didn't want to admit that, not to Benny. Making her feel like she'd caused my relationship to crumble was bad enough, but admitting I hadn't wanted to go through with it in the first place showed that all the work I'd made being a better partner in the years she'd known me had all gone to shit.

I wasn't a better man than when she'd known me and I was ashamed. The best parts of me she'd fallen in love with were now nearly non-existent. It didn't matter if she'd found another love, she still looked at me with loving eyes as if she had sympathy for me, sympathy what had happened between Anna and me. Thinking was becoming a problem for me. What I needed now, more than ever was more liqueur.

❧ I4 ❧

Benny

Ugh, my head was pounding. It'd been so long since I'd had anything stronger than a diet Coke that despite my strong will, I could barely open my eyes. If I didn't have a reason before now that I should slow down while I'm ahead, a hangover was definitely the sign I needed. Why did I think I could handle drinking with a Finn?

Of all the mistakes I've made over the years, of all my greatest regrets, even at my emotional worst, I'd never felt like this. Take a deep breath, Benny. Even though your head is as heavy as a boulder, you still have to open your eyes. Opening your eyes lead to sitting up. Sitting up lead to standing, and standing led you to rehydrating yourself so that you can walk this off. You got this.

I fought myself so much internally, I hadn't realized that in the physical world, something was off. My throbbing forehead hadn't let me feel anything until now, but now that I made myself conscious of my surroundings, the harder it'd been to get up without resistance.

Long, slender arms draped across my body, as a hand came

next to the back of my head, seemingly drawing me in close. My weight cemented Olli's body to the couch, as our legs tangled as if it belonged to a talented weaver.

Had I really been this drunk? To be so comfortable, to cross a boundary I hadn't meant to cross? It was bad enough after I'd come all the way out here, I'd become the boogeyman of Anna's nightmares. Now I lay here, in the arms of the only man I'd actually loved, giving her even more reasons to hate me further.

This made no sense. I wasn't that type of person. I couldn't have done more than get a little tipsy and fall asleep in a less than favorable position. We were still dressed; that was a good sign. But I had to untangle myself to investigate more. Make sure no more lines were broken.

I had managed to pull myself from Olli's embrace with just enough care so I didn't wake him. His face was angelic, pale and child-like as he slept through the shuffle. I couldn't help caressing and admiring that beautiful face before I'd completely pulled away.

It'd only been a few years, but he hadn't aged much aside from light crow's feet near his closed eyes. The weird thing was his oddly attractive features appeared more mainstream in his sleep. To remember what it was like waking up to that face every morning that put me in both a place of happiness and a place of remorse.

I had to put a healthy distance between me and that couch, just so I could stop thinking about him that way. My first thought was to check the first window that came into view, just to see if the weather had let up. Then I remember this is Finland. I shouldn't have been as surprised that not only had the snow not stop, it'd gotten worse since last night.

The only watch I'd had on me read 9:46, so I could only assume it was early in the morning. My plane was supposed to leave two and a half hours from now, but the snow didn't even look like it could be plowed in that small window of time, let alone get me to the airport. With weather like this, the flights were higher than likely canceled.

I was supposed to be leaving my marriage and Olli in my rearview. Out of his life for good. So why were all these strange occurrences happening?

"Urgh." The aggravated groan came from the couch I once lay, and behind it, Olli rubbed his head, standing to his full, intimidating six-foot-four inches.

"You okay?" I called out, as he ignored me and dragged his feet toward his kitchen. The wooden floors creaked, as 198 lbs. of him explored the room he'd found refuge in, and he didn't come out until he brought a jar of strange liquid with him. "I'm not as young as I used to be," he said in English after he'd just swore in Finnish.

"Take this for your hangover," He held the weird yet edible jar in my direction, expecting for me to take it.

With my best attempt at sounding as level headed as I appeared, I asked: "How would you know if I have a hangover?"

His virescent eyes blazed a deep green, as he put the jar in my hand as if no wasn't an option. "Benny, I am Finnish. If I have a hangover, then you have a hangover. I wouldn't be a Finn if I didn't have my own remedy for this type of thing."

If Olli had a remedy for a massive headache, who was I to refuse such a gift. I had ignored the pain for a minute or two, but if it could be gone in less time than I anticipated, I would drink anything to dull the pain. "The taste is off-putting at first, but if you drink it down with no breaks, it's easier."

The unknown jar of liquid hadn't had any particular odor, so I figured it wouldn't be as bad going down. One sip later, I had instantly regret not swallowing it in one gulp, as Olli had suggested. Sensation burned my ears, back of my throat, and hell —nearly all my sinuses, as Olli sat at the edge of the arm of his couch, watching in dull amusement. "You are so dramatic."

Relieved I had downed the last of it in record speed despite a bad first impression, I wiped my tears away and put the jar down. "I drank what tasted like an ogre's toenails, baby vomit, the blood of a virgin, with just a touch of lemon. I think I have the right to be dramatic."

"Well," His tone indifferent, his face as straightforward as I'd known it to be. "It is hard to find good ogre toenails." He ended with a smile that felt genuine despite the circumstance. "How do you feel?"

Despite the taste, the homemade hangover cure had worked within minutes. I wouldn't be surprised if the pain was completely gone by the hour. I gave a thumbs up but didn't speak, as I was still processing the unique tastes that made the cure come to be. "I'd be better if this weather hadn't wasted so much time. I'm supposed to be on a plane in two hours. What am I supposed to do?"

Olli shrugged, his back caving into the couch as his long legs dangled over the armrest. "Nothing." He broke the silence. "Why would you do anything on a day like this anyway? Unless..."

"What?" I asked, my mind trailing off to another train of thought.

Olli just smiled a cock-sure grin, patting his stomach as he recalled the past. "I remember times like this, the things we *used* to do. They fell between nothing and everything." As he asked whether I remembered stating I could never get used to the dramatic weather changes in Finland from Spain, or even the West Coast of the US.

We'd come a long way since Madrid. One minute we were feeling each other out, the next we were married, figuring out our next move. More times than I can count, we'd been stuck inside because of a winter storm, managing our time to challenge the boredom of not leaving the flat.

We'd always made good use of the time, though. Whether we were making hot chocolate, talking about our opposing childhoods, or making love in front of a fireplace, any moment spent was less than boring. "You can tell me if this is too much to bring up but, I can recall giving you the best orgasms of your life during times like this," Olli joked.

He wasn't wrong. He had given me the best orgasms I'd ever had in my life, and not just the time I had been with him. Most times, all we could do was fuck, sleep and eat. But the moment was still raw, I couldn't help but assume Olli joking so candidly was due to the phone call he'd received from Anna the night before. She had been angry, and I understood it. Out of respect, I didn't want to entertain anything that if I were in her situation, I wouldn't be comfortable with my fiancé joking with his ex about. "As much as I'd love to elaborate, I don't want to give your fiancée more ammunition to hate me."

"What fiancée? Last time we spoke, she wanted nothing to do with me. She all but told me to freeze to death in that little cabin of mine. As if I asked for any of it to happen."

"You don't think Anna was just speaking from a place of anger?" I asked. Maybe I wouldn't have reacted the way she might in the same situation, but her anger was just as valid as any woman dealing with her circumstances. "I'd certainly be upset if my future husband was putting me through the same thing."

Olli's eyes softened, and I would have sworn his eyes were smiling at me had anything else had changed about his facial expression. "One thing I've always known about Anna. When she says something, she means it. With her, there are no grey areas. She called off our engagement and she meant it. I think I've said it before, but I'm not distraught by the relationship ending."

He slumped over, catching the weight from his elbows onto his knees, not the least bit frustrated by the consequence of his confession. "I'm sorry to hear that. If I had known my presence would open up so many wounds, I would have just asked you to fax the documents and let you be on your way."

"Don't feel sorry for me. I asked you to come because of what you meant to—mean to me—that with all we been through, you deserved more than a letter in the mail. I've done my best to convince Anna your arrival wouldn't threaten our relationship, but clearly, you brought out an insecurity in Anna neither of us could have helped. That says more about her and less about how you've handled this situation."

Olli babbled on—something he never did, being a Finn—that how in their four years together, nothing he did ever seemed to satisfy her. Most times, he wasn't even sure why she had wanted to marry him outside of financial security.

"I'm sure you love her, though."

"I love things *about* her. It's clear that I am attracted to her." I sensed a slice of shame at what he was about to admit. "And there was never a reason not to marry her. She fit well into my life. Sex was good, maybe a bit vanilla for my tastes, but not every woman is adventurous." He eyed me with an intent that made me consider he'd likely compared his companions in kink to his vanilla lovers often, even if not intentionally so.

"I do care about her and what happens to her. Sometimes, I wish in the time we'd known each other that she would've shown herself more. Shown me that she can be vulnerable."

He sounded so unsure about his reasons for proposing to Anna, without thinking, I'd asked him why he'd asked to marry her in the first place.

"I asked Anna to marry me for a different reason than I'd asked you. You'll think I'm foolish for even admitting it."

"No, I won't," I argued. And I wouldn't. I could never see Olli as a fool.

"I asked her because she asked me to." The confession wasn't intense, but not as romantic as the reason any woman would have liked.

"So, why did you propose to me then?"

Olli locked his gaze to mine, and the need in his wide eyes appeared heavy and honest. "Because my fear of losing you outweighed my insecurities as a man who didn't feel worthy of you."

I remember the day we married one another like it was yesterday. I had always secretly hoped for a well-planned wedding, one meant to make me feel like a princess for a day. Neither one of us could have afforded such extravagance so early into our formative years in the workforce, but marrying the man of my dreams had made a simple justice of the peace ceremony just as special as any dream wedding.

It brought me to tears knowing Olli had loved me enough to not want to risk losing me. It hurt, even more, hearing it in the present. I wasn't sure how I had started, but as I was overcome with emotion, a cross between a sob and a laugh was the only coherent thing I could express.

My life had been far from perfect, but I'd managed to make myself whole again with the birth of Olivia. But coming back to Finland, I learned I was missing an essential piece of my puzzle.

I'd only returned so that Olli could remarry and move forward from a time we were carefree and in love. It hadn't mattered that I hadn't been completely over that time spent, but I wanted his happiness, and if that meant letting go of the idea of one day recreating a life with him, I was prepared to sign anything to make his life easier.

It was the closure I *needed*, but I wasn't so sure it was the closure I'd prayed for. I could move on as if it were even a possibility. But as Olli spoke of times that once were, it flared up my heartache, and I wasn't so sure I wanted to let go of our memories together. But from Olli's responses, I wasn't so sure he was ready to give them up either.

Even now, all Olli could do was peer through me with those piercing green eyes, that could read my entire soul but not give an ounce of material to reveal in return. "Are you crying because you are sad? Or are you crying because you are overwhelmed?" He ran the outside of his index finger along my jaw, leaving a trail of warmth behind. "With you, it's always been hard to tell. Even last night served as a challenge. You kept bringing up going home. You brought up your daughter, and in time that made you weep. I didn't know what else to do, so I just held you. Like I always did before."

And he always did. He always took care of me when playtime had brought me to their intended heights. That's often what happened during a scene. Reinforcing such intense power dynamics, especially our dynamic made things interesting. A lot of our play required him to tame me, so by the end of it all, it wasn't uncommon for overwhelming cries to continue past the scene. Even in our vanilla life, my emotions ran high. Crying seemed to be the only means at my disposal to express my everchanging moods.

Due to his Finnish background, it took a while for him to get used to what he originally referred to as an American response to everything. He soon discovered the way he handled my aftercare blended well into our vanilla life too. Comforting me. Making me feel safe. Holding me reaffirmed his role in my life, as well as re-establish my role in his. I pulled myself together, though. Just because he'd made me feel safe this one time, didn't mean I'd have a chance to feel that security again.

"I apologize for taking so much of your emotional energy. I guess I just miss my daughter. To be honest, this has been the longest I've ever been away from her."

Olli put his hand to his chest, sincere in his stance. "That I am sorry for. Had I known I would be keeping you from something, or someone, I would've suggested you bring her. And anyone else you may have missed during the duration of your trip." As the hint of a smile changed the stern appearance in his face.

I couldn't help thinking if I had brought Olivia, it would have been like looking into a mirror. It wouldn't have mattered if she presented as mostly Black, the facial structure she'd inherited from him, I wouldn't have been able to explain away. Walking away from his love had been one of the hardest things I'd done. Would I really be able to deal with explaining to him he fathered my daughter?

"I think I've caused enough trouble. I understand Anna's behavior toward me, but I don't think I could have been the bigger person if that same behavior would have been extended to my child."

"Benny, if you hadn't come, I am positive Anna would have found another reason to be upset with me. I've really tried to be a good partner. But I don't think I've ever been the man I was..." He trailed off, and for once, I was curious about what he would have said.

"You don't think you were ever the man you were *what*?" I asked, hoping he'd call my bluff.

A look of danger but also something that completely eclipsed the sinister aura in his eyes. Shame maybe. I posed my question again, and to my surprise, it was just the answer I'd secretly— despite the implications—been dying to hear the moment we first locked eyes again for the first time in eight years.

"I was going to say that I don't think I've ever been the kind of man I was, as when I was with you. Seeing you again, it makes me forget that I'd lost you. That I should've never left, or at least shouldn't have agreed to be apart. We were oceans away. But it never changed how I felt about you."

He stood this time, closing the inches between us, until our breaths nearly mingled, his body leaning over my own as he pushed the back of my legs into the couch.

"That I miss dominating you," he spoke in a seductive whis- per. "Fucking you." He leaned in to kiss me, but I pulled away right before our lips could touch. He knew I wanted to. I knew I wanted to. But I was playing with him, bringing out that familiar side of him he'd likely been holding in since my absence in his life.

He liked control, but he preferred to take it. I loved the way he took it when I didn't give in so easily.

The vulnerability in being at the mercy of him was what he'd come to value about my submission to him. We'd had weeks of conversation establishing just what we liked, what we wouldn't do, what we could live with, and everything else that brought us to this point. It wasn't so easy enjoying that behavior in my vanilla life, but in my sub-space, I'd never felt more like a woman than when my body was his to use as he felt fit.

Olli gave me one look over and snapped his fingers to see if I'd object. We had a number of signals that would communicate that we were both ready to enter the scene, and that had been one of the ways we both understood what was happening without having to ask or break the mood. Since we didn't do many scenes where talking wasn't allowed, it served us well to stay in our appropriate spaces.

Neither of us had played with another partner in years, so it had seemed like a decent way to re-establish that signal instead of assuming. To Olli's surprise, he would find no objection in me.

Olli grabbed the back of my head, gently enough where I wasn't in pain, but rough enough where I'd made a mistake and that it was his role to show me my place. He pressed his lips against mine, as it brought out all the love, safety, security, and arousal that apparently had never left.

His mouth parted mine, leaving a rush from the warmth of his slick tongue massaging my tongue. His teeth caught my quivering lip, and the power it had on me sent me back to a place I could have only experienced through him. I felt whole. If I never felt anything else again, I was glad he could make me experience this.

All of what I loved about him coursed through each nerve, surged through every bone in my body. His touch sent shivers through even parts of me I neglected, parts of me I hadn't known could get aroused. Every fiber of me was ringing and seconds from detonating if provoked.

With one last kiss, Olli finally pulled away and it was as if I'd lost a larger piece of me, one I couldn't function without. With a look that screamed discipline and masculinity, sex, want and need, as he stood to his full height, perched his crouch in front of me and without breaking his eye contact said, "Now get on your fucking knees."

❧ 15 ❧

O^{lli}

I was a bit rusty when it came to this kind of thing. At my best, I would've made Benny place a pillow from the couch on the floor in front of me and place her knees onto the pillow, instead of simply demanding that she "get on her knees." But the fire building between the two of us was stronger than any command, and I needed her submission more than my need to be the perfect Dom.

The perfect Dom. I remember what it felt like to be that to someone. The work it took, the sacrifice and communication it required to be everything a person needed. I had courted her, close to six weeks, before I dominated her, and the preparation had made every single second of our first play session explosive.

Domination had been an interest of mine since I traveled around Europe. It were as if I'd always had the need to dominate, but I'd never known what to call it. The whole world around me felt bizarre in its normalcy, but in my exchange with normalcy, it made me feel like the freak. It hadn't been until I met Mistress Alice, that I'd known what to call that urge in me, that wouldn't die down.

It wasn't as if I needed it all the time. I learned where and when it was safe to explore my sexual fantasies, and in the right courtship, I could perform both. Kink allowed me to relieve the stress of being boxed in from society's expectations and to my delight, I'd found the perfect woman, the perfect lover, in a woman like Benny.

Neither one of us had been new to the lifestyle, but her experience helped shape me into the Dom I was today. She'd been so amazing, that moving on from her had proved quite the obstacle. Even though our forms of communication hadn't changed, neither one of us had picked up the phone, requested a friend on social media, or sent an email just to reach out. With as much as she'd meant to me in the past, or how much I thought I'd meant to her, it was as if we were dead to each other since our last encounter.

It wasn't as if I'd wanted to end our relationship; when I moved back to Finland, I did so under the pretense that despite what we'd agreed upon, we might one day reunite. Our biggest obstacle had been mainly money, and I kept thinking if I could make a success for myself, we'd be okay.

Those things happened, but not in the way I'd planned them. In fact, I received separation papers not long after I'd secured my current title, but long before I'd gained any significant wealth. Without Benny's encouragement, nurturing nature, trust or vulnerability, I'd lost my way. In moments of weakness, I'd think up things Benny might tell me to push me forward. Maybe she'd disagree with me; maybe she would share with me words that would lead me to the lost the Dom in me.

But imagining her inspire me helped me move on because even though I'd lost her, it made me feel like all things were possible. Now, I had this sweet, beautiful woman I thought I had lost forever, inches away from my crotch, ready to submit at the promise of my command. One thing I wanted to make clear: I planned to rock her world, but if I did, this was not going to be a one-time thing.

If I experienced her now, there would be no goodbyes. There would be no divorce, there would be no separation. If she submitted to me at this moment, she was mine. Mine forever, and I'd never let her go. She waited, curious eyes peering at me, awaiting my simple instruction. Now was the time to practice greater patience. Now was the time to masterfully use my words.

"Little girl, I want you to unbuckle my belt and then my trousers. Can you do that for me?" I didn't expect an answer other than a yes.

"Yes, Sir," she answered through innocent eyes, and it made all the blood in my body rush to my cock at the sound of her calling me *Sir*. It had taken time, but over the course of several weeks, we'd agreed on titles and language we planned to use in our D/s spaces. I'd been referred to as Master, but it had been more as a preference to that particular submissive and not because I'd actually mastered any skill set required of a Dominant. "Sir" was simple and commanding. It stood out on its own, especially from the pet names Benny gave me as her boyfriend. She eased into the role of slut, a plaything that was merely a slut for her Sir.

"Rub the outside of my pants and stick your hand inside." The jiggling of the metal on my belt clinked as Benny snaked the leather through each belt loop, careful in unzipping my slacks and creating just enough friction between her palm and my cock to get me hard.

If there was a way to be both embarrassed and unashamed at the fact my cock stood fully erect, I'd say I was at that place right now. I wanted nothing more but to shove Benny's mouth onto my length and see if her throat remembered how far my cock used to go back there, but I settled for letting her fingers disappear down my slacks.

Benny had the type of eyes that made me wonder what was running through her mind while performing such naughty tasks. They were dark, nearly black, unless one peered into them from only an inch or two away. When Benny's gaze was fixated on mine, she was able to give off the innocence and softness that made every hair on my body stand on end while still giving off the aura of a fully realized sex kitten.

"Pull my boxers down and gently kiss the head of my cock." Without pushback, her dark, slender fingers were soon consumed by my waistband, as a tuck and pull later, a thick, swollen cock sprung from its cotton restraints.

Benny's fingers gently tugged my member as she took it in both hands and kissed the head. A drip of pre-cum ran down the frenulum, coating the shaft with a milky line of semen. In the past, I would have pulled Benny close enough to smear her lips and face, just to mark her in any way I could. But Benny must have been missing this dominance as much as I missed her submission because like a good girl, she brought my cock to her mouth, spread the liquid along her lips and proceeded to lick it off.

It had likely been years, but Benny never missed a beat. Dare I say, despite how close I'd been to happiness, I'd never quite gotten as close enough to it with other flings. Even my last relationship left an emptiness I hadn't known how to fill. Benny was everything I had been missing in my life, ten times over. She knew what I wanted past a basic level, and eight years hadn't seemed to tamper with that.

Tired of waiting, I took hold of both sides of her face, slid my length into her mouth and began to lightly thrust. I wanted to savor it, not tire her mouth and tongue out faster than I could experience disappearing in her warmth. She looked up at me with hungry eyes as it prompted me to thrust faster to make her work a little more. "Does that slutty mouth like the taste of her Sir?" She blinked her eyes once for yes, another form of the non-verbal communication we'd established when her mouth was unable to speak a safe word.

"That's a good little slut. Make my cock wet, so when I slide inside of you, I feel the remnants of your mouth and your pussy at the same time." Those words of encouragement seemed to press Benny to take me further inside, deeper in her mouth than I'd planned to go. When she tried to stick it further down her throat, she choked up saliva, letting go the deep breath she'd held onto trying to accommodate my cock.

If only she knew how sexy her mouth and chin looked as saliva trickled down her face. I reached down to bring my mouth to hers, messy lips, dripping face, and all. The moisture made the texture of her lips feel softer, and I couldn't help but wonder how I'd gone so long without this, without her, in my life.

How had she been the last woman I'd ever been vulnerable to or felt such vulnerability from? I tried to fill her absence with work, money, other women, but neither had made me feel so alive. "Stand on your feet. Let your skirt fall to the floor and pull your panties to one side," I instructed as she was quick to follow suit.

She stood, busying her hands at the waist of her long skirt. It was only seconds, played out in slow motion as beautiful, smooth legs peeked out of red cloth. Sable, nearly iridescent, skin was on display as the skirt hit the floor. As Benny pulled her panties to one side, my mouth watered at the revelation of her dripping sex waiting for me to suck it dry and make it pulse with pleasure.

I bent to my knees—something I'd only do for a woman granting me her submission—taking in her scent, as I blew a cool breath across her bare skin. I could see the walls of her sex clench, as I slapped the outside of her cunt, watching her jump in anticipation. "Does this slutty pussy deserve to be eaten?"

Benny bit her lip. "No, Sir." As she admitted while she had been without a lover for some time, she hadn't stopped touching it in my absence. I kissed the hood, spread her lips to reveal her clit, and kissed it.

"Good," I whispered. It only took one more kiss to part her lips as I ran my entire tongue between them until it reached her clit. A light swear escaped her lips, but since it had been so long, I hadn't thought to punish her harsh language. I longed for it; lived for the ways I made her lose all decorum. Easing her thighs apart, I placed one on my shoulder. Her free hand reached behind my head to ease me closer to her sex. This wasn't her moment; it was mine. Don't get me wrong; I wanted her to cum, but she was getting too comfortable. It was time she knew her place.

Grabbing both her wrists, I held them behind her back so she couldn't direct me. Her panties obeyed, displaying her mounds of sensual sweetness, as I brought my mouth to her glistening clit.

Her moan melted my resolve, bringing me back to our first encounter, and wondering if her beautiful voice sounded as good in bed as it did when she spoke. I'd been in such awe of her, there wasn't a single thing she'd done that didn't impress me. I'd wanted her body, her heart, her soul, and most of all her submission. Who would have thought years later, I'd be reminded of that magnificent feeling?

My mouth sloshed, licked, and sucked Benny's pussy, her lips, her clit, and everything in between. The scent of her lovely folds tasted like the nectar of the gods as they molded to the texture of my tongue. I hadn't given her permission to cum, but she was going to explode her womanly juices all over me, whether I granted her permission or not.

With her bent knee resting against my shoulder, it trembled and flexed, matching every moan that left her mouth. My tongue followed a rhythm so deliberate, it wasn't long before her pussy tightened and contracted all over my mouth. Her clit hummed and vibrated against my lips, and trust me when I say I felt Every. Single. One.

I hadn't even given her the adequate time to recover before I sucked her clit dry, as her attempts to close her legs and stop the intensity just made me want to make her suffer more. Benny had always been a bratty submissive; her mischievous nature brought something out of me that felt so pure, so real, that the Dominant in me relished in the moments I'd get to punish her to show her how mine she was.

Her pussy had had enough, despite the fact I could have gone on for hours. Once I had my fill making her weak for me, I stood to my full height and pressed my mouth against her, still slick and creamy from her juices, so she could taste herself all over me and know the reason I could be between her legs forever.

"Did I give you the authority to cum, you little slut?" My hand had found itself firmly gripped around her neck. I tilted her face up just enough to where she was forced to look into my eyes when she answered me.

"No, Sir."

I pressed my mouth against hers again, parting my lips as I massaged my tongue against her teeth. The body underneath her blouse was calling to me, begging for me to strip her bare both figuratively and literally, as I ripped it open to reveal ample naked breasts. I bent down low enough where my lips and her nipple could meet while maintaining eye contact.

"I fucking spoiled you. Now you just cum when you want. We'll have to do something about that." I took turns kneading and kissing each breast. The sensation was more for me than anything else. I hadn't had her breasts between my lips in nearly eight years. I didn't know how I had lasted this long without them.

"I'm sorry, Sir," Benny said, biting her lip, trying her damnedest not to show how good my mouth felt to her. "I just wanted to cum. It's been so long since I have. Everything you do makes me so wet and so weak."

I pushed her forward against the couch. Forcing her back to the right angle, where it arches just the way her ass was in the air and her pussy was open to me, I rubbed two fingers between her legs and caught just enough of her nectar to rub against my harder than steel cock. She wasn't going to learn her lesson unless I made her learn it. You don't get to cum on my watch, without me giving you the word, without adequate punishment.

"Since you came like a slut, how about I fuck you like a slut?" As I thrust myself into her as hard as my hips would allow and spread her thighs wider so I could see my dick lose inches inside her pussy. Squeals and screams in succession to one another matched each of my calculated thrusts.

The remains of her last orgasm coated my cock, as I pulled my length outside of her, spread it around her anus and lips, before shoving my throbbing member back inside at a rougher pace. "Are you a little slut?" I asked between thrusts.

"No, Sir." She answered back in a pained moan.

"Then what are you?"

"I'm your little fucking slut," She squealed, as I lost all control and fucked her harder. I'd forgotten how tight her little hole could be, as my thick length stretched her and accommodated to me. The combination of her dripping wetness and slick resistance made everything about right now go numb. My cock was ready. It was seconds from reaching the point of no return.

"Your tight pussy is going to make me cum so fucking hard inside of you. Tell me you want my warm, dripping cum deep inside your tight pussy."

"I want your warm dripping wet cum deep inside my tight pussy, Sir." She screamed.

"Tell me how much you want me."

"I want you so much, Sir."

"Tell me you still fucking love me." As I pulled her hair, breathing hard against each thrust, to the point I could barely breathe.

"I still love you, Sir. So fucking much." With that, my body finally let go of its tension. The problems of yesterday, the fear of tomorrow, and the confusion of right now, all gone with three final pumps of passion, ripping my body apart. My dick throbbed inside of Benny, gushing, out in streams of white cream. I reached over and grabbed her face. She met me to kiss me deeply and loving and it was the first time I'd felt right about anything in the last few years.

I was so busy trying to ruin her while she was too busy ruining me.

❧ 16 ❧

enny
The sweet feel of Olli's soft lips pressed against my shoulders caused me to wake up in a fit of shivers. As I opened my eyes, it gave me comfort to see Olli's pale fingers travel up and down my deeply toned, naked skin, even more so when he angled my face toward his to give me the gentlest morning kiss. With his hand softly gripping the delicate curve of my hip, I felt no reason necessary to get up from this heaven to spoil the moment. It was like I was in a dream all over again. When Olli and I first met, I wasn't even sure he was capable of meeting all my needs, in both a boyfriend and a Dominant. Even now I was impressed with how far he'd come in becoming the person I needed; it wasn't hard to see why I'd fallen for him in the first place. It had always been like a fantasy, a dream come true when Olli had come into my life. Now he was making good on his early promise to me that I would always be his.

"Good morning, Mi amor." He laid another kiss along my neck, making me whither in pleasure with how good it felt.

"I miss it when you speak Spanish." He continued worshipping my body like the goddess he always made me feel.

"It's not like you ever wanted to fully learn it," I accused. Before he'd met me, he was heavily into his online, tailored lessons but the moment I'd come into his life, there went his desire to fully conquer the language. "I always had you to translate when someone didn't speak English. Besides, I like it that sometimes I can't understand you. You know foreign women have always been my fatal flaw," he said with that coy smile of his. It was a smile I wasn't sure even existed anymore in the archive of his sexiest expressions. It was a smile that only became unlocked when I misbehaved and he was raring up to give me some of his favorite forms of punishment that my submissive heart yearned for. Was I naive for thinking I was the only woman who could get him to smile like that?

Turning to face him, I basked in all of his Nordic beauty, from the way his jaw flexed when he liked what he saw to the darkening of his green eyes when that same want turned into the need to devour you whole. As much as I loved him looking at me like that, it was quite possibly the most intimidating thing I've yet to experience. How could you be attracted and yet so terrified of a man so handsome, was a situation I'd found myself only experiencing with him.

"Stop looking at me like that." I playfully laughed as I covered my bare face. He climbed on top of me, gently prying my hands from over my eyes. Olli could be playful when he wanted to be and personally I'd found it equally sexy as him taking control.

"Looking at you like what?" he smirked, knowing damn well what he was doing right now. "The face you're making."

"I don't know what you mean." He made his voice sound more heavily accented than normal, a thing he did to tease me to pretend he didn't understand something. Maybe because I'd found it so adorable, there were a lot of things I purposely let him get away with when he did that cute little thing he did. Of course, it was always when I begged him not to go all out on my birthday, or worse, when he'd beat me to our old apartment just to clear my time of therapeutic cleaning rituals so we'd have more time together. It was sweet but I really looked forward to that cleaning time, even if it did make things easier on our date nights.

"When you look at me as if you're going to eat me alive," I confessed and with that, his lips lowered down to my breasts as he alternated kissing them.

"You only have yourself to blame for that. If you stopped looking like breakfast," he said with a kiss to my stomach, "then I wouldn't have to eat you." He smiled as he continued to explore my body further with his lips. When he got to my thighs, his long fingers traveled along the stretch marks on my legs, ones that had formed over the years due to unplanned weight gain. While I'd never felt that self-conscious about it, his taking the time to draw out my imperfections had made me feel like they were unwillingly on display.

"Stop tracing my stretch marks. It tickles." There was this flood of tenderness I'd always experienced with him after a night of dirty, rough sex, reminding me that I was just as soft as I was strong. Maybe many submissives didn't require that, but I did. I loved the way it reiterated my divine femininity. It was nice for someone to touch you gently like you might break, but I had to admit those light touches did tickle.

"I like them. They lead to my favorite parts of you." His hand caressed the fleshiest part of my thighs, tracing the outline of my hips until finally, his mouth had found other ways to torture me. First with his kisses, which accounted for the reason I was soaking wet right now, and then with his tongue, the same tongue that managed to lick every area around my pussy, causing my clit to swell in anticipation at being ignored. Even when we had our vanilla intimacy, he was good at making me beg for it.

"Please Olli, I need you," I panted, pushing my pelvis involuntarily closer to his mouth only to have him grip my hips and ground me to the bed. "What do you need from me?" His breath was warm against my wet, aching folds pleading for him to taste me. The look in his eyes told me everything I needed to know about what he wanted from me and he wasn't going to give in to my request until he got it. In a scene, I was often punished for asking anything of him I didn't earn or deserve but when it was just the two of us, with no set rules, no protocol and no roles to play, he loved it when I talked dirty to him. Especially when I was clear on what I needed of him.

"I need you to lick my fucking pussy, baby." At my declaration, I could see a light flicker in his sage infused eyes. Not wasting any time, he parted me open with his fingers now covered in my wetness and brought his mouth to my already pulsating clit. My toes instinctively curling as my legs tightened around his neck and shoulders at the way his tongue moved skillfully along the apex of my thighs. It damn near brought me to tears that I could hardly keep my eyes open to look at him. When I did and he saw that he finally had my attention, he went into his nasty mode, lifting up far enough for me to see his tongue licking up every fucking ounce of wetness my body had to offer.

He pulled back the hood to my clit, giving me a better view of just what magic his tongue was doing to me, never once taking his intense gaze off me. Before I realized it, I was riding his face begging him to make me come and when he changed up the rhythm from licking to sucking, I knew he had every intention of doing so.

"Are you going to come for me, little girl?" he asked and when he did, my body became a lifeless vessel transported to a field of euphoric bliss. An orgasm ripped through me in one large gust of energy that I couldn't have stopped if I wanted to. He laid another kiss on it and managed to get in a short-lived tongue massage before I pushed his mouth away from my sensitive privates as he wiped away the excess moisture from his face before his large frame reached up to kiss me.

I anchored him close, feeling his hard erection at the base of my stomach. With the taste of myself still fresh on his lips, I pulled him in another kiss, guiding his eager cock to my willing entry point, only to have him hook his arms around me and flip me over so that I was riding him. I loved being on top of him. Maybe even more than he loved me being in control of how his body felt. The faces he made as I expertly bounced up and down on his hardness was more than enough to bring me to orgasm a second time, but at this point, it didn't even matter. I only longed for our closeness and how good it felt for his cock to assault my entrance at this angle. When he took hold of my hips and slammed into my core from underneath me, I couldn't even hold back. As he came, I did too, in one simultaneous moment of weakness.

I leaned in and kissed him as my fingers raked through his silky smooth strands. The warmth of his arms and hands spread across my body like a blanket as he pulled me deeper into his embrace. He knew how to kiss me. How to hold me and of course he knew how to make love to me the way a body deserved. The fact that I lived without this man for all this time made it perfectly clear why it was so hard for me to move on from him. His role in my life was hard to top. For so long I'd used the excuse that no man was good enough to be a part of my life, as well as Olivia's. The truth was, Olli had set the bar so high that I was never sure if any other man I'd been with had truly loved me. I was sure I'd never experience that type of affection as long as I lived, but I'd been wrong.

Olli had the power to make me remember what it was like to fall in love for the first time. I only wished I hadn't brought all these complications in his life.

"Are you hungry?" he asked, advising me to lift up from him so he could peruse the kitchen. I wasn't sure what he'd find in there but I let him up anyways, his hand making contact with my bottom in one hard smack. "You shouldn't start things that make me want to misbehave," I said, sprawling out to make myself more comfortable in the bed. The second he looked back at me, I was certain he was going to make his way back to pull me over his lap and throw in some more but all he did was lean down to press a light kiss to my lips, all sweet and gentle, just how I liked my morning sex kisses to be.

"Make a threat like that and I'll see to it that we never leave this room." He kissed me again before scurrying off into the hallway to do his best to find us some food.

Everything about this weekend had had me on cloud nine. I forgot how fucking good it felt to feel wanted and needed the only way a man could make me feel. To submit. To love. To devote all my existence into being the woman that I'd always been but kept hidden was what Olli was bringing out of me. Was I wrong for wanting to lose that? I so badly wanted to tell the man that I loved about the child we helped create together but it had a fifty-fifty chance of having a neutral or negative impact, one I wasn't quite willing to deal with right this second. If I wanted him back, he needed to know but what if at this stage of his life, he didn't want children? Having gone all these years without having another, I wasn't trying to force parenthood on someone who didn't want it but I knew once I told him, this whole magic carpet ride fantasy had the power to be over. And I so badly didn't want it to be over.

His phone buzzed on the nightstand, which normally wouldn't have caught my attention, but seeing as how we were trapped, I reached over, not wanting to ignore it in case Olli made arrangements for outside help, but I really wished I hadn't. His phone's background had been a stark reminder that perhaps this moment of bliss was really just that. A moment of bliss. The photo was of him and Anna looking like a star couple if I ever saw one. What if she changed her mind? What if whatever she said to him about ending their relationship was just speaking out of anger and all it would take for them to patch things up was a brief conversation about how much more they fit for one another, and just like that I'd be out of the picture? I did sign the divorce papers, after all.

Once they were processed, Olli and I will be officially free to pretend like this weekend never happened.

Seeing them together brought out the harsh truth of knowing in this situation, I was the other woman. As much as I tried to bite back the guilt in realizing this eventful weekend shouldn't have happened, I couldn't help feeling that once it was over, I'd be forced to face an impossible truth. The more I poured my heart into this, the worse it'd feel once he decided this wasn't for him and that decision would absolutely crush me. I'd gone through that once before. A second time might give me enough reason to give up on love altogether.

Olli

Bringing back whatever I could carry in a nearby basket, I filled it to the brim with whatever there was inside the cupboards and fridge. Some fresh bagels, cream cheese, and thin-sliced smoked salmon had led me to believe that someone had been here recently. My parents, perhaps. Maybe even my cousin Helena and her friends on holiday since she was away studying in China and came back every so often to our home away from home. Either way, the food was fresh, so I was grateful that we wouldn't starve.

As I entered the bedroom, Benny wasn't present. I assumed she'd gotten up to use the restroom or take a shower. I was to be next in line. My body felt sticky from the many times we'd managed to make love in our short stay. It was a good feeling to be covered in her essence and consumed by her love. Until last night, I wasn't sure I could ever have a good time like that again. And this morning was just as memorable as we lazily made love in the earliest hours of the day. There had seemed to be some good coming from being snowed in. It meant Benny was mine again and opportunely, I felt honored to be hers.

In the time she was away, I'd managed to slice four bagels in half, spreading the cheese and salmon across them in a restaurant-style presentation. When she finally returned, hair disheveled and wearing a long tee shirt, I invited her to sit with me.

"Come." Without reluctance, she sat on the other side of the plate I prepared, her expressions somber. To lighten the mood, I leaned in and kissed her, paying special attention to her smooth neck and responsive ears, my hands exploring them both. Despite her reciprocation, there was something different in her kisses. Hollow and empty, lifeless and distant. It was clear she'd been upset about something but for the life of me, I couldn't decipher what.

I pulled away, feeling as if she wasn't going to tell me what had changed from this morning until now over breakfast but I contemplated delving a bit deeper into what was going on. I didn't want to overwhelm her with a multitude of questions as I had no right to pry...fuck that. I had every right to pry. She was still my wife, and after we got out of here, I was tossing those divorce papers in the shredder as we collaborated on a way we could be together. I would move my entire life back to the States because I knew her life was with her daughter, and I refused to not to be a part of that life. Maybe eight years ago, I'd felt home-sick but in just this short time, I'd learned that Benny was my home. After today, I couldn't be without her.

"Benny, eat. Please," I practically begged when I noticed even after the kiss, she hadn't bothered to touch the food. It satisfied me as she took the required bites to finish half a bagel, promising me that she'd eat another one in a few minutes. I decided that was fine by me as long as I made sure she ate something. That was how I preferred things. For me to take care of her and for her to let me.

Then

SHE'D HAD SO MANY QUESTIONS ABOUT WHAT OUR FIRST PLAY session would be like, something I both appreciated and adored. Even with all the answers I was able to provide that still didn't prepare you for being in the moment. I predicted the time I'd have with Benny to be memorable but what we'd experienced tonight was beyond any play time I'd ever had. She'd been in her element and that made me come alive to embody the dominance she needed. We'd decided that the first time we slept together would be the first time we had our first scene in an effort to antic-ipate the feelings that blossomed from it. It wasn't my typical way of initiating sex as more often than not, relations happened first and then I'd worked everything in little-by-little. But with Benny, in the few weeks that we'd gotten to know each other, *that* had been the priority. Making sure we truly knew enough about each other. Learning what both of us wanted both sexually and emotionally on an intimate level.

Not having sex at the beginning of a partnership proved to be difficult but not too difficult to where it wasn't worth the wait. After all that transpired from this night's scene, she'd been the good girl I'd spent weeks praying she'd be, and as much as I loved breaking her and putting her back together, the part of playtime I'd always looked forward to the most was the aftercare.

Helping her down from her sub drop was just as important as making her my slut but the truth was that Benny was beginning to be that person I wanted to call on every day. The way she looked in my arms right now, cozying up to my kisses to her fore-head, to call her anything less than magnificent would have been clearly undeserving. And to think, she'd chosen me to be her anchor.

"Olli?" she looked up at me with her deep, mysterious eyes, filled with innocence and admiration. "Yes, baby?" I replied, smoothing her perfect, thick hair in a delicate way that didn't alter or disturb its beauty.

"Could you make me some food?" she cooed, snuggling deeper

into my grasp as if it were possible to hold her like this and cook for her without leaving this bed. At that moment, I could have stayed right here, holding her in my arms forever. I wanted to but knew that providing her what she needed after an intense first session was something I'd never skim on offering. Besides, it wasn't as though I wasn't a little hungry myself.

Now

"Do you need anything?" I asked as I threw on some trousers. She stood and sat back down then back up again halfway into her last action. Her expression was unsettled and maybe even a little plagued from exhaustion. Such a change from just a few moments ago.

"You know what? Do you mind if I have a little time to myself?

"Sure," I answered without argument. I understood the wonders it did for the soul to have some much needed alone time and with all that's happened in the course of a day, I couldn't pretend to know what was flowing through her mind. If space was what she needed, I had planned to give it to her. Even if it was something I wasn't entirely prepared to do.

"That will give me time to shower," I casually remarked. "But don't hesitate to call for me if you need anything. I'll only be a few rooms away." I disappeared into the hallway but not before giving her a soft kiss on the lips.

❧ 18 ❧

B enny

A little quiet time never hurt anybody, right? I wanted nothing more but to have the man I'd fantasized about, to hold me in his arms and tell me everything was going to be okay. But being alone together; that's how we got to this confusing point, to begin with. What did I think was going to happen the moment we were alone, with nothing more to fill our time? We were either going to talk or fuck, so imagine my surprise when we'd done a combination of both.

Maybe I should have, but legally I didn't have to worry about feeling like his other woman; technically we were still married, and it had been a relief to hear Anna had ended his engagement moments before our frisky reunion. I still had doubts but it felt so good to be kissed, and fucked, and loved, that I'm ashamed to admit I would've let things move in that direction whether things had turned this way or not. Olli hadn't been my first, but he'd definitely been the last I'd had since Olivia's birth.

I'd tried dating again, but no man ever excited me or made feel as though I could see only him, and no man had definitely dominated me since the last time I'd been with Olli. I was wrecked for any man that had come after him. Some opportunities to find the love I'd intentionally sabotaged, while some men hadn't been comfortable with the fact I had a daughter, so, despite some subtle changes, I hadn't found luck in love. Lust hadn't even been an option. I couldn't lust after anyone I didn't feel passion for, and despite having attractive suitors seek out my time spent, none of them ever made my panties wet.

Not like Olli. But we hadn't been together since he left the United States. We'd co-existed close to a decade without each other, and the only reason we reconnected was that he'd planned to marry another woman. Was I destined for Olli walking in and out of my life for another eight years? What if after clouds clear, he decides he made a mistake and doesn't plan on investing in us as much as I planned to?

I was still a woman; I had needs like any red-blooded woman who desired sex and wanted to feel owned. And being a mother didn't change that. But I had a daughter to think about. One whose needs came before mine, and I couldn't forget that just because I'd gotten the things the feminine energy in me still craved.

I still hadn't shared with Olli the link between us that was flesh and blood. But what if I did and he rejected Olivia, a child made through our love? Would the love he asked of me be one-sided or conditional for lying to him?

I'd lost him the first time, being young, naïve and selfless, but could I survive him walking out of my life again? Especially since we shared a child, and walking away from me was like walking away from her, too.

I loved Olli with all of my heart and soul. I needed him now, more than I ever needed him, but my daughter needed me more. Olivia needed him, too. But how was I supposed to tell him that months after he left for Finland, that I'd birthed his child and hadn't told him or reached out in any way?

The door between Olli and me should have never been reopened. Now that it had, how was I ever going to deal with the consequences when it all blew up in my face?

"Are you alright in here?" Olli's intimidating frame lurched into the room unannounced. So much for having time to think of what I'd do if this didn't turn out the way I planned. Olli joined me on the mattress, folding one of his legs underneath him while resting the opposite on the floor.

"Talk to me," he demanded with poetic eyes. "I understand you better when you talk." Perhaps, I should have been grateful he wanted to be so open. We'd come a long way since when we first met, where he struggled with even the shortest conversation of small talk. An unintentional smile crept into the corner of his mouth, making me defenseless against his charm. It was strange; in the past, awkward silence had never been a weak point for him, nor had been leaving me to my own devices when I needed space.

But he sensed something wrong, which was good considering how dormant he's been if he hadn't had a submissive after me. The ability to read a submissive's mood could have been a natural gift, but any good Dom would learn his submissive enough to know her request at needing space were cries for attention.

"It's too much to explain right now—" I tried to buy myself more time, but he interrupted me before I could come up with anything that might drop the whole subject for now.

"We are snowbound in a cabin. Right now, all we have is time." He objected. I didn't have a reply nor was I going to weave myself into a lie, so I said nothing, hoping he'd take the hint and bring up something unrelated to our current moods.

Olli crawled in beside me, trapping me in the warmth of his long arms. He kissed my shoulder, and when our eyes met, we shared a glance so intense it wasn't long before our lips were tangled in a battle of wills. "Why are you being so distant?" He whispered, as our melded breaths, lips and bodies pulled away but brought out another obvious insecurity.

We sat facing one another until I found the courage to speak. "I can't help thinking that had I not gotten wrapped up in all this, you would have very well gotten married three days ago." Olli didn't flinch and wasn't quick to defend himself. Nor did I assume he'd say anything after stealing my gaze for what felt like an eternity.

"Yes, I probably would have." His eyes breaking our contact wasn't immediate. He studied me and how I reacted to his truth before looking down and reaching to comfort me by stroking the outside of my hand.

"I guess that's part of why I've been so distant. I can't help thinking most of what happened so far has been in the moment," I admitted. "I just don't have the confidence in us like I should, ya know? Especially since you've made this completely new life for yourself, without me—"

"So, you don't have a entirely new life you've created without me?" Olli interrupted, an unexpected pain in the back of his throat. "Do you know how much it pains me to see that you've successfully moved on from us. Moved on from me?" he admitted shyly, all traces of his Dom side non-existent.

Olli was unaware of just how little I'd actually moved on. So much of my current life was created by him. I couldn't have moved on from him if I tried. "I never stopped loving you. That's why it surprised me when you sent separation papers. I figured you had met someone. And I didn't want to stand in the way of that, but I was ashamed of myself. Ashamed that I'd been such a coward when I left. There were times I'd wanted to call you, ask you how you were doing. Maybe even reconnect. But I felt like less than a man asking for a warm bed when I had less to offer you in return." We had both wanted to be where home *felt*. But in admitting such, we'd forgotten where home *was*.

"I wanted to be able to provide a healthier financial environment for us, but it seemed more challenging than I anticipated. You were working all the time, and it seemed like you resented me—"

"I never resented you," I interrupted. I hadn't even known he'd observed that much of our situation in the past.

"But it showed in more ways than words, Benny. I wanted to move back to Finland, and you wanted to stay here. You'd never wanted to be apart from me until that time in our relationship, so when we agreed to go our separate ways, it felt like you were asking me to be released. In more ways than one."

Looking back now, if he'd seen that as our biggest challenge, he'd been right for feeling that; in the end it was the moment that broke us. I'd backpacked all through Europe, and Spain was only meant to be a four-month trip to reconnect with the country of my birth, speak a language where my culture had been born and wanted to see through adult eyes. By the time we'd met, married, and moved to the States, I'd already been homesick for close to a year.

Olli's work visa had only been temporary, and with his earning potential, he hadn't wanted to take just any job. In time, I felt like my love for him had been holding him back to reach the goals he kept to himself. If he felt like I'd resented him, the feeling had been mutual. In time, our relationship appeared to hinder his success than help it. And I wasn't sure I wanted to go from the most important thing in the world to him, than the one person he blamed more than anything for his inability to reach his goals.

"You have a child now." It was an admittance that sent a shiver of fear down my spine. "You've likely been in love with someone else who wasn't me. I blame myself for everything that's happened since the day I left. Everything would be so different if I hadn't."

He reached out to me, trailing a single finger down my arm

and the small of the skin on my stomach. "So, where does that leave Anna?"

There was so much guilt, so much regret for my role in all this. I was relieved to know she'd broken things off with Olli. Not that it gave me permission to do all the things we did, but I certainly felt better about knowing that at least he hadn't stepped out on her just to dominate and fuck me. They'd broken up because of our past together, but that part couldn't be helped.

"Benny, I will not lie to you with things you want to hear. I do love Anna. It is a very different from the love I have for you. With her, our situation was convenient. We loved enough about one another to consider spending lives together. We made sense on the surface. Maybe even a few more things made us work. And I would have been content with a life like that because it would've helped me from remembering what I'd lost."

Olli took a deeper breath than normal as if in all he'd admitted had prevented him from breathing. "But Anna accused me a long time ago of not being over you. I had tried to make us more honest. Tried my best to make us freer. I knew that it would never be the way with what I had with you, but admitting my past to her? My past with you? All it did was make her withdraw."

Anna had never wanted any part in kink or BDSM, and despite his fear of wanting her to know that about him, he admitted it anyway. She hadn't taken to it well. Even accused him of wanting a controlling relationship. He hadn't wanted that at all, he'd just wanted to share with her something that, before her, had been important to him.

"She didn't want me to know her in that way. She was perfectly happy with making me guess the things about her that could have been resolved with open communication. Most of all, she resented that I once had a life without her. Especially one so intense, so detrimental in shaping the man I was today."

"So, when I say I love Anna and I say I love you, they are both true. But they do not mean the same thing. I know you love me because you used to tell me and show me. I knew when I hurt you because we were open and honest. Most of all, I tried to be a better man for you, because you told me *how* I can be a better man for you. I would have settled for anyone less than you, but if you're telling me that in this day and time, that we have a chance? I don't want the love I have with Anna. I want the love I have with you."

The words from Olli's mouth sounded like the poetry I so desperately needed to feed my soul. He could have been telling me to go to hell, and after that confession, I would've still found his delivery poetic. But that didn't mean I still wasn't terrified. If he felt so strongly about everything he said, would those words still hold true after learning of our shared daughter? The daughter I kept from him for seven years.

That there'd been no other man I'd been in love with all this time, but that I'd been raising the daughter I never told him about. I was trying to imagine him embracing the idea of being a father, but couldn't picture it without some lingering resentment.

He took his hand and caressed it all along my face. The calluses of his palm glided against my skin underneath and reminded me how soft I was in comparison. "You are everything I want in me. Filling holes to the parts of me I'd lost since we'd parted so long ago. Now that I have you, how can you expect me to survive without you?" Olli pulled his hand away and readjusted himself to rest his arm around my waist.

"Even if we *could* make this work," I later insisted. "I can't just pack up and move my entire life to Finland. I have a daughter, and she's situated—"

"Did you expect that I'd want you and not consider your daughter, too?" I froze at the sound of *your* daughter. That was enough to push my words to the deeper part of me in fear I'd admit the wrong thing.

"I would have no issue being a second father to her if you wanted me to be. I've been in the works to secure a deal that'll allow me to retire soon. Even if I hadn't, I earn more than enough to provide for you and your daughter. When I retire early, I could devote all my time to you two. Make sure she's in the best schools, make sure your mother has the best care. I want to provide for your family because I want them as my family, too. Since we're still married, they are my family. I finally feel whole. If that's a concern, I would do anything just to be with you."

A tear fell down my cheek and without any control over myself, I couldn't stop crying. Olli saw this as his opportunity to console me in any way he could. I wish I could tell him these tears falling down weren't tears of sadness. But he wouldn't understand, not completely, why they were tears of joy. Hearing him say all those beautiful things; one can only hope he still meant them after hearing the truth.

"Is there anything I could do that would make you feel better?"

※

WHEN IT'D BEEN CLOSE TO A DECADE SINCE YOU MADE LOVE, five times in less than twenty-four hours felt like a practice run. Fine-tuning old habits, perfecting newly developed ones, discovering new skill sets that you never thought possible. One of Olli's many talents was he was just as skillful in good, old-fashioned vanilla sex as he was when the intensity was higher in a scene. Some Doms struggled when you took them out of their element; the opposite could be said about vanilla men who didn't have the creativity to satisfy the average woman.

Olli had mastered the art of both, proving with each thrust, caress, and kiss his lips and cock fed me to make up for my eight-year dry spell. I'd climaxed four times before we even approached round two. My pussy was so sensitive from losing control that I would've stopped Olli if I hadn't been convinced I had another orgasm in me before he'd admit defeat.

"Baby, if we don't stop, we'll probably die of dehydration," I joked.

He hooked both my legs against his chest and shoulders, sweat dripping down his torso and forehead from the work he put in and the heat of the fireplace we'd centered ourselves in front of.

"Dying between your legs would be the ideal way to die," he joked and thrust with wild abandon. My phone began to ring and despite my circumstances, I reached to grab the phone. Olli pulled me an inch away from it, as his hips came to a slow and he wiped the sweat running down his face.

"Don't pick it up; it'll only take you out the moment."

"It might be my mother. I don't want her to worry." We were snowed in, and I'd already missed my flight back home. He was between my legs; we weren't going anywhere.

"Just know, if you pick up that phone, I will still continue to fuck you. Do your best to refrain from moaning, though I'll likely give you a reason to." He let go of my arms and let me reach for the phone in my shirt pocket.

"Hello?"

It didn't take more than a few seconds for Olli's pace to come to a quieter steady one as he concentrated on slower, deeper, penetrating thrusts, reaching one hand to rub my clit, the other to pinch my left nipple.

"Oh my God!" I screamed instead of moaned, hopeful it sounded as convincing over the phone as it had in my head.

"What is wrong? You do not sound well," my mother asked concerned from her end of the line.

"Nothing, Ma." My body contorted to the rhythm of small contractions milking Olli's cock in my juices. "I sprained my ankle trying to help cut wood and build a fire in the fireplace," I lied. "I guess trying to walk on it is harder since I can't get to a hospital, or anywhere else for that matter."

"You know what you do?" Mami ticked off as if I were really about to perform all these tasks in tandem. "You put ice on it for fifteen minutes, then as high as you can, rest your foot above your heart to help stop the swelling." My mom's advice would have been dead on if I'd actually needed it. But much to her suggestion, my feet were already as high above my heart as they could possibly be as they rested on Olli's shoulders. If I actually did sprain my ankle from now until I hopped on a plane, at least I'd know the perfect activity to keep me off my feet.

My throat strained of a satisfying pain when Olli forcefully thrust into me, something he only did to keep my focus on the fact that he was fucking me as well. My mom was none the wiser. On her end, it just sounded like I'd tried to walk a distance I shouldn't as she made suggestions on her end that were home-made treatments that might help with the inflammation.

I was relieved to know Olivia had been taking a nap when she called; I don't think I could've played the homesick mom and the wife getting fucked over the phone at the same time. But I had to admit, the way Olli's body used me, without a care in the world, made me wetter than the first five orgasms had.

Olli folded over my body until I was horizontal from his view and jackhammered the shit out of his hips as he came harder than he ever had since the time that we started. I could feel his warmth coat my walls, and I climaxed with him once more as my mother wished me safe travels and hung up the phone.

In his native language, a silky swear left his mouth as he gently kissed the top of my nose. He pulled out of me and I could feel the milky liquid it left behind. I can't say I didn't love the way he wrapped himself in a tangle of limbs with mine, soothed by the sound of crackling embers from the fireplace. Our sweaty bodies slicked and melded as one, readjusting when needed. Olli pulled at small tendrils of my hair, as I watched his curious green eyes in his afterglow.

"Do you think your daughter would like me?"

❧ 19 ❧

O^{lli}
Then

I'D SPENT ALL OF YESTERDAY ON YOUTUBE GATHERING UP recipes to impress Benny for our dinner date tonight. Luckily, a portion of the ingredients were so easy to find here in Madrid. Back home, I'm sure it would have proved to be difficult. I spoon-fed her a portion of the homemade Pescado con tres salsas, something I thought she'd love and appreciate. I was probably the last person who could tell what a good Pescado con tres salsas was supposed to taste like, but judging by the way Benny closed her eyes and orgasmically moaned at the flavor coating her tongue, my guess was that I'd done a decent job.

"Wow, this is *really* good." Her smile warm and genuine. She reveled in the savory aftertaste of the second serving that made me feel good that I could please a woman in a way often men neglected, with food. "Here, try some." She took the spoon from my hand, collecting a healthy sample with one heft scoop. The warm, spicy blends of garlic and hot peppers danced on my tongue. Like her, it was foreign. Different but exciting to try and satisfying enough to keep coming back for more. She looked so lovely this evening.

"Do you cook a lot back home?" she asked. I did but never food this extravagant and about half as much time spent. But I wanted to learn, especially if it had the power to put the two of us in a good mood. Food had the ability to do that.

"Enough, but I can always stand to cook more. How about you?" She smiled, almost embarrassed to admit that she ate at her mother's house almost every night before she moved overseas. "It's not as if I'm a bad cook. I'm actually pretty good; it's just hard to compare *my* cooking to a woman who's been cooking longer than I've been alive, you know?" she said taking another few bites of the rice.

"What about your father? Did he cook?" Her eyes cast downward, a somber expression altering her soft features. Of all the dates we'd been on, I'd never seen her that unhappy about something. It was evident that her father was an untouchable subject, but as someone who'd planned on learning all about her, there was no subject I'd found to be off-limits. "Actually, my father's not really in my life right now. Never really has been."

"I didn't mean to pry," I said, sensing the sudden shift in her mood. As sweet and considerate a person she was, I couldn't imagine anyone choosing not to be in her life. Perhaps my father hadn't been the sort of fathers you saw on TV with their unconditional understanding and openness they expressed toward their children but he was a presence in my life I hadn't once taken for granted. Without him, I wouldn't be the person I was today.

"I'm sorry to hear that, Benny." My fingers stroked her face in a comforting caress. My sweet Benny. I wanted to give her so much, even if for now it was just my free time. "It's not really a big deal, Olli. I've healed from not having my father around a long time ago. He's still in Equatorial Guinea. When I met him for the first time, I was sixteen. It became relatively clear that some men just aren't ready to become fathers when women are ready to become mothers." This early in my life, I hadn't given a second thought about fatherhood, but I did know that if I'd unknowingly fathered a child, it would devastate not knowing who they were or coming to discover their existence. I'd want them to know me.

"I could never do that. Not to my child. Not to the mother of that child. Family is important and a healthy one is essential to one's life. I'm sorry you don't have a better relationship with your father." She offered me a final spoonful of my prepared meal. Although we were in the early stages of our said courting, while we were on the subject, I couldn't help but imagine how stunning she'd look, glowing with child. My child. If we made it that far, the idea could manifest more than just an idea, but a necessary step in the future we could have together.

Now

BENNY BIT HER LIP. BENNY ALWAYS BIT HER LIP WHEN SHE WAS nervous about something. Was she thinking about how I'd fit into her newly made life? Even if that wasn't what was troubling her, I sensed something was wrong. Her face said everything without a word leaving her beautiful mouth. Under her wish, we slipped back into our clothes, despite my desire to admire what I had missed over the years when it came to her irresistible body. I was beginning to feel a little worried.

First she needed space, now she carried the weight of the world on her shoulders. Whatever discussion would take place in the next few minutes was so urgent that apparently, we couldn't have it without being fully clothed.

"There's been something I've been meaning to tell you. Really since the moment I got here." Her complexion cast a shallow undertone that made her appear almost distorted. Scared even. As if she'd bared witness to a horrid act and couldn't unsee it.

"Obviously when we spoke about my coming here, I didn't expect for us to be having these heavy conversations about you and me getting back together. Or even being in each other's lives past this weekend. If there's anything I've realized today, it's that I've always loved you. Maybe I never stopped loving you. There was always something around keeping you in my thoughts, which makes it that much harder to admit that I haven't been completely honest with you."

I prepared myself for the worst possible development that could affect a future that included the two of us together. Perhaps, she had a fiancé back home. Maybe even a live-in boyfriend. I didn't imagine her child's father being that far away from his family. Without knowing the severity of her admission, I came to all these conclusions of what could be so damaging that she'd chosen to be dishonest with me. If there was one thing I took pride in our past history together, was that honesty between us was never up for debate. We told each other everything.

"You say what you want is to be with me. But once I get this off my chest, I'm not sure you'll still feel the same. Going forward, I don't blame you if you decide that you're making a mistake by wanting to be with me."

Now it was I who felt fear as I'd never known it. There were a lot of things I could live with. I didn't have the pleasure of just turning off my feeling for her. In short, there wasn't anything she could ever say to change how I felt. With what I put her through, she'd earned my giving her the benefit of the doubt.

"Please, Benny. Do not torture me any longer. Say what you have to say. I can't promise to understand but I'll find a way to." I finally confessed, which only caused her to furrow her eyebrows and fight back tears that would surely come depending on how I reacted. I prayed that I would have a handle on myself. On my emotions. I just prayed it wasn't as terrible as her claims.

"It's about my daughter." She took a deep breathe, trembling as she struggled to get the words out. "I found out just days after you left the US for Helsinki that I was going to have a baby."

"What?" My expression faltered, confused about what that was supposed to mean without the entire context of her confession. "I wanted to tell you, Olli. I really did. But you were so unhappy, and I didn't want to stand in the way of doing what you needed to do to find happiness."

Now, I was getting upset. That still didn't tell me what I needed to hear. My leaving. Her pregnancy. How did this all tie together? "Wanted to tell me what, Benny? Stop dancing around it." She took another deep breath, looking directly into my eyes with sudden newfound courage. I wasn't sure I wanted to know the truth as her confession drew near. The nerves in my stomach knotted up to a point of unmovable tightness. The truth, I sensed, was a truth I wouldn't believe until it left her sweet lips.

"My daughter Olivia... that's her name, Olivia" She hesitated. "I didn't have her with another man. She's yours. Ours." She corrected herself last minute.

Life flashing before my eyes. I believed that only happened when you were close to death and reminded of all the things you'd done, good and bad. I had no control over the life that was racing past me. I'd become a father. I'd become a father and hadn't been told. I'd become a father with the woman I never stopped loving. A woman who kept this secret from me.

For a moment, I sat there, lost for words or fully formed thoughts. It wasn't until she called out to me that made me remember where I was, what I was doing, and what I'd just been told.

"How could you keep something like that from me? All these years...all this time. You could've called. You could've written!" My tone rose with every sentence to the point where I didn't recognize my own voice.

"Olli, we'd both moved on. Every year that passed, it got harder."

"You're talking about details that could've changed my decision to leave. You suspected you were pregnant when I left, and you just let me go!" My nostrils flared, Benny suddenly feeling smaller as I approached her, backing away, cautious.

"Yes, I did, Olli. And I don't regret it," she boldly stated.

"How do you think it makes me feel to know I wasn't there? I could've helped you. We could've figured a way to work things out."

"You were a mess when you left. Always fucking miserable and questioning every little thing you did. I tried to be there for you. I tried to be supportive but nothing I did was ever good enough. You were taking your shortcomings out on me and I was not going to risk bringing a child into an unhealthy environment. Children have this way of keeping two unhappy people together, and I didn't want that for myself. I didn't want it for her either."

As much as I hated to admit it out loud, a great deal of her argument had been correct. When I left, I was in a state of depression I didn't know how to come back from. I'd felt the weight of what it was like to devote your life to taking care of someone and coming up short with how to provide for her more than the bare minimum. I wanted so badly to give her everything other Doms were able to give their significant others, and while I struggled to find my way, I neglected my duties as a Dominant, but worst of all, as her husband. That still didn't change the hurt I felt now. Hurt that came from being the father to a child who didn't know who I was. Did she think I just abandoned her? Not knowing the answer was what pained the most.

"Does she know about me? Does she know where you are right now? Does she at least...does she at least look like me?" I asked as a final attempt to fight back unwanted tears. Benny pulled out her phone and brought up her phone's photo album. There was only one labeled "Olivia". To whether or not she looked like me, I was to be the judge.

Shifting through the album, this time, I'd found it difficult to hold back tears, so I didn't even try. This little girl, our little girl, was nothing short of amazingly beautiful. She didn't outright resemble me with her warm brown skin and dark hair. Underneath the surface, I could make out the distinct blend of features that were both mine and Benny's.

Her eyes. Her dark eyes were that of my father's. Looking in her eyes was like reveling in my own comfort as a child and being happy whenever I got to spend time with my father doing only the things that we shared as father and son. But the shape of them, all wide and curious, I marked as my own. Even her nose and ears were mine, but her lips, that beautiful smile was and could only be from that the love of my life Benny's. She was so big. And to think I didn't even know what her voice sounded like. Or what her favorite color was. I didn't know anything about her. Of all the secrets Benny could have kept hidden from me, why did it have to be this?

"Olli, tell me what you're thinking." Her voice followed me as I ventured the cabin looking, sometimes even *relooking* at the countless photos she had stored on her phone. I was so lost in thought, I hadn't realized I was already back in one of the cabin's bedrooms. The one we'd spent all night making love and making such a beautiful mess in. Benny kept on probing, and I kept on focusing on the beauty of this seven-year-old treasure who shared our DNA. It was difficult to keep my mind in the conversation Benny wanted to have with me.

She'd had seven years to live with the idea of how becoming a parent had the power to be life changing. I just wanted a moment in peace to admire a few photos; was that so much to ask of her?

"I need some time to gather my thoughts, Benny. Can this conversation wait just a little longer?"

She frustratedly threw her arms up in the air. "Take all the time you need. In a few hours, I'll probably be long gone anyway. That will give you all the extra so-called time you need." It was then that I finally put the phone down. Benny, if anything, knew how to force a conversation out of me. She knew me well enough to predict what my next move would be. She wasn't going home, not without resolving any of this. In my mind, it was already settled.

Before I could inform her what I'd mentally decided, the call of voices in the first room prompted me to perform a quick run-through of the house. In the living room stood three men in heavy utility gear, shovels in their hands.

"*Is everything alright?*" one asked in Finnish as another conversed with me about how my home staff, worried when I informed my butler of our snowed-in status, had sent a rescue team as soon as the weather allowed it. As a courtesy, they'd even helped shovel my car out, an act for which I was grateful since it would have taken me all morning by myself.

Benny emerged at my side to experience the wonder of us being able to leave here soon. If the stars aligned, she would be making an afternoon flight without her rescheduling. What I didn't confirm was that her trip back would include an anxious plus one: me.

❦ 20 ❦

Olli

The rescue couldn't have come at a more confusing time. All those chances. All these years. All the moments I looked back at what we'd been through together. She'd kept from me a truth that shouldn't have been kept hidden. I was the father to her one and only child. She'd had remnants, reminders of me sprinkled in her life and all this time I was forced to move on when I thought I'd had no choice to. Didn't I deserve to know?

She hadn't even given me the chance to decide on my own terms if I would stay or not, despite my frustration with my lack of success in the US. I *wanted* to go home. *Needed* to go home, but if Benny had told me of the news of our baby, I would've never chosen to leave her. I knew how her father left before she even got the chance to know him; she didn't talk much about it but I knew how much it affected her with how slow we moved in our courting phase. Her trust had taken longer to earn, something I credited to no man truly valuing her role in their lives the way she'd deserved to be treasured. And I'd done just that by abandoning her in her greatest time of need. All she had to do was tell me and I would've taken the first plane back to California. All she had to do was tell me...

The roads were icy and slippery, forcing me to drive slower, even slower than last night, so Benny's attempts at conversation got ignored to the point where she stopped talking. Silence was always the one thing that hurt and confused her any time I'd been upset about something. When I willfully ignored her, she knew that was just my way of punishing her for how badly she'd fucked up. Some people yelled and screamed; others said awful things in the heat of the moment, but I'd found that neither one of those methods had ever worked for me. Silence was where I found my solace—and retribution. Processing this. Processing that. Processing anything and everything that could've been. I wasn't sure how she had expected me to behave once she broke the news, but if I was certain about one thing, I knew she realized I wouldn't be happy at the thought of losing years of the life I could've had. This life, the only life I wanted with her from the very beginning.

"Look at me," I commanded as we approached a stop light. Shame and sympathy etched in her features and made being upset with her a very difficult task. Her dark eyes looked empty as if finally letting go of her concerns were the source of their light. My expression softened as I tried to sympathize with her at this moment.

"Benny, how have you been taking care of our child? What have you been doing for money?" I knew how most single women struggled in her country as I knew her mother worked several jobs to support her to put her through school. Life couldn't have been easy; both working too much and spending less time with our daughter or engaging in the complete opposite, giving her more of her time but living paycheck-to-paycheck. I didn't like either scenarios, but I still had to know.

"Olli, I've been handling my financial situation to the best of my ability. I had the opportunity to teach when Olivia started school but unfortunately, the job had insane hours despite the pay being more than I was worth, based on my level of education." A car beeped its horn at us when I didn't drive off at the sign of the green light. Holding up my finger, I signaled for Benny to wait on her explanation as I rolled down my window and signaled for the driver to go around me.

"*Are you stuck?*" he asked in Finnish. Sticking my head out the window, I yelled back, *"No but I don't plan to move, so if you're in a hurry, go around!"* Taking my advice, the driver drove up far enough to go around us but not without giving me a strange look for the sake of it.

I turned back to Benny, motioning for her to continue her story with a wave of my finger. I thought it best to park the car and turn on my hazards.

"That's when the ski instructor job came along. I'd always known how to ski well and the certification was easy enough. The job paid enough to support the two of us and send her to private school as long as we lived someplace cheap and didn't live above of our means.

"I'm not going to sit here and lie to you and tell you we haven't struggled sometimes, but my mom helps me a lot. She watches Olivia when I need to pick up extra shifts, and I get state assistance for food. That also really helps."

As hard as it was for her to tell me all this, it was just as hard to hear the reality of her financial situation. These were all things I could've helped with, whether or not Anna and I were to be married. I would've made her understand the life I had before agreeing to marry her. If I'd known about Olivia even four years ago, I may have never even met Anna. But to learn my family had struggled while I lived a fulfilled life where money was hardly ever something I thought about I couldn't help but feel like a terrible person.

"And this job? Do you like it?"

She shrugged, a look of defeat in her eyes as she tugged at the skin of her fingers. "I did. Due to the company's cutback, they had to let me go, but I don't really see it as a setback. I've been down this road before, and I always get back on my feet. Olivia has never had to worry about me taking care of her, and I always protect her from my own failures. She doesn't even know I lost my job."

The thought hit me. The settlement I'd offered her. Why would she turn it down knowing it would rectify her circumstances, even if only for a short time? By now, I had so many questions but no words formed in my mouth to ask them. She'd always been stubborn, but I didn't realize she was *that* stubborn. "The settlement, Benny. Why did you turn it down if it could've helped? You were so eager to sign your love away. To end my marriage to you. But even if you hadn't told me the truth, the money could've helped."

"Olli, I felt so guilty for not telling you. You moved on. You seemed happy. Causing trouble in your life was never my intention but this whole weekend, that's all I seemed to do. I didn't take the money because I didn't want to feel like I was exploiting you."

"We have a daughter," I uncharacteristically barked at her, causing her to cower in stillness. It was rare when I ever got that angry and even rarer when I took it out on Benny. That fear in her eyes had been likely the reason she hadn't told me. It was why I wasn't ready to speak about it until I got my thoughts in order.

"I apologize for yelling at you. It's just, it's my blood, too, that pumps through her veins. Do I not share that responsibility you've forced yourself to do alone?" Now that I knew, I couldn't just go on with my life knowing there was a child out there that shared my DNA. Benny wouldn't be returning home alone; my next move was to accompany her on her flight back to California.

"I'll have my assistant postpone my plans for the next few weeks. I'm going home with you. I want to meet my daughter," I said with finality and not asking permission. If Benny understood anything about me, it was that once my mind was made up, nothing would stop me from doing what I intended to do. As expected, she didn't argue with me, and we hadn't spoken another word to each other the entire rest of the ride home.

I pulled into the driveway, reassuring Benny that I'd only be a minute to grab the few essentials I needed for the unplanned trip. I was relieved she had taken the hint with how upset I was and let me venture the house by myself while she waited in the car. Even if it were only a few minutes I had to myself, I wanted the time to think things through.

My mind wandered back to all those years ago when I'd hit a boiling point with our current dilemma with me not being able to find work. Had she given off hints of her being with child? Did I ignore the signs due to my depression and unhappiness? If I could go back in time, I would've put Benny first instead of getting lost in my own disappointments, because now I'd found myself in a predicament that depending on how we dealt with the matter, someone could wind up hurt and unhappy and then we'd only find ourselves in the same place we were eight years ago.

Just as I finished gathering all of what I would take with me on my sudden trip, Anna materialized at the door of the closet we once shared together. Clearly, she still had the keys. It didn't really surprise me to see her. The way she threw temper tantrums, I was sure I'd hear from her sooner or later with accusations of her being overemotional at the time and not meaning what she'd said.

"Anna, say whatever you have to say quickly. I'm on my way to the airport, and I don't have time to get into a heavy conversation." Her face softened.

"Olli, I've been worried sick about you; those things I said over the phone, I only said out of anger. Surely you know that I'm here to apologize. When you drop your ex off at the airport, I'm certain we can get this all straightened out. I understand now. I was being childish." My nostrils flared at the thought of her thinking her threats were the reason I was distraught. In all honesty, our weekend conversation was the furthest from my mind. She was the last person I'd given thought to since hearing the news about my seven-year-old daughter.

"Anna, I'm a complete mess right now. Your threat to call things off was something I took to the heart. You and I are over. You said so yourself. It's best if you just forget about me. Forget about us." Somehow, I hadn't even noticed the documents she held in her hand. Had they always been there? Blinded by my own frustration, perhaps, they'd always been there. The divorce papers that marked the end of my and Benny's marriage. I'd forgotten all about them being trapped in that cabin together.

"The papers are signed. You're taking your ex to the airport. Things between us don't have to be over. Maybe I had an ounce of doubt in you before, but I trust you now to make the right decision for you and to make the right decision for me." Anna stepped close enough to me to touch her, handing me the papers as if she'd known exactly what I'd do with them. A smile crept at the corner of her mouth as if saying "thank you for choosing us". But now, with the papers in my hand, I did the only thing I could think of to get the message through to her this time that this journey between she and I had ended. The past was now my future and the future, my past. Inserting the twenty-five-page file in the reigns of the paper shredder that sat on my desk, the divorce papers disintegrated into dozens of even threads of unreadable minced spirals. It was the first time I saw her often sweet face turn into something almost unrecognizable. Ugly even.

Of all the years she whined and fought to get her way with me despite the little she offered in return, she would finally understand that what you say, even in the heat of the moment, had consequences. And while I didn't like being the cause of her pain, learning I had a child with Benny would be the last test our relationship couldn't pass. She would never accept Bendición had earned a permanent spot in my life as the mother of my first child. That would be the news that would be the final decider of our fate.

"Anna, things are different now. I love you and I wish I didn't have to hurt you this way, but I have unfinished business that involves my past life with Benny. I hope one day you can find it in your heart to understand. Perhaps even forgive me." With that, I carried my small bags out the room only to find Anna on my coattails, yelling hysterically to get in the last word. In her native Swedish, we fought from the second floor, down the steps and even out to the front door. Finally, we'd reach the car I was taking and leaving at the airport to catch our late afternoon flight to Benny's side of the world. If I let her get any closer, I feared she'd plant some idea in Benny's head about her and I getting back together, and I didn't need that hanging over an already fragile problem brewing between us. So, I said the first thing I could think of to get her to back off.

"You were right, Anna," I spoke to her in her mother language. "I'm still in love with Bendición, and that's why I cannot marry you. I didn't want to tell you like this but...you've left me no choice." Like a deer in headlights, she stopped in her steadfast tracks. Anna knew the worst thing about me, and that was that I told no lies.

Outside was so frigid that even with the blink of an eye, you could see the air at just the slightest of motion but the look on Anna's face was colder than any drop in temperature winter could ever bring. Without a jacket, she stood there like an ice queen, unaffected by the sharp winds that surrounded us, in her own way defeated.

"Be well, Anna." There was nothing else I could say to make this better for me or for her, or even the nearby Benny watched us just a few feet away in the passenger side of my vehicle. Tossing my overnight bags in the backseat alongside Benny, I climbed back into the front seat and backed out of the driveway. Anna was still standing there, in the blistering cold weather, lost in thought. As much as I worried about the longing effects of what my truth might cause her to do, I couldn't help but be overwhelmed with anxiety as I made my way to the airport on the way to meet my daughter for the very first time.

❧ 21 ❧

Benny

Olli made his way back to the car and didn't waste a second pulling out of the driveway. Olli offered me nothing but a frontseat of silence. Maybe it was his intention to make me consider all I'd hid from him, but it ramped up my anxiety not knowing what he was thinking, what he'd said to Anna, and what we were going to do once we got to California.

Anna never liked me, and after last night she had all the more reason not to. I'd been with Olli in all the ways a husband and wife should have been, and it didn't help that emotions had been amplified with the reintroduction to our D/s selves. Had they been arguing about that, on his way back to the car?

Olli wasn't a liar; since Anna had called off their engagement, I'm sure he'd at least been honest about how we'd spent being snowed in together. Since they had only gone back and forth in Swedish, I couldn't have leaned in even if I'd wanted to. But based on body language and other tells, they'd been discussing something big. I couldn't help feeling I'd get stuck between my feelings for him and reconsidering our divorce and trying to figure out if Olli had been serious about ending things with Anna.

The sight of them together? I admit it made my heart drop into the pit of my stomach. I knew why I'd come here, but Olli had dominated me, made love to me, fucked me, loved me. I had a lot to make up for, but ever since I got off that plane and saw him, I couldn't help but feel like the man I'd loved had never meant to leave my side in the first place. I'm sure I didn't see their true relationship in all its forms. But so much has changed since we were rescued out of that cabin.

Olli knew. He now knew more linked the two of us than a simple marriage certificate. Even if we hadn't spent a day learning each other the way that we had, I would've told him after he left, I found out I'd been six weeks pregnant. That I was scared, and didn't want to leave California but hadn't wanted him to leave his home either. With so many mixed emotions, the weight of being pregnant with only the help of my mom, the lingering shame of a failed marriage, I had convinced myself if my mother could do it, I could too.

When you thought you'd never see a person again, everything seemed like it'd make sense if you took things one day at a time. But I got off that plane and saw him and told myself, he *needed* to know. Even if he and Anna hated me forever, even if it put me in a place where I was in his life in a way less than ideal, I would've told him. Because Olivia back home deserved to know. Because of above all, Olli had made me feel being snowed in proved he had deserved to know from the beginning.

I'd made a mess of the situation, but I didn't have the past. I only had now. I couldn't help thinking what the omission of truth had done to Olli's life. Olli was vulnerable in more ways than one. In the course of 24 hours, he'd dealt with his courtship with Anna being tested. He had reconnected with me in a way I didn't think we could walk away from. And most of all he'd learned he'd fathered a child. *Our* child. There was no way to tell what this all hitting him at once made him feel.

If Olli was another man, it wouldn't have surprised me if he had come back to this car and reminded me that while being snowed in had been fun, now that we had gotten it out our system it had been time to return back to our lives where we didn't exist to each other anymore. But Olli wasn't another man. Learning he'd become a father—learning I'd hidden the fact he was one— took some processing, but I couldn't help feeling I'd pushed him further from the life he'd made for himself as well as push him further away from me.

☙❧

I KNEW MANY OF THEM WOULD BE HARD TO ANSWER, BUT I wished he'd had more questions. Anything would've been better than Olli keeping to himself the entire duration of the drive to the airport. I internally reminded myself that I'd rocked the boat enough. We'd been apart close to a decade, but I knew what he needed just as much as he with me.

When I had asked him for space, he'd been happy to give it. It'd be best to award him the same courtesy. I had owed him that much. It wasn't up to me to convince him he and I deserved a second chance, especially since I hadn't been as good as I could've been making sure he wasn't missing out on his daughter's life.

I had to face facts. He wanted to see Olivia, but he might be so upset with me, I may have to come to terms that I'd ruined any chance at us having a future with all three of us involved. Maybe, in the beginning, I thought if I'd called him, we could be a family. But the more I got used to his absence, the more I convinced myself I'd only cause pain and grief if I had called.

I hadn't wanted Olivia to ever feel rejected, and even though it *was* Olli's responsibility as her biological father, there had been this fear that he'd want nothing to do with me either way and then I'd be worse off than I was now.

At least now I knew he had a genuine interest in what I had kept from him for so long. My phone vibrated in my pocket.

Almost as if she knew I'd been thinking of her in this very moment. My caller ID read *Home*, but I could almost guarantee the person on the opposite end would be Olivia.

Olivia wasn't used to us ever being apart for so long in a short amount of time. From the time I'd carried her to giving birth—even now—never more than a twelve-hour day a work shift ever kept us apart. She'd missed me, but the feeling was mutual. Mami was missing her just as much as the other way around. Olli wasn't speaking to me; what could it hurt to just let her know I was on my way home?

"¡Oye, bella!" Kissing sounds made from my end of the phone seemed to catch Olli's attention. I know he was avoiding me, but the sound of Olivia's laughing voice brought me out my pit of darkness wondering what to expect next from Olli.

"Mami, where are you?"

"I'm on my way to the airport, baby. You know your Mami misses you, though!" I whined through the phone, and I noticed not all parties were as happy as I was listening in on my conversation. I tried not to notice every tell Olli's body reveal, but his knuckles turned white, clenching his fist at the use of the term *Mami* being thrown back and forth. He knew who I was talking to; I just hoped he didn't think I was trying to throw it in his face. I know he'd only just known about her, but she relied on my presence, my call, my voice to assure her she felt safe. Even him being upset with me felt small and insignificant in this moment.

His hand loosened its tense grip the longer he listened in on our conversation. Our conversation was a mixture of asking about my time here, what she's been up to in school, as well as a lot of nothing. Even he had to know that despite his feelings about me, we shared something bigger than both of us in common.

Olivia.

As his hands and facial expressions softened against the backdrop of our conversation, I felt guilty knowing there'd be no passing Olli the phone so he could receive the same affirmation and love I got from this call. That made me feel the most guilty of all the things I'd been responsible for in my short time here.

"I love you, Mami."

A mixture of a laugh and almost-cry combined with my reply. "I love you, too, baby." Both us of fought to hang up the phone on our ends. I waited for the call to drop and put my phone screen in its lock screen before placing it back into my pocket. We reached the entrance driveway of the airport and I tried to only think of how long it'd take me to get home. Anything beat having to think about how long it would take for Olli to speak to me.

Focus on Olivia. If I focused on my daughter, I wouldn't have to focus on Olli. I wouldn't have to think about him as my husband, or that in time he could become my ex-husband. The worse had already dome, but if there was worse to expect, at least I'd be prepared for it. We exited the car after Olli parked in the nearby garage and fetched our luggage from the trunk. It'd be another few minutes before we reached the first gate. Olli fixed the collar of his jacket.

"Are you coming?"

❧ 2 2 ❧

Olli

With an eighteen-hour trip between layovers and delays, I was sure I'd be able to balance my worrisome mind with other things. It wasn't looking to be the case so far. All I could think about was how afraid I was. I couldn't know, or even plan what I would've liked to say. From Benny's recollection, the daughter I never knew, knew nothing about me either. I don't think I had ever been this nervous. Except...for that time I was on one knee proposing to Benny.

What if I made the wrong impression. What if I said the wrong thing? What course of action would I take should Olivia not want a father? What do I say to make her feel good about my absence all this time? All these hypothetical situations frightened me. It was a relief I hadn't been showing any signs of it to Benny.

I had to exude strength when I felt like I had none. I was glad Benny had gotten rest in the times of our many stops, but I envied the fact she'd had less to worry about. From listening to their phone conversations, she was well loved. One can only dream of building a relationship that strong.

Once we reached California, something in the air changed. I

tried not to notice it, but it was there, eating away at not just me, but Benny too. I rented a car so we would be able to move from destination points much faster, and let's face it—in a place like California, the only way to travel was by car. Benny managed to convince me to make a pit stop to get coffee, and I didn't object because I could've used the caffeine. I'd gotten two hours of decent sleep, tops. I wanted to be alert, but if she offered to drive, I wouldn't stop her.

It wasn't long before the destination was in the rental's GPS and challenged with an hour and a half drive to her place. A quiet drive didn't bother me; I quite enjoyed the ambiance of the sound of other cars on the road, forcing yourself to learn the vehicle you'd have a connection with for the limited time you had with it. But once we reached the general area of Benny's living situation, I can't say that I was pleased.

Benny hadn't mentioned much, but she had shared that she would be moving in with her mother soon, and I couldn't help but wonder if she were struggling financially. The neighborhood we drove through was probably safer than it looked, but it didn't feel right knowing Olivia and Benny had been living in poverty, all the while in Finland, I'd been doing the complete opposite.

The GPS lead me to a modest apartment building, a two-story house, which I'm sure they occupied one of the floors. "You sure you want to do it so soon?" Benny protested. "You're running on an hour and a half of sleep and—"

"If I don't do it now, I fear I'll lose my nerve," I interrupted. "I've waited long enough. I think I deserve to see my child after learning of her existence."

Benny quietly agreed, sensing how withdrawn I'd been the last few hours. From the look on her face, I'm sure she was surprised I was finally showing some sort of emotion. The animosity between us? It was going to be there until it wasn't. But I'd say introducing me to Olivia would be the start of something evolving.

Deep down, I knew this was gently punishing her. She wanted

inside my head, and I couldn't give her that right now. Nothing but opposing forces controlled my emotions right now, and a part of me needed the space. Without it, I couldn't be the Olli she wanted me to be, *needed* me to be.

What felt like hours had only been a mere thirty-four seconds from the time I pulled up, to the time we got out the car. She led me to the entrance, a dark red door with light brown outlining. The apartment itself didn't look that bad. In fact, I'd call it charming if the house next door didn't have boards on one of the windows. But I nearly bumped my head on the front door's low entrance height. Some places got it right in the US, but I'm sure I was spoiled from most of my homes being built from scratch and accommodating my tall frame.

"Do you mind hanging out in the living room at first? Just so I can have a moment to explain things better?" Benny whispered, forcing me to lean down to her height to hear her better. "You're her father, but you'll still be a stranger as far as she's concerned. Give her more than a chance encounter, okay?"

Benny took my nod for an answer, disappearing into rooms foreign to me in her home. If I had been present this whole time, I'd know exactly which room was the kitchen, the place I'd prepare coffee and morning breakfast. It pained me to know I wouldn't even know which bedroom was ours or Olivia's. That is if she even had one. I couldn't imagine moving in with someone based on convenience and things being accommodating. Benny's home may as well had been a labyrinth. A maze of frustration and wonder that could only lead me to feel even more insignificant than I felt. I should've just followed Benny. Get the moment over and done with.

But I'd waited this long. What were a few more minutes?

Several voices could be heard from a distance, both mature but one significantly older. Benny's mother, perhaps? Even if I had been close enough to eavesdrop, it wouldn't have mattered. Since

Spanish was Benny's mother tongue, why would I expect her to converse to her mother in any other language?

I understood some, but I should have made a stronger effort when I'd had a patient teacher. In comparison, Spanish had always come off more assertive than my natural language, so I wasn't able to tell the tone in the way they spoke enough to consider it a heated exchange or healthy conversation.

A soft, kind, younger voice joined in. Surely, that was my daughter unless someone else lived here. Her understanding in Spanish was minimal, maybe even less than mine, and I couldn't help thinking we already had something in common.

"I'd like for you to meet someone, Olivia." My heart skipped a beat. Were my palms getting sweaty already? There was a tightness in my jaw I couldn't relax if I tried. The moment was here. Whatever happened now would make or break me.

Every detail in the way this meet up ended would give me insight on what's to come for the rest of our lives. The sound of footsteps made a brick form in the back of my throat and I just hoped as the door opened, I'd be able to speak. Benny led Olivia, hand-in-hand, as she stole a look before directing her attention back to her mother. Even in person, it was hard to ignore her warm brown skin and thick curly hair. Other than that, she'd grew much more than I call tell from a single image shared through phones. If I had seen her walking by before Benny's reveal, I would have certainly had questions.

"This is my friend Olli, the one I was telling you about?" Her attempt at reiterating whatever she'd shared about her several minutes before. Olivia was reluctant to speak, but I knew why. There was fear in her body language but more curiosity than anything. Was she smart enough to piece together why this encounter was so important?

I hadn't casually been around children save for visiting family on holiday so sometimes I forgot just how small a little human could be. I took the awkward silence as an opportunity to introduce myself. "Hi Olivia, my name is Olli," I smiled, hoping she caught the nod to her name with mine. "I'm sure your mother told you we knew each other from a really long time ago, but as soon as I saw her again, she wanted to tell me about you."

I couldn't believe I was staring at her, face-to-face. She didn't appear as happy to see me, but that didn't matter to me. She already seemed more independent than I thought she'd be. Studying my appearance closely, it didn't take long before she turned to her mother and asked, "Can I talk to your friend by myself?" Benny had done her best to convince Olivia that her presence would've helped answer more questions. But Olivia was firm. Her insistence forced Benny to excuse herself into the next room, but not before reassuring her she'd only be a room away if we needed her.

Once Olivia was convinced Benny had gone a considerable distance, she revealed just how perceptive she really was. "I kind of look like you." As her lip curled, not quite disgusted, but trying her best to figure me out.

"You look like your mother, too." She hadn't given me much to reply to, but her next words confirmed her suspicions about me being here.

"Are you my daddy?" She hadn't wasted any time, surprising me with her overfamiliarity. How could this not be my daughter? She was to the point with one of her first questions. She didn't favor me all the way, but she looked enough like both of us to come to her assumption.

"Biologically, yes," I admitted, trying not to patronize her. "Would you believe that I didn't know about you until now?"

"I don't know," She spoke in an indifferent tone, like she was challenging my lack of emotion. "Mami never talks about you. I didn't even know you'd be..." Whatever she'd wanted to say, in a moment of choosing her words more carefully, she'd chosen not to finish the sentence.

"Be what?" I asked to counter her hesitation.

"White?" She admitted shyly. It'd almost come out like a question. Like she wasn't sure she was allowed to say it.

"Yes, I am white but I am also Finnish."

She looked confused. "What's that?"

"It is what you call a person from *Finlandia*," I smiled back. "The way you are an American because you are from the United States of America, Finland is where I am from."

Olivia's lip curled to one side, taking in me and all my words. "So I guess that's why we've never met. Because you live so far away?"

"Olivia, if I had known about you, there would have been no reason I would have lived so far away. I am sorry for how much time I've been away. I would love to make that time up if you'd let me." I made it clear that I wanted to make time for her, but only if she were interested in rehashing our relationship. As her demeanor changed, her emotions became unreadable to me. She gave me one last look over and created a distance between us, despite never losing conversation with me.

"Sometimes it just seems like all the girls at my school have a daddy. I used to wonder why I was the only one without one, but I guess you were too far away. I wish you'd been around more," As an ocean of guilt washed over me. So much, I thought I'd drown if what she said next was turning me away. "I guess you're here now right? Is it for good this time?"

"Olivia, look at me." I bent down to meet her height and saw the many things she shared physically with Benny. Deep brown eyes, thick eyebrows, and a curt smile. "I know I can't make up for yesterday, but I'd like to make up for today, tomorrow, and forever if you let me. I'd understand if you don't forgive me, but I want a daughter-father relationship with you. How does that sound?"

"Sure," Olivia shrugged, and for some strange reason, it made me laugh.

"Just, sure?"

"Did you want me to say no?" Before I could even answer, Benny stormed through the room. Her main intention was to have Olivia mind her manners, presuming the tone she's used to be sharp in nature. I hadn't come to that conclusion myself, but even if I had, I would've encouraged Olivia to speak freely. She didn't owe me her immediate respect.

Benny instructed Olivia to get herself cleaned up for dinner, as I stood in the middle of the room, disappointed our first encounter had been cut so short. "I shouldn't have expected her not to come to her own conclusion of who you were." As Benny gave off the impression that she was ridden with guilt over unintentionally admitting she'd been listening in. "I'm sorry if you felt like she should—"

"I don't want her to apologize for speaking her mind. It wasn't an ideal first encounter, but I didn't expect one based on the circumstances," I interrupted.

It was no one's fault we were in this situation, but it would've helped if Olivia would have at least known *something* about me. Even a little bit of information would have better prepared her for a situation like ours. We were different in some of the things I could tell from the surface, different upbringings, different mannerisms. But considering, I couldn't have expected a better outcome.

"It just felt a little too grown for my taste. You'll decide for yourself if and when you consider Olivia to be overstepping boundaries of parent and child, but until then, I just want to make sure she's respectful." She went on to admit how naturally curious Olivia had been before the exchange, but she hoped we could've all talked about it together. She'd been doing it alone all this time. I wasn't shy about admitting I'd appreciated a one-on-one attempt at conversation.

She wouldn't have to do things alone anymore. She wouldn't have had to if she hadn't been so fearful of picking up a phone to call me. But I wasn't going to argue that factor. What we needed now was unity. Olivia deserved that much from us. "I am confident that this way was better than other possible outcomes. It didn't blow up, as you might say."

I could tell that Benny had wanted to explain the idiom better, but thought against it in the moment. "I should go—"

"Go?" Benny asked confused. "Go where?"

It'd slipped my mind that I'd booked a separate hotel room a few exits from here before we got on the road. I hadn't done it out of spite, but I'm sure it appeared as such. I no longer felt the anger I once did having met the daughter I never knew. But I still needed time to myself to think. "I won't be spending the night," I admitted. "But I'm a phone call away if either of you need me."

"Olli, I hope this isn't about—"

"It isn't about anything," I interrupted. "I just need...time." Benny appeared to have an understanding of my decision not to stay here despite the obvious. There may be a time I accept her invitation, but tonight wouldn't be one of those times.

23

Benny

Here are the rules regarding your current punishment.

1. *You are not to text me, with the only exception being in regards to Olivia.*
2. *There will be times I text you, and if it doesn't require a response, you are not to reply.*
3. *Olivia is to be dressed and ready by seven-thirty when I pick her up to drop her off from school.*

I will arrange to pick her up, too, and will text you if I plan to spend the afternoon with her, in any case, this form of communication will not require a reply.

For the duration of my stay, should you happen to break any of my rules, your punishment will be prolonged. Make me proud.

That was the text I received the night Olli and I had flown in to California. Since we'd come to the States, we hadn't had a real conversation and while it was for my own benefit, the lack of communication between us worried me. The only time we'd really talked was when he admitted that whatever papers I'd signed back in Finland had been destroyed, and when he thought there'd be a better time to discuss it, he'd let me know.

That meant he and I were still technically married, and I had no idea how to feel about that. I guess I should've been happy. After all, being reunited and sharing my truth with him about our daughter made me realize that he had been the only man I've ever loved. But a part of me felt this overwhelming guilt of not getting in contact with him sooner. It only made it harder that non-communication was his favorite form of disciplining me. Verbal communication was how I worked through my issues and non-verbal was how he worked through his.

As much joy it brought me to see and feel Olivia's excitement after seven years of not not knowing who he was, she'd finally had a father, I wondered just how long he'd planned to torment me in the process. What was on his mind? What was he thinking? What exactly was it he was feeling right now? I didn't even have a hint of knowing as he isolated most of his free time focused on making up on lost time with his daughter. Unfortunately, all I seemed to receive were the regular check-ins, so it surprised me this morning when he texted me this morning asking if we could spend time, all three of us as a family, he called it. I wanted to see him but only after the torture was over. I loved my Dom but right now, I just needed my husband.

His Lexus RX rental pulled up at exactly nine A.M. and because it was the weekend, I'd let Olivia pick out her own clothes today. I'd even spent the morning doing her hair in an intricate design of intricate braids and loose ends because she, in the week of getting to know him, was obsessed with impressing her daddy. I pulled my own hair back in a low ponytail, choosing simple over eye-catching since in a way this day was for Olivia anyway. There wasn't really a point for me to go all out when Olli saw me the exact same down as he did when I was dressed up.

Unless under his request, I decided what I wore but I did miss the times when we lived together and he'd spend an hour of his free time setting aside clothes he thought I'd look good in. Even then I was able to put my faith in him to help me put my best foot forward. His guidance had always been a thing I craved.

My heart was a pool of emotions as Olli approached us, and Olivia leaped into his arms. He spun her around as she screamed in delight and even gushed when he complimented her hairstyle, just as I knew he would. He put her down and gestured for me to follow them to the car.

"Iskä, can I sit up front with you?" she asked with joy welling up in her soft brown eyes. The second day they spent together he'd made it known to her how much it would mean for her to call him Iskä, the Finnish term of endearment for daddy. I was sure he'd let her do anything she asked of him, as long as it followed with Iskä after it, so it surprised me when he bent down to meet her height and politely told her no.

"As much as I would love that, Olivia, I'd like it if your mom sat up with me today. Is that alright with you?" He brushed a gloved finger along her chubby cheek, which caused her to blush and smile. She nodded as he helped her into the backseat as I readied myself to the passenger side of his rental. It wasn't like I expected to be banished to the backseat but seeing how he wasn't talking to me in our normal way of functioning, I didn't see much of a difference if I had.

Before I could make it to the door, Olli had finished helping Olivia in and was at my side to open my door and even helped strapped me in with the seatbelt with this knowing look in his eyes, that despite me being his version of disobedient and him taking disciplinary action as a result of it, he still found a way to let me know I was precious and cared for and that it'd all be over soon when he was ready to discuss what we'd do in the long run of decision making.

As he returned to the driver's seat and started the car, he

interlocked his strong, long fingers in mine, bringing the back of my hand to his sexy full pout to kiss. It wasn't the affection I was hoping for, but it still felt good to feel his touch again. Inhale his skin again. Rejoice in the rush it gave me to have his sexy mouth against me. Maybe I hadn't been great at earning it these days, but I was happy to see at least in the eyes of our daughter that it looked like we weren't fighting.

"Missä olemme menossa?" I asked, the conversational Finnish I knew coming back to me as he pulled out into the road. That was one of the first things I learned to ask, moving with him to Finland. I'm sure he got tired of me asking where we were going because I pretty much asked every time we left the house.

"Tulet näkemään," he answered me back in his low native tone. *You will see.* And while that was the most he'd managed to say to me directly all week, it didn't take away the pride I'd felt at that moment. We were on our way to spend our first day together. Not just the two of us but as a family.

❧

I should have assumed our first family outing would be someplace in the wilderness. I, for one, was a city girl and didn't care for the great outdoors but Olli being from a country that prided itself on its scenic forest trails and legendary sights, he loved a day spent outside bonding with nature. With so many state parks to choose from, he'd chosen Julia Pfeiffer Burns State Park for its waterfall and beautiful beach promises. I was amazed at how much Olivia was enjoying the steep path leading to the legion of landmarks this park was famous for. Before today, I'd always worked so much that when I did have the time to do our mother and daughter things, we did a lot of things I thought she liked, like going to the movies or going shopping. The few weekends I got off, I'd try and take her to theme or amusement parks. But seeing her take after her father with his love of animals and fresh air made me realize that quite often, I neglected spending time with her in a way that truly forced us to unplug from everything in our city life and just enjoy each other's company in a way the city never gave us the chance to.

As both of us flanked her sides with her hand in each of our own, she began with her own little questioning. Things I hoped I'd have a few years with getting her used to the idea of us both being around, but perhaps there was no fooling her.

"Iskä, how did you meet my mami?" Olli's eyes cast a teasing glare, all wide-eyed and mythically greener in the presence of natural surroundings, as he turned to look at me. A small smile formed at the corner of his full pout as if somehow seeking my permission to indulge her how we'd really gotten together. Up until last week, she hadn't even known what he looked like, so I choked on the thought of preparing myself for this situation should it ever come up. I wasn't asking with my eyes for Olli to lie, but that didn't mean I wanted him to be one hundred percent honest.

"Well," he started, "I met your mother on a blind date." That was actually the truth, I laughed to myself. "What's a blind date?" she tugged at our arms, signaling for us to lift her over a thick collection of branches that her short legs would have surely tripped over. She happily squealed as if she were taking off for flight.

"Well," he paused, "it's when you're set up with someone through a friend you mutually share and respect who thinks you might like each other despite not having the opportunity to see each other's photos first."

Olivia laughed. "Why would anyone agree to go on a date with someone when you don't know what they look like?"

"Because you trust your friends to know what sort of people you like. When your best friend thinks you might like a new TV show, don't you trust them to know what your television preferences are before they suggest something to you?" he asked in a way that helped Olivia understand without asking a dozen follow up questions.

"I guess so."

"That's how a blind date works."

"Did you like my mom when you first met her?" He shot me a second look that was mysterious as it was playful. When I look back to that time, I wasn't really sure what was going through his mind at the time, all I knew was how *I* felt. I'd never been more attracted to someone my first time meeting someone.

"Very much." Was all he'd managed to say but in his own little way was like saying it was love at first sight.

"And did she like you?" He swung the hand he'd had interlocked with hers forward. "You'll have to ask her." Olivia turned to me, cheeks blushing and an innocent, goofy grin on her face. Olli knew how I'd felt but it didn't stop him from putting me on the spot. If anything, it was good to show Olivia that feelings were there in any case Olli was serious as I thought he was about getting back together. She'd never seen me interact with a man in the same way I was around Olli. I hoped she'd internalized that as putting value in relationships that were special and not just the ones that were available for the time being.

"I did like him. He was so sweet and quiet. When he stood for the first time, I had to adjust my neck because I didn't realize he'd be such a tall person. Maybe most would have been scared of him, but I thought he was very kind and polite." We walked a small distance in silence until Olli decided to be the one to break character and add his own version of our story.

"Your mom was wearing this all-white dress, and back then, she used to style her hair the way she does yours. She was like no one I'd ever met before. She got me to smile within the first five minutes of knowing me. Besides you, your mom has been the only girl with the power to make me laugh. We talked to each other every day after our first date, even if it was to tell each other good morning and good night." His take on the interpretation had sent a rain of shivers down my spine. He remembered such small details about our past and it warmed my heart knowing he was sharing those sweet moments with Olivia. I always wondered how his brutal honesty and straightforwardness would translate as he embraced the path to fatherhood but he'd somehow managed to stay true to himself without coming off as unloving. It would've been so nice to have him around in Olivia's formative years. Although she was still so very young, a lot was bound to change with the possibility of her father being more present.

"Look at the beach." Olivia broke free from our reigns as she darted at her own youthful speed at the landmark up ahead. "Olivia, stay at a distance where both of us can still see you. If we can't see you, you're too far away." Olli demanded but it was the first time all week we'd had any moment alone where Olivia wasn't an earshot away. I wanted, no *needed* to know how long it'd be until he was speaking to me again.

"Thank you for all the sweet things you said to Olivia." Adjusting the gloves on his fingers, he stopped and glared at me with a bout of awkward silence. It wasn't uncommon of him to resort to staring if he'd felt the last thing said to him didn't require a response. He knew how much it meant to me to have conversations and express myself openly, so freezing me out was an effective form of discipline to correct my misbehavior. And I hated it!

"When are you going to decide to stop torturing me, Olli? Haven't I been punished enough?" This time he'd broken his vow of silence just to give me a sliver of what I wanted from him. And that was an explanation of when this thing might be over soon. I just wanted to be his again.

"Not until I say you have. There are lots of things I've wanted to say but have chosen not to in fear that in my anger, I might misspeak. I promise you it is better we talk when I'm ready to provide you with a well-thought conclusion to my feelings about our unique scenario. In the meantime, it's satisfying that we can be pleasant in front of our child while we figure out the issues between us. She spent seven birthdays not knowing anything about me. The last thing I want her to think is that her parents argue all the time or don't get along."

That, I appreciated. She was just a kid. A kid who'd gotten a father after years of praying for one any time she had a holiday wish. I wanted to display a united front, and unfortunately, this was just Olli's dominant way of presenting that. Eventually, he would stop being angry with me but it wasn't now and I had to respect that.

"You should see the way her eyes light up at the thought of me loving you. She knows her mother deserves love and happiness. Just like I do. But today isn't for me or for you. It's for Olivia. We'll discuss it further when I decide that I'm speaking to you." He brushed my cheek with his bare hand before he excused himself to join our daughter in her excitement of the gorgeous sight up ahead. A smile formed on my face as I watched the two of them splash around in the running water with threats to take their shoes off to see how deep the water went.

"Olli, please make sure she doesn't get her hair wet," I begged as he nodded and hoisted her up on his shoulders only to have her scream about her being afraid that he would drop her.

"I would never drop you. My job from now on is to keep you safe. That's if you want me around more."

"I do want you around me," she yelped the further he walked into the deep end of the water.

"Yes? But like every day more or like every week more?"

She rested her chin on the top of his head and guided him through the water by his ears. It was so precious. "Every day more. I'd miss you if I didn't see you all the time like I see Mami."

"I'd miss you, too." And it was in that second that I took out my phone and wanted to capture this tender moment between them. Olli had years to make up in photo album memories. I couldn't have thought of a better time than now to start.

"Hey, you guys. Let me get a picture of you two."

"No." Olli shook his head with a playful smile.

"C'mon; *please*," I begged, but his mind didn't budge. Was he really so upset with me that I couldn't take a picture?

"If you want a photo, take your shoes off and come in with us. The only way I'll let you take it if you're also in the photo." He provided a more thorough explanation. I stripped out of my socks and shoes and got waist deep in the water, clutching my phone tightly so that I wouldn't drop it. With her still on his shoulder, he wrapped his arm around my shoulder and together we captured our first, in what I'd seen as many more, family photos. My definition of the perfect day.

❦ 24 ❦

Benny

One positive thing about today? At least I knew the way Olli was treating me was temporary. I admit I wasn't pleased with the lack of attention I was so used to getting from him in better circumstances. But I was humbled by the fact he was spending it with our daughter. It was hard being jealous knowing I'd racked up years of memories with Olivia; at best, he'd had a few days.

He was developing his own way of bonding with her, completely separate from the way I bonded with her, or even the way he bonded with me. I'd had my own careless reason why I hadn't told Olli in the first place, but it was seeming to matter less and less.

I knew now that Olli would've likely done anything just to keep food on our table, even taken work that didn't meet his skill set. A life like that would've still been happy; but a selfish part of me liked the way Olivia seemed so impressed by him, knowing he had the means and wealth to spoil her at any time, and likely would be based on his seven-year absence in her life.

If any kid deserved it, it was my Olivia. *Our* Olivia.

I watched from the backseat as Olli attempted to teach her useful words in Finnish as he went on to tell her he'd picked up a little Danish and Swedish from his travels in Scandinavia, while still managing to master a conversational level of German. Should I have been blushing this hard? My cheeks were warm and tingled just a bit from their exchange about what musical genres and musicians she liked—or at least the ones I let her listen to, as he flubbed at the names of American acts like Bruno Mars and Taylor Swift.

It was like watching a movie on my favorite channel. It came as no surprise Olivia hadn't wanted the day to end. "Aw, do we have to go inside?" she whined just moments after Olli had pulled up to our house. We'd all collectively unbuckled our seatbelts and Olli reassured her they'd get one more memory before we exited the car.

"I will walk you in and make sure my girls are okay. Is that okay?" Olivia nodded and I swear the sudden rush to my cheeks would've been noticeable if I'd had lighter skin.

"I wish that we could hang out longer." Olivia pouted, despite her father reaching in to hold her hand and lead her toward the building. She was wearing that sour face too—that look that rarely worked on me, yet through the looks of it, was clearly melting Olli's resolve.

"I would enjoy that, too." Olli only looked in my direction for a half a breath. He wanted to be able to make decisions or reservations considering Olivia but still wanted to respect that my authority was still important. "But I will only do it if your mother is okay with it. I do not wish to overstep her boundaries."

Olli wouldn't normally ask my permission for something he felt just as entitled to, but it was clear I'd already set rules for Olivia, so I appreciated that he respected that. Things could change in the future. I wouldn't expect Olli to follow my lead forever when it came to raising our first daughter. But right now we were taking things day by day.

"I'm okay with you two spending time with each other, so long as you're home by a decent hour." I directed at Olivia. Olli nodded as we walked up the stairs to our floor. As promised, Olli got us there in one piece. I assumed he'd know he had an open invitation inside the apartment I now shared with my mother, but he was polite. He wanted to be invited in as there was no reason for him to wait in the hallway while Olivia changed for dinner.

Mami must've been cooking. There was a lingering scent of peanut sauce fragrancing the entire living room. If I didn't know any better, I'd say contrichop con arroz was on the menu. I should've called her ahead of time to make enough, should Olli have wanted to stay for dinner. Mami stepped out of the kitchen, mouth agape, surprised Olli was standing in the living room.

"Buenos días, Ms. Obiang." His tone soft, his hands gestured in front of him as if he were about to bow.

"Hello, Olli. I'm assuming you are staying for dinner, no?" For reasons known more to me based on my relationship to her, it seemed like an invitation to mock me, more than genuinely invite him. She wanted nothing more for him to be the father mine had been to me.

"I'm afraid not, Ms. Obiang. But thank you anyway; everything smells amazing."

Mami was not expecting him to be so cordial, faking a smile while making a backhanded comment in Spanish too intelligible for more than herself to hear. When Olivia ran into the living room, Olli met her with a bent knee to reach down to her height, as she climbed into his arms to give him one last finally hug. They already loved each other.

"Can we go out to eat?" she asked him, knowing I'd intervene.

"Abuela is cooking. Don't be so quick to ruin your appetite."

Olli surprised me when he brought his gaze in my direction, nearly hypnotizing me to say yes to anything he'd ask. "Is ice cream fine?"

I knew that any answer that wasn't a yes was likely to make me the bad cop in our co-parenting dynamic. It wouldn't have mattered though; when he paid attention to me, there was never a time that I'd say no. "Yes, but in moderation. That's fine."

Olli twirled Olivia around in a playful manner I'd never seen him behave before now. "We're going out for ice cream. How does that sound?" Olivia giggled, alerting the entire room at just how excited she was to be going out for sweets that went beyond the traditional sweet plantain or rice pudding that was always waiting for her at home. Olli walked over to me and awkwardly kissed me on the cheek. Once it was over with, Olivia gained his full attention as I followed my mother into the kitchen.

I'd silently thanked her by pressing my palms together and mouthing *gracías*, for keeping the animosity down, especially keeping her opinion to herself in the company of Olli and our daughter. She held nothing back in my company, however.

"Maria Bendícion, why is that man still here? Did he not get what he came for?" Referring to the divorce papers she assumed had been the reason for his trip. I never went into detail what had happened in Helsinki, and with his absence, she had right to her suspicion. But I'd never actually known what happened between her and my father. For all I knew, their fallout could've been the very thing that stood between me and Olli a few days ago. But because I'd never asked for any details, accepting my father wasn't interested in taking care of me, she was in no position to judge. Especially since Olli was stepping up.

"What he *came* here for, is a relationship for his daughter. Which he does have every right to."

"Since yesterday?" She challenged.

"Since Olli and I are *still* married. I should've made that clear the moment I got here, but Olli and I have decided a divorce wasn't best for us right now."

Mami's eyebrows furrowed, as it was met with lips curled based on the confusion. "So, wait; I am confused. Was he not to marry another woman? Was that not the reason you flew all the way to another country when responsibility plagued you here?"

Mami knew which words to use to trigger me to defend myself, but I'd be cautious to admit the things that were *not* her business. "Ma, all you need to know is that Olli wants to get back together so much, he was willing to shred the already signed divorce papers, uproot his entire life to California, just to be the best father he can be to Olivia. Would that be okay with you?" I was on the fence of whether I wanted her to hear the sarcasm in my voice or not. She was used to being blunt, but her harsh words were rarely rooted in sardonic humor. I loved her, but who was she to argue with what was right in front of her? At every turn, she looked for cracks in Olli's armor to prove he wasn't perfect. To prove he was more similar to a man I barely knew than different.

"So if you two are still married, why is he staying at a hotel?" Mami wanted me to have no answer. It was obvious from the start she'd wanted to one-up my recent reveal. Even if I gave her a reason, she wouldn't be satisfied with the truth. That Olli was still upset. With me. The trust I so easily gave away during our reunion, would have to be earned back on my end. I was patient enough not to force it. I wanted forever to have a lasting effect.

For now, I'd just let Ma believe in my naivete. She was just protecting me from pain and heartbreak, but I didn't need protection from Olli. I needed his protection. Olli wasn't my father. He was his own man.

The same man taking our daughter out for ice cream right now. The same man that welcomed news about his daughter with dignity and humility, instead of punishing her with my mistake.

Maybe things weren't going the way I'd planned them to, but I was sure they were going the way Olli planned them to. And I'd be selfish to ask anything more of him.

❦ 25 ❦

Olli

Her hand felt so small in mine. The smooth feel of her cinnamon complected little hand. Even as we waited in line for ice cream, I was impressed with how well behaved Olivia was in comparison to the other children around us. Up ahead there was a little boy who'd dropped his cone for being too impatient to listen to his mom's instructions of eating it slowly. But my sweet girl stood quietly by my side, tugging my sport jacket with the occasional question about how many toppings she could get once we were the next in line. So sweet and polite like her mom. I gave her arm a little shove, her gaze centering on me with wide-eyed innocence.

"Did you know Finland is the world's fourth consumer of ice cream? This means where I'm from, we eat far more ice cream than you do here in America."

"But isn't it cold all year round? I looked it up online and every site I went on says that Finland is always covered in snow. That some people even bring out their skis just to go to work and school." That idea made me laugh. Olivia said some of the most charming things and I loved every second of her wild ideas that involved my native land.

"I don't know about skiing to work, but it sounds like fun. And to answer your question, yes it is cold most of the year but it is why we appreciate summer when it comes. Even so, not even five kilometers of snow could keep us away from our beloved ice cream. Do you have a favorite flavor?" As we approached the beginning of the line, the chalkboard behind the long glass case displayed the two dozen or so kinds of frozen treats they had available for the day. The colors ranged from an assortment of tastes, textures, and flavors that even I was uncertain to what I might choose. I decided I'd let Olivia decide for me. After all, if she were truly her father's daughter, she would choose wisely with a flavor I was sure to love.

"Umm...I like caramel. Oh and cookie dough," She blurted out as if remembering the moment she got close enough to get a quick refresher course on all the flavors. "Actually, I sort of like them all; it's just those are my favorites. Do you have a favorite, Iskä?

"I like caramel, too." I offered a warm smile. Caramel was what I'd get. The things Olivia and I had in common were almost frightening. We shared the same love of nature and for that, I couldn't wait for her to see my home in the spring and summertime. Similar sense of humor. Quite often, I had to break down clever things I'd said to the unwilling recipient, but Oli always seemed to get when I was trying to be funny, and it always put a smile on my face when I could make her laugh. I loved seeing that toothy smile. If I were to look back at my own childhood photos, I was certain she and I were missing the same teeth, so it wasn't hard *not* to see my seven-year-old self in her.

And now, she and I could bond over ice cream flavors. Everything I knew about her I loved. To think I'd convinced myself I could never love another the way I did her mother but I was wrong. These women in my life were the death of my unhappiness.

There were things about her that reminded me of her mom. Her ability to strike up a conversation with people she barely knew. Her desire to have long debates about everything and sometimes nothing at all. The traits she inherited from the both of us truly defined what it meant to be the best of both worlds and I looked forward to every moment we got to spend with each other from this moment on.

Finally reaching the ordering counter, I let Olivia persuade me into getting the largest size available of creamy dulce de leche but only if we could sit down and enjoy it together. She'd come to learn that her father didn't do anything on the go. I liked to take my time to enjoy things, the thing in question being more of her time. We carried our bowls to a nearby booth with plush red seats that squeaked when we sat across from each other. A medley of Benny's striking beauty and my unique oddness, I couldn't help but admire how beautiful this girl really was.

"How do you like the ice cream?" I asked popping a spoonful in my mouth as I watched her savor a frozen bite of hers.

"It's really good."

"You know there's a place in my city that has the world's best ice cream." She pointed her little spoon at me, offended I'd even suggest a better place than here.

"In your opinion."

I nodded. "Yes, it is in fact, my opinion. But I'll have you know they have dozens of flavors you'll never see here. Tastes you'll only experience in Helsinki." I flirted. "Perhaps one of these days we can go sometimes. If it's okay with your mom. But you have to like the snow," I teased. Her eyes lit up at the mere suggestion of snow.

"Are you kidding? I love snow. I wish we didn't always have to visit mom at her job just to play in it."

"So, you don't mind the freezing cold? Having to bundle up to stay warm?" The man-made snow I assumed she spoke of could hardly compare to the late winter in Southern Finland but to my delight, her answer was like music to my ears.

"Everyone thinks I'm weird. I prefer snow to the warm weather."

While I did have a preference for Helsinki's short summers, the winter hardly bothered me. I was happy to discover it didn't bother her either. I had so many places I wanted to show her. "Do you think you could see yourself living in a place where it snows all the time, like where I live?"

She shrugged, this time looking her own age instead of the seven-year-old going on thirty-five attitude she usually displayed. "Yeah, I could. Even if it were just to see where Santa Claus lives." That ounce of knowledge made me smile again. "Word is, there's a place called Lapland, and that's where Santa really lives. Not the North Pole like I've been led to believe this whole time." She finished her statement as if I were unknowledgeable about that very subject.

I rested my chin in my hand, ready to unveil a well-kept secret. "I hate to confirm but it is true. He makes it a priority to visit the children on his Finnish list first. Another plus to the holidays where I am from." I smiled and in turn, she rewarded me with a smile in return. She took another spoonful from her large bowl of ice cream, and it was evident that she was much faster at enjoying her frozen treat than I was. I actually liked the milky mess it was becoming.

"Can Mami come, too?" she asked as if sensing our rift from today's nature trail. "Of course she can. Your mom loves it there. I know you'll like it, too."

"Iskä, do you love my mom?" I hesitated, feeling bulldozed and backed into an inescapable corner. At seven, it was hard to believe she even knew anything about love the way adults expressed it but she must have known something; otherwise, she wouldn't have asked such a provoking question. Perhaps she was more mature than I'd come to realize. This being our first in-depth conversation about something she wasn't able to see with her eyes, but that greatly impacted her life.

With me being around more, things were set to change for her and I didn't want to start our relationship with my sugar-coating the past I shared with her mom. She deserved to hear the truth about my feelings. "Olivia, I love your mom very much."

"But do you love her or are you in love with her?" she asked with an adult perception.

The only answer was that I was in love with Benny, maybe even the only woman I'd ever loved. "Olivia, when I look at your mother, I get knots in my stomach. To answer your question, I am both in love and love her as a person."

Her lips pursed to one side, looking more like Benny when she made her quick last minute decisions. "I hope you don't get mad at me for asking this then. If you loved my mom so much then why were you gone for so long?"

Another complicated subject that required time to process my thoughts on the matter. If I wanted to teach my daughter anything, it was openness and honesty in a way that was not compromising. "Well, let me explain to you in a way you'll under-stand." I started. "Your mom and I were together but then we broke up a long time before you were born. Sometimes, there comes a time when you take on more responsibility than you can handle, but the problem is, when you're in a relationship with someone, you don't have just yourself to worry about. It's your partner that counts on you, too.

Back then, I tried to be a good partner for your mother but failed at being a great one. I loved your mom so much that what I was going through, I didn't want her to go through with me. Have you ever worked on an assignment at school where you had to work as a team with one of your classmates, and no matter how much work either of you put in, you still received the same grade?" I explained and to my relief, she needed no further break-down on my example.

"That's what it's like to be married to someone. When one person fails at it, both of you suffer as a result. I didn't want your mother to do more work just to be left with the same outcome. This is why I left. I wasn't sure I could take care of her, the same way she took care of me and I hated myself for that. Time went by and I went on to meet someone else. I was happy for a while but the idea of meeting you made me happier. Does that make sense to you?"

She nodded, taking the very last bite of her bowl of ice cream, the spoon lost in her mouth as she licked it clean of the last caramel swirl that remained. "I think Mami really likes you. She spends a lot more time getting ready when she knows she's going to see you and she's always sad when you don't give her any hugs." It was sweet that Olivia cared so much about her mother's well-being. I'm sure it was hard to watch her mother alone with no one taking care of her the way she took care of others in her life. Benny's empathy and compassion were so admirable but when her kind face transformed into desolate emptiness, I sensed some-thing wrong deeper than taking the bite of her once full bowl of ice cream. I didn't like seeing her unhappy.

"Is everything okay, Olivia?"

"Yeah." She shrugged. "It's just when Mami is sad, she typi-cally says no to everything I ask her. A few weeks ago, she promised I could go to one of my friend's slumber parties, but then she got back from traveling, and her mind changed. All of a sudden, I couldn't go."

She meant when her mom returned with me from Finland. I could see how Benny's mood could have shifted from that event. "And you think it's because she's sad," I questioned. "I don't know but could you talk to her? I'm going to be the only one out of my friends not there and I already don't get to go to all the things they invite me to because they live so far away." I thought back to the whole week and a half I've been here and not a single moment had I spent a moment alone with Benny. I genuinely missed her. The way her scent consumed me. The way her taste revived me. Even the way her voice sounded after a long night of sleep comforted me like a pleasant lullaby that eased my stress away.

I wanted to spend the night making us both feel human again. I was ready to put this dispute to an end and cherish the woman I valued most in my life. I'd given myself plenty of time to think about it, and I was ready to forgive her. No more grounding.

"How about this? As of now, you can go," I said knowing I'd have to have a long talk with her mom. "When I drop you off, I'll talk to your mom about it to bring us to the same page, but also mention that it would be tragic for you to miss the sleepover of the century over something so trivial."

"But what if she doesn't listen to you?" she whined.

And that's what she didn't understand about her parent's relationship. Benny always listened to me. "She'll listen."

"Yeah, but what if she takes back your permission."

I gave permission, not her. Another thing our unsuspecting daughter wasn't keen to. "She won't."

"But..." she started. I pressed my fingers to her small pout, quieting her from further worrying.

"You let me deal with your mother, okay? You are only allowed to focus on the fun you'll have with your friends tonight." Overjoyed with happiness, Olivia's fingers moved in record speed to text her friends she would be attending the night's festivities. And now that left to my own planning. How I would make it up to her mom for going over her jurisdiction. Olivia, she wasn't the only one who'd had fun marked on their things to do list. Except mine involved more screaming and fewer clothes.

AS I ARRIVED AT BENNY'S APARTMENT BUILDING, I WAS relieved to see the text I sent earlier had gone through telling Benny to meet us outside. I walked Olivia to the door and her mom greeted her with a hug with an outcry of all the fun we had at the ice cream parlor. I bent down to Olivia's level, insisting she go upstairs to get ready while her mom and I talked a bit. I knew there was a chance Benny wouldn't be happy with my decision but I knew she'd be thrilled to know her punishment was over.

Like a good girl, Olivia did just as I asked as I took her mother's hand and led her to the rental car door. Once I secured her inside, I made my way to the driver's side as I turned my body to face hers. She did look remarkably more put together than earlier, so I suppose there was truth to Olivia's confession earlier. In all fairness, she was always a vision of heaven in my eyes.

"I gave Olivia permission to go to her friend's sleepover tonight." I got straight to the point. Her brows furrowed at the suggestion as confusion lined her feminine features.

"What? Olli why would you do that? You had no right to tell her she could go."

"So I have no rights as her father? Is that what you mean to tell me?" My comment silenced her, causing her to press her lips together as if holding back what she really wanted to say to me. "She seemed visibly upset she couldn't go. I was afraid your current feelings about us were affecting your recent decision making. Or at least that's what I got after speaking to Olivia about it." A smile adorned her face, as she began to laugh hysterically before collecting herself to address me.

"First of all, Olli, she played you. I can't believe you fell for it. Did she happen to tell you why I told her she couldn't go? Her last progress reports were *terrible*. I told her until she brings her grades up, she didn't need any more distractions. Texting her friends all day is the reason she takes so long to do her homework *now*. I didn't want to reward her, especially because I know she's capable of better." I nodded, impressed with how good an actress our little Olivia was. If she was failing school maybe it was because entertainment was in her future.

Benny looked lovely and yet stressed, I knew this would only add to it but there was no way I was going to go back on my word with Olivia. "I will see to it that Olivia spends the next quarter of her studies pulling her grades up to a more than satisfactory level. Even if we have to hire a tutor. But for now, I still want her to go to that sleepover. My decision still stands."

"Give me one good reason she should go to that sleepover, Olli!" she spat. This time frustrated that I hadn't faltered in my decision even after hearing out her reasoning for Olivia's punishment. "Because I miss you. And I'd like to spend the night kissing and fucking you. I've had days to plan out our next play session. It is better if Olivia was someplace you deemed safe but wasn't our concern for the night."

A small smile formed at the corner of her pouty lips as she let go a deep exhale at the dismissal of her sentence. With the crook of my finger, I signaled for her to come closer, declaring the punishment over with a kiss to her sweet lips. The kiss was gentle, soft at first, eventually graduating into a tangle of tongues and lips as if we hadn't seen or felt each other in ages. When she backed away from me, we were both drunk with lust and breathless but I suppose that was to be expected after twelve days of no sexual contact.

I pulled out my wallet, her curious eyes following my every move. "I had my credit card companies overnight me cards with you listed as an authorized user. Before the night ends, I want you to buy the prettiest dress and the sexiest lingerie and heels to go with it. Do whatever makes you feel pretty." Her hands traced over the risen letters of her first and last name on the weighty plastic as she secured the three cards in the back pocket of her tight blue jeans.

"Do you have a color you'd like to see me in, Sir?"

My cock grew hard at the sound of my triggering nickname.

"It doesn't matter. You won't be wearing it long," I said with a light brush to her smooth dark cheek. Minding my manners, I remembered the key I'd gotten earlier for the hotel room she'd be staying in for tonight's play session. The card I gave her next was the hotel I planned our play.

"That's where I'd like for you to meet me tonight." She flipped the card over in her hands taking in the address before placing it along with the cards she stuck in her pocket. "Be ready by eight. I'll contact you later with the rest of my details," I said as I offered to walk her inside for one last chance to let her know I couldn't wait to see her tonight. I took her arm as she attempted to walk inside.

"Don't try to walk away without kissing me." And at that, she leaned in to give me a small taste of a kiss. A kiss that wasn't mine yet but would soon be once I brought her to her knees. "Try not to wear anything too short," I advised with a slap to her ass that had her sashaying off in defiance. She was going to wear whatever she wanted. But I was going to do whatever I *wanted* to her for being the brat that I loved her to be. As she disappeared into the building, I couldn't wait for her to see what I had planned.

Benny

How many times was I going to check myself out in the mirror? Maybe as many times as it took to realize the woman I was staring back at was me. I looked like me, but it'd been so long since I put in this kind of effort. While I always practiced proper haircare techniques, tonight I went out of my way to hire the best natural hair stylist to recreate my nostalgic curls.

Stretching and straightening my hair was just easier over the years, especially since I had Olivia's hair and my hair to think about, but since Olli wanted me to experience a pampering I wasn't accustomed to at any point in my life, I took it upon myself to allow my Dom to worship me in all the subtle ways that weren't traditional interaction. I'd gotten my nails and toes done, tried on a dozen outfits before I decided on a cherry red, curve-accentuating sweater dress that complemented the heels I'd splurged on because I'd never known a nude, open-toe heel that was *my* deep-brown nude.

A good skin regimen here, a little mascara there, and I was nearly unrecognizable. Striking even. My natural hair did that for my appearance, so I can't remember a reason why I'd stopped wearing it so free. There had been times where I put in more effort than just jeans and t-shirts, but never like this, and never for someone as special as who I was pulling all the stops for. All eyes were on me, and for the first time in a long time, it felt like a good thing.

With so few brown faces, I definitely stood out in the upscale bar Olli and I planned to meet each other. Being the center of attention made me feel alive, and desired and wanted, despite how introverted in nature I'd grown. Ladies either gave me stares of envy or compliments at how beautiful my skin tone comple-mented my dress and that was tame compared to what all the men had to say.

By the way the men at this hotel approached me, you'd think I was a famous actress or something. "Can I buy you a drink?" A white man in a grey suit and peppered hair asked while wondering if I had a room at this hotel. He wasn't my type, but he thought he was by the way I'd flirted before telling him I was waiting for someone special.

"Can I get a drink for the lovely lady?" A man with a nice tan and crisp poplin shirt and slacks later asked. He was a bit sleazy, wondering if I *worked* here and if I had a certain price for what he was interested in. Killing him with charm and kindness was all I had. "I'm not a hooker if that's what you're implying," I smiled, biting my lip. "But I bet you couldn't handle what I had in store, so while things are civil, it'd be best to just walk away while your dignity is still intact."

For a long time, I didn't really worry about my safety. Not that I haven't been a woman all these years that I've been single. It's just between juggling motherhood and gaining a few extra pounds, it'd been so long since I'd felt sexy. I remember being that age where men would go out of their way to chat me up and because I didn't know how to say no, or feared it, I'd force myself to grin and bear even the worst male attention.

I should have been afraid of this guy, but I wasn't. Just knowing Olli might be somewhere, watching. Made me feel safe enough to have the courage to turn even the most tasteless of men down. Much of the men that approached me wasted no time bringing up that they were doctors, attorneys, hedge fund managers, businessmen of every field. They only wanted one thing, and it killed them that I was turning every single one of them down.

Olli's instructions were clear: Appear available. Charming. Irresistible to the point no man could walk past without taking a second look. If they seem like someone you might like, feel free to flirt and make them think they have a chance, but in the end, turn them down.

It was all a part of the game he wanted to play, our roleplaying. He loved the idea of other men wanting me, every man wanting to fuck me. Each man that approached would be expecting something from me that I wouldn't be giving up tonight. Or at least not to them, and not to just any man for that matter. I could have my pick of any man, but I would *choose* to go home with him.

One of my favorite scenarios of our blissful past was just what he'd plan for me tonight—a scene I could never turn down. I'd go into a place and tease him; I wouldn't know he's there, but my presence alone turned him on, so the version of me who put in effort was bound to blow his mind. Any man who sparked conversation I was welcome to give it to them, so long as I gently sent them on their way after the expectations of sexual encounters were off the table.

It worked him up and challenged him to see me flirt with other men, plus teasing him on top of that? He would have his hands full with whatever punishment he had in store for me, and as a woman whose faith was recently restored in love, but submission too, I would gladly take it.

"You've been here a while," a handsome stranger stated and sat down next to me and his dark eyes smiled with him. "I hope someone as beautiful as you wasn't stood up." He was attractive, my age or a little older, with just enough naughty in his smirk to suggest he was gentle but could handle a woman in the bedroom. When you were kinky, you just knew if a vanilla guy could satisfy a woman by his body language alone.

He was confident yet gave a comfortable distance that implied he wanted to be near me but respected my boundaries. In a normal setting, I may have even given him my number if I were single. If I had been horny enough, I would have suggested we go up to his hotel room and get to know each other a little better.

None of those details mattered once Olli came into view. Securing a seat at the end of the bar, his virescent eyes locked on mine, daring me to bring attention to him. His signature slicked-back hair appeared close to brown in the dimly lit room, but even in the darkness, his fierce shade of arctic green eyes glowed in the distance. I wasn't sure if he'd gotten so riled up, he could no longer hide in the distance while other men adored me.

But he nodded, giving me his stamp of approval to carry on and entertain my current guest. "No. Not stood up. Just looking for the motivation to head up to my hotel room. The way my night is looking, I might head up early." The stranger smiled, and with that revealed a dimple in his California tan that normally would've had me curious.

"Well, I guess it's a good thing I came over. Can't have you turning in early before I got the chance to talk to you," he flirted. It'd been so long since I got this kind of attention, I laughed at his attempt to humor me and flirted back. Olli positioned himself so that his elbows rested against the bar's high surface. He took a sip from a modest cup of liquid, which from this distance looked like vodka, but could have been water to keep himself hydrated.

I wanted to make sure he was paying attention, so when I had an open invitation to lean into my bar mate, I did so just enough to draw attention to the cleavage I hadn't hidden. Despite how respectful he'd been during our encounter, he was weak to full, shapely breasts within his eye shot. The cut of my bust was high enough where I wasn't spilling out the dress but still provided a nice view. Hell, if I weren't me, I'd probably be staring at my breasts.

A gold pendant rest against my throat, a collar I'd bought just to show Olli I hadn't forgotten what I was, who I was to *him*. Even though I entertained my guest, all I could think of was Olli. Wanting his attention, wanting his affection. My pussy clenched at the sight of Olli flinching at the sight of my sexy stranger's finger lightly rubbing my hand. He must've said something as his reaction hadn't reflected how well things had been going up until now.

"Did you hear what I said?" Clearly frustrated, the stranger turned around, not being able to ignore the Nordic prince who was demanding my attention. He wore a pained grimace before thanking me for wasting his time. All I saw was the back of him while he left the hotel bar and never looked back.

Olli smirked, intrigued and eagerness shining through his dangerous eyes. He pretended to be a stranger just like everyone else, pointing first to his drink, then to mine. Now I finally felt comfortable taking that drink.

He snapped his fingers to catch the attention of the bartender, as the tapster disappeared into the back, returning with an expensive bottle of wine. Olli pointed to the red wine—a clear nod to my preference over white—and took the two glasses the barkeep offered. It wasn't long before he made his way over to me.

Normally, Olli wasn't the flashy type. In the time we'd reconnected, he wasn't one to flaunt his resources like a squanderer of money. But when he sat down, it became perfectly clear the person he'd agreed to be for the night and I was about to enjoy every second of it.

"I couldn't help but notice that it looked like you needed a drink." He poured until it reached an adequate level in my glass and handed it to me but insisted on me drinking the water to my side before I indulged. His dark grey suit was pressed, cut and tailored to fit his body in the most delectable way, his carefully knotted blue silk tie matching the handkerchief that peeked out his breast pocket. I wasn't picky about what turned me on about a man's style but I didn't think a woman alive could resist a man so beautiful in a three-piece custom suit. At this point, it was going to take more energy to turn down his efforts as I did with the others. Even my eyes screamed that I wanted him. Sometimes I had to sit and remind myself that no matter who he was playing in a scene, I was still the luckiest woman alive who got to call this man my husband.

"Thank you. Wine just happens to be my favorite." I said taking a sip, admiring the strength in his hands as he poured himself a glass. "How are you tonight?" he said in his heavily accented English. He scooted his chair in closer as my heart rate quickened at the act of him being so close to me. It felt like it had been forever since he was this close to me.

"Better now." He laughed a low laugh. Bringing the glass to his lips to take a sip from his drink. "I take it you're not a regular here?" He leaned on the table, invading more of my personal space that would've been uncomfortable with a complete stranger but was fine since it was only Olli playing a role.

"Why, do I look familiar?" I asked, cocking my eyebrow.

"Honestly, you don't look like anyone I've ever seen before. I think that's what made me approach you. I'm sure you've heard the saying that if you stand in front of a piece of beautiful artwork long enough, there's no way you can leave without going home with it." He said with an arrogant grin, his eyes taking turns glancing between my eyes and bustline.

"Are you saying you want to buy me and hang me up on your wall?" I flirtatiously asked, in an attempt to make things more interesting. Keeping up with my pace, he answered with a coolness that made my clit swell with an eagerness. How long could I keep this up for?

"Perhaps not hang you up but I can think of a number of things to do to you pinned against a wall. Does that mean you're for sale?" He said, again with that cocky grin that was so out of his usual character.

"No, it doesn't. But thank you for the wine." I held up my drink and put down the glass pretending to be offended. It couldn't have been furthest from the truth—if anything it exhilarated me to hear Olli speak to me that way. He was always the perfect gentleman but that other side to him was one of my favorite things about him to experience. He eased up, leaning back in his chair, giving me considerable distance from the moment before.

"I'm not the kind of person who apologizes for saying what's on my mind but I get the impression we got off on the wrong start. Perhaps we can start over by introducing ourselves," he recommended.

"I'm Carmen."

He repeated the name back, a large emphasis on the 'r' that was reminiscent of the rolling in my native Spanish. "Nice to meet you, Carmen." He shook my hand, bringing my fingers to his lips to kiss. The gesture sent another craving to my clit, aching and needing to be touched. "And you are?"

"Yours."

"Yours?"

"All night if you'll have me." he slyly added as he took another swig of his near-empty drink. If he had been some random stranger, I'm sure I would've thrown my drink in his face by now, but it was my Olli, and he was doing such a sexy job at getting me to leave with him. It wasn't part of his game but I was ready to just get up and go with him right now. Saying all the right things in all the right ways was taking a toll on my self-control and after a week of him staying a few cities away from me, I was aching to let his love consume me. Even if it ended in disciplinary actions.

"Keep me company for the night." He leaned in, his hand traveling up the fleshiest part of my thighs as his fingers settled on the outside of my barely there v-strings. Unable to fight back the moan it induced as his fingers massaged the outside of my panties, his dripping fingers revealed more than my words could.

"Mmmm..." He whispered, making sure no onlookers were keen to what we were doing. "I wonder if I water it, will she bloom for me?" His low, hungry voice growled, forcing my body to tremble and tear apart praying he'd make due on his promise. Pushing my panties to one side, he brought two of his fingers to my mouth, forcing me to never lose eye contact.

Olli ran his fingers on the curve of my lips, plunging them in and out of my mouth until they were dripping just as much as me. He brought his damp fingers between my legs, carefully spreading both lips to expose my sensitive nub. He bit his lip, "There she is." As his slickness mixed with mine rubbed and caressed, a constant tender motion until he was convinced he wanted to taste it.

He licked his fingers clean and teased me with, "Sweet. Just like I knew you'd be." As the vibrating of his cell phone appeared to take him out the moment, his demeanor changing from a patient tender lover, to that of a man in a rush to be somewhere else. "I'm afraid I have to run," He lied through convincing eyes. "Unfortunately, this is as far as things go."

Heat and arousal, a feeling of being on the brink to something explosive, swelled between my legs, my curling toes and my pebbled breasts underneath my dress, at being denied what he'd brought me so close to. Denying my orgasm when he knew damn well any additional movement would've had me bouncing off a wall. This was the game—Olli knew I was going to try and convince him to stay—he worked me up to the point I couldn't function without his touch, and we both knew a little begging could go a long way.

"Wait, do you really have to go?" I whined. "After all that, it would be a shame to not finish what you started." I bit my lip.

That was too much teasing to end things now. Maybe I sounded a little desperate but I was already soaking through my panties and in dire need of him. It was cruel to end things before they even got started. "I'm afraid so lovely." He said with the utmost sincerity in his eyes.

"Well, wouldn't you like to take my number?" Asking as a last attempt to change his mind, but his mind was made up. He wanted to bring me to a point of begging and personally, I wasn't there yet.

"I'm not sure what I'd do with your number. I'm just in town for the night, but I'll tell you what I would take. Your panties."

I laughed condescendingly. "My panties? Why do you want my panties?"

"Well, I'm the reason you're wet right now. Do I not deserve a souvenir on behalf of my hard work?"

I was reluctant to take my panties off in a public hotel bar but by now the crowd was clearing out and there weren't that many people looking in our direction anyway. There was something dangerous about walking around with no underwear on and tonight that's how I wanted to feel. Dangerous.

Without warning, I slide the straps of my v-string down my hips and past my thighs. His eyes watched me with keen delight as I brought them to the base of my feet and slipped the lingerie in his large palm, closing it shut.

"Thank you." He pulled them out to admire them before securing them in the pocket of his expensive trousers. "It was a pleasure." He said as he stood up and adjusted his tie. Without looking back, he walked out of the hotel's bar as I sent him a text on where to meet him next. No answer.

"We're meeting up still, right? I texted again and after fifteen minutes of waiting around to see if he'd even read the text, I was beginning to feel like something had really happened. It was rare when he didn't let me know what was up or would happen next and unfortunately, I didn't even know what room he was staying in. Only the one he'd gotten for me. What happened to me being off punishment? Clearly, something had gone terribly wrong. It wasn't like him to not tell me even the smallest detail of where he may have run off to.

Maybe it was Olivia? No, if it had been, I would've been the first person to know about it. My number was on my mother's speed dial in case of emergencies. Her friend's mom had a list of numbers to call in case I wasn't available and my mom was listed as the first.

Olli, I don't know what happened with you, but I wished you had told me something. I spent the past thirty-five minutes waiting to hear from you, was my last text to him. The time read eleven thirty-seven, and I didn't plan on waiting all night hoping he'd return. Taking one last look at my texts with no new replies, I grabbed my clutch and proceeded to the hotel's lobby, a lavish expanse of empty elegance, to the hotel's elevators. The wait wasn't long as I enjoyed the pleasantries of the music that played as I rode to the second highest floor. This really was a beautiful place to stay if anyone was on business or even vacation. From the museum inspired walls to the still corners and luxurious accents, I hadn't even known I desired to stay in a place like this until tonight. As I approached my room for the night, I pulled out the key card Olli gave me earlier today, the heavy door opening with a soft click as I hurried inside. The room was more than spacious but dark as I struggled to find the switch that powered the lights as I toed out of my heels.

Through seconds of wall searching, light filled the room with the flip of a switch as I jumped back at the image of Olli sitting comfortably on the edge of the room's king-sized bed, taking a swig of something dark in a highball glass. "Fuck, you scared me."

"What took you so long?" he asked, sounding almost irritated. The idea he'd left me hanging had nearly crossed my mind but I was relieved to know he'd been up here waiting for me the whole time.

"I spent the past hour waiting to hear from you." I snapped back, knowing my attitude would further infuriate him. "You could have just told me you were meeting me up here instead of having me wait on you," I added, ducking for cover in the bathroom to avoid the anger building on his cold, menacing features. That was where I made my first defiant mistake. Assuming I'd earned the right to know more than what he told me in regards to his night planned, my second was not addressing him by Sir.

He materialized behind me before I even had time to think, his tight grip around me as his opposite hand cradled the smooth, delicate skin that led to my neck. His skin appeared so pale against mine, a perfect blend of contrast that was both striking but equally mismatched.

"You watch your tone little girl." His eyes intrigued with the way I looked under his needy possession. "You're going to learn some respect."

In one swift movement, he guided me from the bathroom to tossing me haphazardly on the spacious bed. Removing his cuff links, as he went to loosen the constraints of his tie, it became clear just how jealous he was with just a small exchange of words he'd let slip from his rambling.

"Did you know what it felt like to sit at that bar and watch strange men ogle and stare at your tits all night?" He spoke with an intense sharpness that made every nerve ending I had, spark with a stimulant that'd be hard to come down from. "What were you thinking, wearing a dress like that?" He gestured, accentuating my luscious curves as he ran his hands invasively over my hips until he reached my breasts and squeezed.

"Stand up. I want to examine you and make sure you're still mine." At his command, I was on my feet. Without my heels, I was humbled by his towering six-four frame, which I'm sure was his intention from the moment I fell out of them. He crossed his arms at his waist, offering a scolding gaze that wasn't easy to decipher.

He circled me, reasons he wouldn't reveal until he demanded I take off my dress. "Lose the dress by pushing it down your hips and letting it fall to your feet." I followed the first part without pushback. "You are not to be seated until I'm done with you first."

I pushed the dress down until it reached my hips and stopped. Should I want to make it easy for him? Or should I invoke the brat in me and make him work? "I take it you don't like the dress, Sir."

"Did I say you can speak?" The intensity in his eyes grew, forcing him to take my actions as a sign of defiance. I shook my head before the hunger in his eyes grew to the point of mouthwatering need. "Dress off, now. If I have to demand it a third time, I can promise you will not like the outcome." It was the final motivation I needed to follow his command, but if I hadn't been wet before, it wouldn't be long before I was dripping down my legs and I wouldn't be able to hide it.

The real humiliation came from being naked, bare without any adornments or enhancements. I was nude, as in without clothing, but I got to feel as beautiful as he already saw me with my barely-there makeup. My Sir wanted me as bare as we could get away with in the short amount of time we wanted to get to this, and as he watched fully dressed at my body free of clothing.

That meant no bra to perk me up, no panties to hide my arousal. My stretch marks from childbirth, my curves that have been added to my figure over the years. Olli took in everything as he circled my body. Most people were only truly naked during showers and sex. Imagine having to be so while your Dominant silently watched you, all while you're not entitled to what they're thinking.

"As I watched every man walk up to you with the intention of defiling your body, I craved each and every opportunity to walk right up to you and defile your body in front of them," As he cradled my face and burned through me with a harsh stare. "It was infuriating. They needed to know you were mine, but frankly, you needed to know your place too."

His hand glided close enough to my sex to feel its heat but didn't allow me the sense of touch. He was teasing me. And for the love of God, I needed him to touch it. Pet it. Lick it. Make it purr. "But you know what infuriated me most?" He prompted the question, but assuming I couldn't speak, I decided not to provoke him.

"Knowing how much of a slut you are, you probably liked all the attention. Huh, little girl?" He grabbed my chin with a hint of roughness that still felt playful, as he brought my face to his, expecting me to answer.

"No, Sir," I lied and with that fabrication, he held my face in his hand and lightly struck my jaw.

"Get on the bed with your arms stretched in front of you, but keep your ass up in the air," he demanded, but not before slapping my behind before he let me go.

"Yes, Sir." I walked over to the bed, my knees trembling so hard, I couldn't walk straight. I positioned myself as he asked me to, and from a distance, my sense of sound tried to pinpoint what he was doing. A drawer opened and I could hear him rummaging through its contents. The wait was worse than what it'd actually be; one could only assume it'd be my punishment.

He returned, securing my wrists to each side of the bedpost, with restraints that would restrict my ability to move my arms and hands. "That should keep you in place." As he made sure to turn my face the slightest bit, just so I could see him smiling.

"Now tell me, you little slut. How many men came up to you with the expectation to fuck you? And I suggest you answer wisely, as a lie will have interesting consequence."

I took a chance and recalled the amount I remember approaching me an hour or two back. There'd been at least five if you included the handsome stranger, but I wasn't sure how long Olli had been watching from a distance. For all I knew, he could've only witnessed my encounter with the very last suitor, and any answer past that would garner a much more severe punishment. To be on the safer side, I went with, "Two."

Olli laughed. "I told you, lying would have consequences. I counted five. Tell me you can count up to five." He taunted back, confirming he'd been watching me from the time I sat down. He wasn't a hard person to miss but I guess I'd let my admirers distract me that I hadn't noticed him at all. Shit, I should've said five.

"I'm sorry, Sir. I assumed you only meant the one from the moment you came to the bar, I thought he was the only one you saw me with."

"So you knew it was five and you chose to lie to me anyway. That's not very nice of you. I'm going to give you a lesson in counting. For every strike I land to your bottom, you're going to call off the number until you reach seven. If at any time you lose count, we'll just have to start over the process. Maybe then you'll remember how much lying is bad for you. Raise your head if you understand." I raised my head and nodded and without any additional warning came a slap to my exposed backside. Olli didn't always use his hands but of all his choices of impact play, there was nothing that hurt half as much as how good the sting of his hands felt. Then the burn of his palm met my willing ass. That was one.

Another hit to my rear end connected with no time to anticipate it, and another, and another and then another. The next one stung so badly that this time I did actually lose count. Air stopped pumping in my lungs as I questioned what would become of me for forgetting which number we were on in my spanking. "What did I say about losing count? Now it looks like we'll have to start all over." But by now I was almost out of it, drifting off and seeking comfort in my subspace that he could've said anything at this point and no doubt I wouldn't have fought him on it. He untied one of my hands as I circled my wrist at the kinks that formed from it being tied up. I thought he'd untie the other hand but the second he pulled out a wand massager from one of the nearby drawers, I knew he'd planned on giving me more work to do that would only make receiving hits even harder to focus on. He powered it on to the lowest setting.

"Hold this up to your pussy but under no circumstances are you to come without my permission. And let's not forget you still have yet to master the art of counting." The strong vibrations the wand offered my core were overwhelming at first, but by the first slap to my ass, I knew the feeling was going to build up so intensely that whatever permission I needed for an orgasm that was already on its way, would happen before I got a chance to beg for it. The sharp whacks echoed in the near silent room and by a double back-to-back strike on four and five, I almost lost my balance on strike number six.

By hit seven, I was one step to getting the praise I so desperately sought until the orgasm rushing between my legs and all over my body. Even though I'd tried my damnedest to hold back, the waves of pleasure crashed through me like a meteor shower and a repressed cry escaped my lips and shook my entire lower body to where it showed. Sir would not be pleased. He sat down at the head of the bed, unlocking my opposite hand.

"What did I tell you about coming without my permission?" He cradled my chin in his hand, bringing my mouth close to his with the impression that he might kiss me. His breath was a warm, smooth sensation that tingled against my lips, almost like he'd indulged in a mint a moment prior. The sweet, calming effect of the scent drugged me to the point of intoxication.

As he got comfortable against the bed's headboard, he ordered me to turn around on all fours, opposite him. I couldn't see what he was doing, but his fingers gave me clues, as they massaged my rear end, and the force of his bite on my ass, sent shivers throughout my body.

"Whenever I see that pretty little ass of yours, I just want to fill it." The sound of a glove snapping against his wrist became more distinct, so I had to use my senses to guess since he hadn't allowed me permission to turn around. A squirt from a bottle was the next sound I was forced to decipher, as his cold, wet gloved fingers began massaging my anus.

The slippery, slick substance had to be nothing but lubricant. It was scentless and tasteless, but the slick consistency told me he was about to have fun with my back hole. He kissed my ass, promising that if I relaxed, it'd make it good for him, which in turn would make it good for me.

My body tensed at the surprise assault at the glide of his fingers, smooth as the latex glove he wore, as he traveled to my back hole, and gently moved a finger in and out, a controlled motion that had me wanting more. "You're such a good girl."

As his lips pressed against my cheeks, and the double sensation made my knee tremble to the point where I was gathering the strength to keep my position up. "You like my fingers up your little ass, don't you? You dirty little slut." I moaned at his name for me, a name he'd only use when he was about to go harder.

It'd been ages since I did something so wild. I'd always been curious about anal training, but out of any Dom I'd worshipped, none of them had ever made me feel safe enough until Olli. He'd been patient and I'd been willing, and it wasn't long before it was one of our favorite acts to perform.

When Olli fucked me in the ass, it never hurt. In fact, everything he did to my willing ass, felt just as good when he fucked my pussy, and I felt honored that he'd loved it so much. He growled, taking another big bite of my ass cheek. The loosening of his belt I would've missed if it hadn't hit the floor a few inches in front of me. Olli crawled behind me, pulling just enough of his pants down to where his erect cock popped out, as he penetrated my pussy from behind.

"There you go." He lips met my ear in a series of small kisses and whispers. Olli only stopped to squirt more lube onto his fingers, as his thrusts continued to stretch my delicate walls, while his fingers stayed deep inside my ass.

The mix of sensations was a whirlwind of overwhelming feels and emotions. Pain and pleasure. Torture and pampering. As Olli felt himself approaching his well-deserved point of refuge; he ordered me to come so that we could have the pleasure of experiencing it together.

In one shared blissful moment, all my dreams and fears, nightmares and fantasies released on one powerful crash, our bodies colliding into one another's until the point of euphoric bliss. I had never come so hard in my life. Not that I was full of myself, but I don't think there'd ever been a time he had either. Streams of his overpowering masculinity burst inside me, as it's warmth and slick liquid made the last few pumps into me so much easier. Olli wrapped his arms around my torso, laying light kisses against my sweat lined back. We sat there for a moment, tears already forming from the intensity of the play session. It was the most intense scene I'd experienced in a while.

"Would you like a minute to yourself?" he asked, knowing I needed a moment to collect myself as the subdrop kicked in.

"Please," I assured him.

Olli stood to his feet, planting a quick kiss on my forehead, as he let his pants fall to the floor and made his way into the bathroom. The tinkering of a shower head powering on was the number of sounds and sensations I was now aware of now that we weren't in the scene. Heavy streams of water hitting the floor seemed to drown out most of my thoughts and any other sound in the room.

Now that I was coming down, I couldn't remember a time I'd felt this free and sexy, alive and in the moment, while also experiencing an exciting fear that wasn't all bad but was still scary after the moment. Submission was just one of those acts that a lot of people didn't understand until they truly experienced it.

To feel powerless and powerful at the same time. How freeing it was to give someone the responsibility of owning your free will. I was more revived than I had ever been. Even other times I'd engaged in submitting. This time just felt different. It made me aware of the ways I could be better. I wanted to be a better mom but for Olli? I wanted to be the woman he needed me to be. The wife I should have never stopped being.

Olli returned to the bedroom with a soft brush, a hair tie, and a scarf as he aided me in securing my disheveled hair into a low bun. Relief washed over me, knowing his past scarf tying skills had been decent enough to cloak my hair from getting wet. "Come," he commanded as he helped me reached a standing height.

"Let's get you cleaned up." Olli was careful to walk in slow, motionless strides as he led me to the shower and stuck his hand in the running water to make sure the temperature was right for both of us.

The warm water brought me back to reality, as gentle, careful hands moved up and down my dark limbs with soft and delicate care. Olli took care of me as no other man had. Maybe it's why I could rarely date after him. I knew no other man would handle my body with such beauty and skill. How I had ever let him leave in the first place would always be my greatest regret. I loved him so much, I wanted him to be a better him.

Somehow I'd gotten lucky enough to experience him at both these points in our lives, and I was grateful to have the same emotionally intelligent man I'd always loved while being able to have him to myself for all time. I didn't even care about his money. With his promise to retire soon, I just wanted to make up for time lost.

He wrapped his arms around my waist, picking me up to rest on the tops of his feet. While I wasn't the shortest woman, kissing him had always been easier that way.

"I love you," I said under my breath as he breathed in, resting his forehead against mine. His eyes were heavy but stayed open long enough to hear me say those words.

"Why do you love me?"

I could think of a million reasons, and once I reached that million, I'm sure I could come up with a thousand more. The main reason, though? He made me feel as if a love like his was the only option. That anything less than him would be settling. Years ago he'd admitted to wanting to be the perfect man for me.

Over the years, he'd held himself accountable, blossomed into a fully recognized human, he'd spent so much time trying to be what I wanted, that he ended up changing what I thought I wanted. You're always told that as a woman, you can never really change a man. But the right man will change for love, improve the things about himself to be better for you. He'd already deserved me, but he wanted to feel as if he'd earned me.

That's why I loved Olli. To him, the world would always be the start of what he wanted to give me. Even if he gave me everything, he'd never feel it was enough. To be loved that hard. I had to ask myself, was I deserving of him? "Because you make me feel like a princess."

My eyes started to well, tears falling before I could stop them. Olli cradled my face, wiping whichever tears he could catch, as he leaned in to kiss me.

"I'm sorry I kept you away from Olivia. You two can never get that time back, but I promise I'm willing to do everything humanly possible to make up for the time you've lost," I apologized.

"Shh..." He pressed his finger to my lips. "I want you to know that I was never displeased with how you handled things. You did what you thought was right at the time. I'm just sorry I couldn't have done more." As his eyes danced and fought my stare with his intensity.

"Please don't think I was trying to punish you intentionally on the way here. I never want you to feel as though I'm treating you as if I don't see you. I need to channel my anger better, I was just caught off guard knowing I had a daughter, and that I could have done more for her." He'd missed her first word, her first step. He hadn't even had the chance to watch me give birth. He was madder at himself than me. That I hadn't trusted him enough to tell him. That I hadn't trusted he could be there for me.

"You've done everything on your own up to this point. You've always been stubborn, but I need you now to let me take care of things. To take care of you. Could you do that for me?"

He was right. I had been stubborn. Forcing myself to heavy lift for so long, I didn't know another way. I hadn't fought for him years ago, but I planned to fight for him—fight for us—because no one deserved it more than us. "I will." I finally let my guard down. Olli leaned in to kiss me again, sweet this time, a kiss reminiscent of our youth. Our first kiss.

"I want to buy a bigger place," His lips still pressed hard to mine. "Someplace safer, for you and Olivia. A place you don't have to worry about having bars on the windows." Even suggesting if I liked West Covina so much, he'd even consider a safer area, so I wouldn't have to uproot Olivia.

"I'm willing to consider a future in California as long as you need, but I want Olivia to get used to splitting her time between California and Finland, too." He spoke through a smile and a kiss. "My parents will want to know their grandchild better, and I, one day, want her to consider Finland just as much a home as she does the US." I wrapped my arms around his neck, startled by him lifting me into his arms. I wrapped my legs around his hips so I wouldn't fall, and joked that I was fragile, requiring his love and tender care.

He carried me over to the shower's back wall, wearing a smug smile and with eyes glassed over from confidence. "When have I ever dropped you during times we had sex in the shower?"

Even after a deep conversation concerning our future, he still had the hots for me and wanted to hear me scream his name. His cock engorged and hard again from our passionate kiss, rested between us, and I honestly couldn't understand how he was ready to go in such record time. "How are you already hard again?" I smiled.

"I'm always hard for you." Our eyes locked once more before he leaned in to kiss my neck. The tender, damp press of his mouth made my pussy wet with need, and want, but most of all, desire. Desire to be fucked again, desire to be his. Olli adjusted me against the wall and teased my opening, rubbing the length of him against my pussy.

"Oh my God," I moaned back to him. "Do you even have the energy, baby?" As his eyes met mine, narrowing as if insulted, as I knew what happened next would make me regret that assumption. Maybe regret was a harsh word. Looking forward to it was more like it.

"If I have the energy to fuck my submissive, surely I can find the energy to make love to my wife." As his hardness teased my lips and pierced the apex of my thighs in one smooth, clean thrust. The jolt of pleasure and pain made me gasp; I was catching my breath waiting for what came next. Toe-curling strokes made taking him in heaven on earth. As long as this man promised to honor and cherish my body, I would be forever his to make love to.

"I love you, Bendición," he moaned inside of me.

"I love you too, Olli." I guided his lips to mine as my beautiful, strong, protective husband made love to me into the night.

❦ 27 ❦

Olli

Leaving that bed was the hardest thing I'd ever had to do. In fact, the only reason Benny and I managed to pull ourselves away from each other at all, were based on promises of many and more moments like that to come. It was official; we were a family again. Benny as my wife, I as her loving husband, with Olivia. Nothing made me feel more complete than knowing I could finally be the father I wanted to be, as well as being the father she'd been deprived of and deserved from the beginning.

We'd all lost time we couldn't get back, and I was sure that I could give both of them—maybe not a better life—but a different one. For all that Benny had given me, both past present, and likely future, I was ready to give her the world. Our bond was as honest and powerful as any bond could be that it was a wonder I'd allowed myself to enter into so many unhealthy relationships.

Dominating Benny had not only proved I was capable of making her feel safe, feel loved, adored and worshipped, but it also allowed me to channel my frustration and aggression in a way that improved our relationship. I honestly don't know how vanilla couples did it.

Walking through with an air of readiness, all I could think about was how and what I'd provide for Benny and Olivia, where we'd live, what our life might be like with more children. I wouldn't trade my experience with Olivia for anything, but I couldn't help wondering what it'll be like if I had the privilege of being there from the beginning.

That's if Benny even wanted more kids. Now that I'd gotten a taste of it, gotten to be present in my daughter's life, I wanted more of fatherhood. I wanted Olivia to get the chance to be a big sister, and help any that came before her to help navigate what it's like to be a part of this family.

But maybe, for now, I was getting ahead of myself. I wanted to see our family grow now that I was officially a part of it for good, but it was best to live in the now, where I knew how things stood. Those goals could come in time and even if they didn't, the burdens of yesterday no longer concerned me. The sense of calm I felt was rather refreshing.

When I'd reached the elevator of my temporary hotel suite, the ride to the twelfth floor gave me time to process everything that had happened over the last few weeks. It had been a temporary refuge, one I now regretted but found necessary to arrive both at this place in my life and relationship with Benny.

Now it felt wasteful having so much room to myself, so far away from my family. I was going to check out and stay someplace closer, even if it weren't as glamourous. I'd figure out our living situation somehow. For now, I just wanted to be near my wife and daughter.

When I reached my hotel room, I should've noticed something was off; it was quiet and I hadn't heard much from back home. I had so much on my mind, I'd completely ignored my room door was open before I even walked through.

I knew she wasn't one to back down easily, but I figured she'd heard and understood all that I had said in our last encounter. Behind the door, I found Anna, waiting for me in what had meant to be her wedding dress. It was bold but didn't surprise me. I couldn't help having some sympathy for all I'd put her through in this short time. She'd lost a life she'd become accustomed to, a husband and possible father to her future children. Maybe they weren't important to every woman, but they had been important to her. But Benny coming back into my life changed everything. Including the future I'd promised to someone else.

But I had to give her credit. Anna was a lot of things, but a quitter had never been one of them.

⚜

IN THE COURSE OF LESS THAN A MINUTE, MY MIND KEPT TRYING to figure out what she thought this stunt would prove, how she found me, whether this sudden appearance should have me fearful of not only Benny's but Olivia's safety as well. But whatever the consequence for hurting Anna was about to reveal, I hoped only I would pay the price for it.

"Anna, what are you doing here?" I asked. I thought it best to keep my tone stoic; otherwise, she might view every way I answer as a personal attack.

"I told the front desk that I was your wife—"

"You know what I mean, Anna." She fluffed out her dress and showed it off as if revealing it to me for the first time.

"Just showing you all that I have left of my wedding day," As she paced along the open space of the room with a challenging gaunt. "When you left so suddenly, I came to the conclusion that it could only be because of that woman from your past. I refuse to refer to her as anything other than your little whore." She spoke sharply, and I could tell that even after all that, she'd been holding back.

"You left saying all you had to say, without taking into account all that *I* had to say, despite me forgiving you for your transgressions. So, I hired a private investigator and tracked you down, so I could tell you that you're a spineless, cowardly excuse for a man. Being left by you made me the laughing stock of *everyone* I know. If you were going to make a fool out of me, the least you could've done was settle your affairs. Make sure I was taken care of first. But no—you had to go back to that whore of an ex-wife of yours, all because she had your little bastard child—"

"You don't talk about my daughter!" I brought her in close, not to scare her but to make sure she witnessed the fury in my eyes when it came to my family. "Or my wife in that slandering manner. I take responsibility that you're upset with *me*. I hurt you and I'll be forever sorry for that. But what I won't take responsibility for is making a fool out of you. Your family has done that enough."

Anna had been hitting below the belt, leaving me little choice but to do the same. It had always been an unspoken truth that Anna's family had racked up major debt. I knew it. *She* knew it. Everyone we knew, knew it. It came as no surprise that marrying me promised a gateway to solve that issue through her to her family, which was why despite never warming up to me, they encouraged our union more than anyone.

Spending years ignoring random phone calls from cousins, uncles, or other distant family members, begging for loans to soften gambling debts, failed business attempts, even to aid in a Ponzi scheme or two. A part of me knew I didn't want to know what and where the money would've gone if I had given in. But nothing proved Anna had been marrying me for something other than love than that moment just before the wedding as she spoke to her mother. I should've put it out my memory but it'd been hard to. You never forget overhearing your fiancée's parents trying to convince her to refuse to sign a prenup.

But Anna has always been smart. She would have rather had something than nothing at all. Being my wife would've solved most of her problems, even if she hadn't been entitled to half of it, had we gone our separate ways. But we never got that far. I won't lie and say before reuniting with Benny that I hadn't wanted it. A life with Anna. I never expected pure devotion from her, but I knew one thing.

That she needed me. Or at least, needed me more than she *wanted* me. If she could have helped it, there would've been little she wouldn't have put up with to avoid the road her parents and family members went down. The money I earned, the money I was about to earn, would've afforded her that and then some.

"Guilt me all you want Anna." I let her shoulders go, but the tension in her torso still remained far after the release. "But let's face it, you would've never been with me had I not been able to provide you with all the things you love." *Things*, not me. There'd been times where she'd outright have a meltdown when I didn't get her the exact diamond bracelet, or pearl earrings or other wasteful jewelry she never wore but begged me to buy her. And I'd do it; making her happy was all I knew how to. Buy her things, make her feel special and valued. But I needed to feel those things too.

Benny made me feel those things.

I wouldn't ever dare to compare the two now, not when there was no contest between them. But how could I not love the fact all Benny wanted was my love, attention, and affection. Wanting those things and loving me when I had nothing. Anna, I would've been lucky if she had ever loved me at all.

As I took her in from head to toe, Anna looked as if she hadn't been wearing that damn dress, she would've ripped it to shreds by now. And I would've welcomed it. At this point, anything remnant reminding me of that day was one too many. "Just tell me something, Anna. If I couldn't have promised you a comfortable life, do you think you would've ever loved me? *Did* you ever love me?"

Anna collapsed to the ground and in her defeated state, shed tears like I'd never seen before. It'd been the most vulnerable I'd seen her in the entire time I'd known her. "I would've grown to love you. But you wanted a fairytale. A life where everything is perfect, including a wife who—"

"What I wanted was a woman who loved me," I interrupted. "A woman who saw me. One I didn't have to second guess how she felt about me." True words. Real words. Words I had never been able to speak until now. I bent down to face Anna, mascara running down her cherub cheeks, flushed and appearing more damaged than I'd known her to be.

"What I failed to see was that I'd already had a woman like that in my life, that I didn't fight for. But I'm fighting for her now. I don't have to ask myself these things when it comes to her. I owe everything I am to Benny. That woman is my wife."

As I stood to my feet, grabbed the suitcase on the side of the bed, and made my way toward the exit. Halfway to the door, I stopped. There was only so much that I could do, and even now, I wasn't even sure she deserved it. But I wanted to be the better person. There was murky air between us, and if I could do one thing, the time was now to do it.

"Consider your parents' debts paid. I'm not responsible for the rest of your family, but this is only under the condition that you never contact me again. No more calls, emails, surprise visits like this one. I don't want to hear you tried to contact my daughter, or her mother in any way. I want the best for you, Anna. I've said that before, and I really mean it. This is your chance to start over. I hope you take advantage of it. And I wish that you find happiness as I have. You deserve at least that. Be well." And without another word, I walked out that hotel room and out of her life for good this time.

❧ 28 ❧

Olli

Nothing made a seven-year-old more ambitious than the promise of freshly popped popcorn. The timer hadn't even gone off and yet here Olivia was, at my side pulling at my clothes impatiently as if she'd never eaten junk food before. It was her turn to pick the film for the weekly ritual she and her mother shared as an effort to spend time together, but this time I was invited to their routine movie marathon, and it was evident that the girl had been more hyper than usual.

"Shhh...relax, sweetheart. It's not going anywhere." Three consistent loud beeps marked the end of its cooking time as I put Oli to work by insisting she grab a large bowl to dump the popped kernels in.

"Take it in the living room, Oli. I'll be right there." In a blur, she zoomed past Benny entering the kitchen, leaving nothing but the wind in her path. "Well, someone's excited," she squealed, looking casually beautiful in her slim fit leggings and thick knitted socks. Her braided hair was styled in a simple milkmaid design that kept her thick hair out of her face and what I assumed, was easier to cover up at night.

"What can I say? Seeing the journey between Miguel and Héctor makes anyone excited." I hadn't seen the movie until Benny's insistence that I watch it with her. There weren't many movies celebrating her own culture, but having heritage from a place with a shared language and history was reason enough for me to give it a chance. I wasn't prepared for that ending. Tear-jerker endings didn't normally affect me, but there was a first time for everything. "Oli could use a brush up on her Spanish. Olivia, don't forget to sing along." I teased.

We were in the process of considering teaching Olivia to learn conversational Finnish, as my parents would appreciate any effort upon meeting their first grandchild. But that didn't mean I wanted her to ignore her maternal grandmother's first language, so this was just as much education as it was entertainment.

"Hey, if the movie runs too late for you, feel free to get back to your hotel any time before it gets too late." She opened the fridge, grabbing a few bottles of sparkling water as I wrapped my arms around her and planted a kiss on her cheek.

"Actually, I was wondering if I could stay here tonight with you and Olivia. If that's okay with you?" I knew this was her space, and I didn't want to intrude, but nights at the hotel were becoming lonelier since Benny and I were on better terms. It wasn't even about the sex. I just wanted to be with my family and cuddle next to my wife instead of retiring to an empty bed. Okay, so maybe sex crossed my mind more often than it hadn't but still. That hadn't meant that cooking breakfast for my wife and daughter couldn't be *also* part of that.

"Of course that's okay, baby. Do you need anything from me to make your stay more comfortable?"

I looked to the living room to pinpoint Olivia's location but decided to say my next request in Finnish, knowing I could speak freely without her ears being subject to my profanity. She didn't know Finnish yet so...

"If you promise me to sleep naked, I'll reward you with making love to

your pussy at the sign of sunrise. I know how much you like when I make you come with my mouth." Pulling away laughing, she slapped my chest as I pulled her in for a kiss.

"She can probably hear you, you know?"

"Right. Because she learned to speak Finnish overnight?" I teased. *"You'll do it for me or no?"*

She rolled her eyes. *"I'll think about it, okay? Let's just get started on our movie night."* She stepped on the tips of her toes to reach in and give me another kiss as she made her way back in the living room with Olivia.

◈

A HALF OF BOTTLE OF WINE IN AND AN HOUR LATER, BENNY nestled up next to me as Olivia turned back to confirm she was falling asleep. "I told you she was a heavy sleeper." Pressing my finger to my lips, I whispered a "Shh..." as not to wake her. The little one and I had plans. Plans we couldn't risk her mom over-hearing.

"I'm going to put her to bed. Meet me in your room in three minutes." I said as I lifted my sleeping bride into my arms. Their apartment wasn't big, so the walk to her bedroom felt effortless as I tucked her into the comforter, remembering the silk bonnet she kept by her nightstand to ensure her hair looked the same in the morning as it did in its current state. "Good night, my love." Placing a kiss to her forehead as I made my way back to my midnight planner in the bedroom down the hall.

As I opened the door to Olivia's bedroom, she sat on her light blue *My Little Pony* bedspread looking older than her seven years as she flipped through a thick women's themed wedding magazine as if taking notes for her future day.

"Okay, Oli. What did you find out for me?" I knelt down by the edge of her insanely small bed, resting my chin in my hands as I waited for her answer. I wanted to plan something big for Benny, but I wasn't sure how to plan wisely so that she wouldn't expect it. That was where the little one came in. As many questions as she asked, it was a normal thing to expect she had a genuine curiosity. With her black marker and track notes, Olivia handed me a few magazines set on the page her mother took most interest in. They were all lovely wedding dresses. Some I could already picture my blushing bride wearing.

"So when mom looked through these ones at the hair salon. Her eyes lingered on this one. This one *and* this one." She pointed to a simple yet classic design. One I knew just about any designer could accomplish. Another was expertly constructed but wasn't entirely Benny's style. While the last was her taste but wasn't memorable enough. I needed something that when I saw it, it bellowed my wife's name. Any dress that was made for her didn't need to speak loudly with words.

"These are lovely but I was hoping to see a dress that was breathtaking but simple. Some that made me feel the way I did when I saw her for the first time. There aren't any others she liked?"

"Umm...there was one other one but the magazine was like six years old. I'm surprised it's not falling apart by now." She handed me a publication that wasn't just missing the cover, it was missing about half of the pages. But I knew the moment I browsed what was left of it, that the dress of her dreams was the dress I just so happened to open the page to. It was elegant. It was intricate and lastly, it was fit for a princess. With the right call, I could have a dress like that custom made in a weeks' time. Plenty of time as we spent the next few days house shopping, just as I had promised her.

"Good work, Olivia." I held my hand out for her to give me a high five.

"Why are we looking at wedding dresses anyway? Abuelita says you're already married to Mami."

"And she's right. We are already married. It's just that, when your mom and I got married the first time, we didn't have the access for anything large or lavish." Her eyes widened as she shook her head of loose curls from side to side. She looked so much like her mother yet oddly enough like me, too.

"Yeah, but you know Mami doesn't like large or lavish. She just likes things to be special." And special it was. Marrying Benny was the single happiest day of my life but if I could have made it more memorable. I would have. Now I was in the position to provide more and I wanted to give her the wedding she undoubtedly dreamt about. "I have photos of the first time. Would you like to see?" Her face lit up at the suggestion, her curls uncontrollably bouncing up and down with a nod of her head.

I pulled out my cell phone and accessed my cloud history with photos dating back almost ten years. When I was with my ex, I'd promised to get rid of them but never got around to it knowing how dear the photos were to my memories. Even when I thought I was happy, it was hard to let go of a time when things were so much simpler and love led the way. In the same situation, it was easy to rid myself of all the remnants that reminded me of Anna. That stage of my life was over. If I had to do it over to be in the same position as today, I would've suffered those years with her for just one night like today's.

After a few minutes of scrolling, I finally got to the pictures of us on our wedding day, looking a decade younger with the same mannerisms that never changed. I really needed to smile more. I promise myself to smile in any new photos we took, even if it was just a few out of one hundred.

"Here. Take a look." I handed her the phone to watch Olivia's expression shifted to an uncontainable level of excitement. "I like Mami's hair in this picture."

"What did I tell you? She used to wear her hair just like yours."

"You look like a prince and she looks like a princess. What's the point of you doing it all over?"

"Simple. Because you will be there. And Abuelita. And you would get to meet **Iskä's** mom and dad. When a couple renews their vows it means they can tell each other things they didn't get to say the first time." With our families present, it would've been more of what she wanted. More of what I wanted her to have.

"Oh, can I be the maid of honor?" she squealed. "I'm sure she'd feel honored to have you as her maid of honor."

"Cool," she added with a yawn that prompted me to tuck her in and kiss her good night. On the walk to Benny's room, I'd come up with the cleverest way to bring my vision to life. She wouldn't be expecting it and it hit two birds with one stone. It didn't hurt that it would fulfill my promise to provide her and Olivia a safer place to live.

First thing in the morning, I'd make a call to a reputable wedding dressmaker to get started on that but for now, since the first time I'd been back, I would have the privilege of cozying up next to my beautiful and *ahem* newly discovered *naked* wife.

I really should have gone to sleep but who could resist a late night snack sleeping right next to you?

BENNY

Whoever said shopping for your dream house was a nightmare had clearly been correct. I never knew I'd be so picky when it came to shopping for a home but in the three weeks we'd been looking, not one of them featured all the amenities I desired. Safety was first on Olli's list in our search. Where he was from, kids Olivia's age could walk to school *and* home by themselves without the worry of something life-threatening on the way there.

Naturally, there were few places in California I'd compare to the safe streets of Helsinki but over the weeks we had managed to decide to split our time between here and his home in Finland. We wanted something definite before Olivia was off to middle school. She would finish up to the fifth grade in California, where we'd planned to live full-time so she could graduate with all her friends. Beyond that, our plan was to move to Finland for the school year and vacation to the US in the summertime. The school system was an obviously better choice where he was from, and we wanted the best for our daughter.

"Olli, honey. Don't get offended at this but, I only see white people walking around. I feel like this might not be the neighborhood I want to live in." I posed the concern to him from the passenger's seat as we drove away from a very thorough eight a.m. appointment. The house was amazing and I loved how there were children playing outside but my idea of safety didn't exactly involve moving into a neighborhood to be the only mixed-race family. "That is fair, but when we relocate to my hometown, I'm afraid there won't be much of a choice." He shrugged as his features formed a sympathetic grimace.

"I know but I know what to expect there. While we're here in the States, I'd love for us to fit in, even if it's just a little."

"You'll like the next one, I hope. It's a Mediterranean and I know how much you love Mediterranean," he said as I pulled on the listing for the home we were on our way to. Olli was right. I did love my Mediterraneans. Something about their design was just reminiscent of the homes you saw people retiring to. My ideal house had tons of bedrooms. This one had five. While Olivia was our main focus for now, neither one of us were opposed to having another baby. Obviously not right away but more children was something that was on our checklist when we got settled into our new lives together. Plus it was my dream to have enough room to be able to host our families around the holidays and special occasions. In a way, we'd been lucky in the family department. Neither one of our families were larger than a hand count, so already this house was looking like the best out of the bunch of our three grueling weeks of hunting.

When we pulled up to the house, I tried to hold back the

excitement I felt from the outside alone. I was actively trying to hide my solicitous emotional state, but from the moment we pulled up, I was in love with the house. Olivia's response to house shopping had been unexpected; I feared the idea of moving to a new place or new country might scare or overwhelm her. She's never known more than West Covina, and even though she'd have her own space—much bigger than before—she had been disappointed at the move between our apartment and living with her grandmother.

If anything, Olivia wasn't shy about showing her enthusiasm. She was excited that we'd be moving to a big house, but most of all, excited that it'd be all three of us. She showed maturity I wasn't used to seeing with her, and I couldn't help thinking that knowing she had a father that loved her, raised her self-esteem.

"It looks like a mansion," Olivia chimed. It was a nice house, but I insisted it was much more family-friendly than the space a mansion would provide. It was definitely enormous, especially in regard to what Olivia was used to. But Olli brought his gaze to mine and thought I should let Olivia be excited no matter what type of house it was.

Olivia looked as beautiful as I always seen her, only today she stood firm that she'd wanted to wear her best clothes, her favorite holiday dress for good luck should we like it. I'd been resistant; before today, I didn't have money lying around to buy a new one, should her dress get a hole or damaged, just so she could wear it as we went house browsing. But Olli stepped in. He reminded me that I'd said I'd let him take care of me, which meant he'd take care of Olivia. Olli could afford to get Olivia an entirely new wardrobe if she wanted. So, it wouldn't hurt anyone to let her wear the damn dress, even if no home impressed us.

At this moment, I had to refresh my memory at the idea I wasn't Olivia's sole parent. It would take work. The years of me being stern were being challenged by the fact Olivia already had her father eating out the palm of her hand. But they'd already developed a bond I couldn't break and sometimes it didn't feel like my place to want to ruin that.

Olli was already encouraging her to pull up her grades, offering his time to aid in her assignments while limiting her social privileges. He couldn't keep up his wall for long, but I was pleased that he could be both kind and disciplinary, without making his daughter resent him. She was Daddy's little girl, and I'd never regret it happening the way it did.

Olli opened the door for both of his girls as he picked his daughter up out the car. She screamed, naturally afraid when he tried to place her over his shoulders. But when she asserted that she could walk for herself, avoiding the fact he was too tall for her to feel safe about him carrying her, she trailed especially close to him, like the sidekick she'd become.

"Before we go in, I must confess. Olivia and I have a surprise for you." He smiled softly as Olivia looked like she was seconds from blurting out the surprise. "We ask that you keep your eyes closed until the big reveal. Olivia insisted on it being a surprise." As his smile shifted from sweet to unreadable. It was clear he didn't want to give off any signs to the surprise. I couldn't anticipate something I had no time to prepare for. We'd only known a week ago we'd be coming here to view this place. The two of them were keeping secrets, acting shifty and keeping me in the dark. I had a half a dozen reasons why they'd hide something, but *what* was still a mystery. Olli placed his hands over my eyes and lead me forward as Olivia's small hand found mine to help guide me through.

"You guys, we have to be quick. The realtor is scheduled to be here any minute, and I don't want them to assume we value our time more than theirs," I lamented.

"Fine," he replied, a playful annoyance in his voice. "You can open your eyes now." As his voice suddenly came up from behind me. He uncovered my eyes, forcing my blurry vision to adjust to the sight in front of me. I wouldn't have been surprised by the living room in a normal situation, as I expected it would be spacious. It was three times bigger than our last one, and the mother and wife in me already fantasized about the plans and possibilities for the décor of the room.

But even with all that running through my head, that wasn't what knocked the wind out of me. The golden triangle of the room nearly stopped my heart from beating, and if Olivia wasn't screaming *"Do you like it?"* over and over, I would have sworn I was in an alternative universe.

A magnificent white wedding dress was held up by a mannequin just at the room's center. The stunning majestic gown wasn't like any other dress I'd encountered, tried on, owned or even window shopped and wished for, assuming I'd ever remarry.

The dress that I had married Olli in was essentially the same color, but surviving on a shoestring budget, it had been thrifty and stopped at the knee. The gorgeous frock not only had a train that went on for days, but it also featured an off-the-shoulder sweetheart neckline, a detail that wasn't short on lace and silk embellishments, that was as long as any royal gown I'd seen. To make matters worse, that wasn't even the best thing about the dress.

The bodice was elegant and fit for a queen, guaranteed to make any woman feel like nobility. It's slight dropped waist provided the perfect transition into a full ballroom skirt. Endless layers of romantic tulle made the dress appear as it was floating mid-air. Olivia pulled in for a closer look, and if she hadn't, I wouldn't have even known the mere sight of the masterpiece had cemented me in place.

"Why don't you help your mother into the dress," Olli smiled. "We'll follow through with what we talked about when we meet outside, Okay?" he said without explaining himself, as he disappeared into another part of the house and Olivia pulled me closer in the direction of the dress.

"Olivia, what's going on honey? What are you two keeping from me?" As she kept repeating *"It's a surprise"* and I slipped down to my underwear. Olivia must've known this was going to happen. She had a stool and everything, assuming she'd have to zip me up.

I don't know how it was even possible, but the dress was made to my exact measurements. Granted, Olli knew my body, but he wasn't keen on US measurements, and blatantly ignored my obvious weight gain. He claimed to him I looked the same as eight years ago with just a little bit more to touch. A dress of this caliber should've taken weeks to make. I had reason to believe it cost a fortune just to have it to try on.

Olivia helped get the back, buttoning and zipping wherever needed. She helped me with a tray of pearls left behind, and with a mirror being the only real object in the room, I had a chance to glance at the woman staring back at me.

This woman...she looked vibrant. She looked happy. The woman my eyes laid upon looked like she went for all the things she wanted and deserved every one of them. There were a million other things I could've said about her, but the only other two that mattered surfaced.

The woman in the reflection looked in love. This woman looked complete.

"Now see why we didn't tell you?" Olivia whined. "If we had told you, you wouldn't have been as happy to see the dress." She smiled a full-toothed grin before asking if I liked the dress.

A soft laugh rumbled in the back of my throat. "I love it."

"Come on, we're supposed to be meeting Iskä outside." As she continued to pull my arm before I was ready. I took one last look at myself in the reflection, amazed at how far I'd come. I glowed despite not having an ounce of toner, or blush, or makeup of any kind.

"You look pretty, Mami, now let's go!" Olivia said, ordering me with impatient enthusiasm. It took some work on both our ends, but we managed to travel through multiple rooms, as she led me through the spacious house. Glass sliding doors were at the end of the destination and I had reason to believe it was the home's backyard.

The astonishing site out back alone should have been enough to make my heart stop. I was confused but curious about what was happening, why it was happening and what all these secrets led to. Finally, all the clues started to have some ounce of clarity.

Outside, the tree branches were decorated with a weaving stream of twinkling lights and ornaments. Lanterns accompanied by verdant garlands made everything look votive, with the intricacy of something that had been planned for months. Photos of the two of us hung by white satin ribbons along the bodies of each tree and throughout the trimmed lush of emerald green, including the shrub fence behind it.

Hundreds of white petals formed a horizontal line that led straight to my Olli, who on his end, had appeared to don a dark blue custom-tailored tuxedo. I don't know how he'd gotten dressed so fast, but boy was my man dapper. He was as handsome today as the day I met him, ripped from the page of a fairy tale, where he was always and only suited for the hero or charming prince.

I took a deep breath before making my way past the trail of rose petals, fighting back tears with each step I took. I was drowning in them, unable to keep a straight face, as the end led to Olli, and he took my hand in his. My family was here; his family was here. I was trying to gather strength but this moment was too emotional. I don't think I could have ever predicted this could happen. Not in a million years.

"Benny, I am sure you are wondering what all of this is in front of you." I nodded, unable to form words, coherent sentences or even the most minimal forms of communication. Compelled to do the next best thing, I stood back and listened, hoping it'd all be explained.

"Today, I wanted to surprise you. It is exactly eight years from the time that I met you. From just that simple moment, I knew you were destined to be my one and only." He wiped a tear away and lent me strength as he continued on. "I kept thinking how flashy or difficult it might be to bring both of our families together for a moment so important. But it wasn't long before I put those pessimistic thoughts away. This was the type of wedding you always deserved. And in front of you, our daughter Olivia, your mother, and my parents, I want to admit that my biggest regret was walking away from you and our life together."

He didn't have to apologize anymore; I'd already forgiven him. The moment I stepped off the plane from West Covina to Helsinki, I'd forgiven him ten times over. But it meant a lot that in front of the people who mattered most to us, that he wanted to own up to his mistake. It showed a lot of humility and growth, and I knew my mother would respect him more for doing that.

"Everything we built had been irreplaceable. It was good and special. Most of all it was right. We were so right. We *are* so right." His words weren't helping me keep the waterworks down. By the time I'd stopped crying, I was halfway through his speech before his voice cracked in a similar whimper.

"Lots of people speak about this feeling of wholeness. That feeling you have when you meet the person that was meant for you, and only you. I hadn't realized how true that was for us until I tried to live without you. Without you, I couldn't function as a full person. I owe you every dream I've ever had, every goal I'd ever accomplished. But most of all every memory you've ever given me. You gave me something I didn't ask for, and frankly something I don't even think I deserve. A family." He pulled my fingers to his lips, gently placing a tender kiss on the back of my hand.

"The only way I even know how to pay you back for the immense value you've added to my life is to love you unconditionally, wholeheartedly, and take care of you and our family for the *rest* of my life. Maria Bendición Tuominen, will you marry me all over again, and let me be the man you've deserved?" Overwhelmed by Olli's word, the only thing I could think to say was "*Yes*".

"I love you so much Olli." As he didn't let me say anything else before a ring materialized from his pocket. I looked into his eyes, consumed in overwhelming joy.

"I love you too Benny. This ring, this house, and my heart? They're all yours." As he whispered I'd be his princess in public, but not to think for one minute I wouldn't be his slut behind closed doors. To be honest, I couldn't see it going any other way.

EPILOGUE

Benny

The blend of hot steam and hearty aromas hit my face like a warm summer day. Although my feet were beginning to swell from slaving away in the kitchen, it almost made it worth it to let the smells convince me that this could be the best meal ever. Rosemary and sage were my favorite additions to anything and although a much-needed break was in order, it warmed my heart every time I decided to make my family's favorite holiday meals. Combining ideas from both my husband's Northern European background and my Central African one was easier than it sounded. We both loved fish, so it wasn't hard to see that we were a fish family.

A sense of relief washed over me as Olli entered the kitchen and wrapped his arms around my shoulders. He reached in to place a soft kiss on my neck that still managed to give me butterflies.

"Would you like help, mi amor?" That was the thoughtfulness of my Olli. He always sensed what I needed, and more importantly when I needed it. I wasn't sure how I could even be this lucky. Despite our less than conventional start, in addition to a rocky middle, Olli had always been the one to prove to me that a good man steps up and does everything in his power to give you the absolute best version of himself that you deserve. He was such a great husband and ever since he retired from his work due to a life-altering investment several years ago, he's been an even better father, highly dedicated to his family. Not once had I ever worried about how everything would work out because, in our little world, everything was close to perfect.

Olli kneeled down and opened the oven door as the baked salmon, at his request, filled the air with much-needed, festive joy as we counted down the days before Christmas. For the entire month of December, it had been a tradition of ours to end our week with memorable feasts and being that we and the kids spent eight months of the year in Olli's motherland, the snow, the weather, and even going into the city made it feel a lot more like the sort of holidays you saw in movies. This one felt especially special.

I ran my fingers through his thick dark hair. He looked up to give me one of his mischievous little smiles that I never got tired of. "Is there anything I can do for you while I am on my knees?" he asked, biting his lip and switching to English. If the kids weren't coming in soon, which I predicted they'd be swarming in, testy from the sweat they worked up from playing outside, I might have just taken him up on his offer. But we had an army to feed. I leaned down to meet him, cradling his face as my lips felt at home on his.

"The kids will be in soon...but maybe when everyone is sleeping..."

He pressed his lips to mine a second time, giving me a taste of what could come. "You know how good I am at getting everyone in bed by nine." He really was, I thought, laughing to myself as I attempted to walk away to finish setting the table, only for him to pull me closer for one last kiss on my fairly new three-month-old baby bump, acknowledging the presence of our fourth child together.

"Hurry up and get out of your mother's tummy so I can meet you." Olli kissed my stomach again before he stood to his feet. When I looked back on our relationship, I couldn't believe I was already on child number four. We hadn't wasted much time after he surprised me with the renewal of our vows, we honestly couldn't keep our hands off each other long enough to lose excitement from the last one being born. Olli was so good with them and never failed to get excited any and every time I announced being pregnant. As long as I could keep having them, he would welcome every child we'd bring into this world. But really, I just wanted a small break in between the next one. Four was enough for now, and I was looking forward to *this* version of our family.

As Olli wrapped his arms around me, I couldn't help but notice all the kisses we exchanged despite none being done under the traditional mistletoe. I was such a superstitious romantic.

"You know, in old Nordic culture, it is said that mistletoe was often shared after murdering a colleague or a loved one." He said setting me straight. "Perhaps it is best if we avoid the mistletoe altogether. It is however, bad luck to refuse a kiss from the person who promises to spend the rest of the night making you feel good." He kissed me on the cheek and at the sound of collective merriment and light teasing, in unison our eyes darted towards the kitchen door to see our babies bundled up and ruddy from the blistering cold winter wonderland of outside to the cozy, warm environment that was our home.

Olivia, who was now twelve and already as tall as me, was the proud mama bear, being the big sister I never imagined her being. Yet, the role had fit her like a badge of honor. She loved her baby bother Olli Jr—or OJ—as we called him. Despite the fact that she was seven years older, the two were like two peas in a pod. She was always helping him with everything, and I hoped he showed that same eagerness towards Marja, our youngest, who was only a year and a half younger than him.

Olli ran over to them, showering them with hugs and kisses as he scooped young Marja up into his arms. She was so tiny in his arms, and it was funny to remember how at one point, they were all once that small. They were growing up so fast, I couldn't stand it.

"Hey, you guys, you want to help Iskä finish up dinner and set the table? I'd be grateful for the help since Mami's going to lie down for a while." With excited eagerness, all three were ecstatic to be assigned tasks to help dinner approach faster. With one last kiss from my beloved and youngest daughter, I made my way into the living room to find a comfortable spot on the sofa to rest my poor, tired feet. I wanted to turn on the TV but decided that listening to my families' joy and laughter was just the entertainment I needed to ease the stress of a long day.

Finally, Olli and I had everything we wanted in life. All I ever dreamed of was a man who strove to be a great father to my kids. A man that would've moved heaven and earth for his family. One that only wanted the chance to see his kids grow up and to be around for all of their moments. While some things felt a little hectic every once in a while, this life, *my* life, was much more than I ever could've asked for.

The End

Did you enjoy this story? Do you wish more stories like this existed? Consider leaving a review for <u>Meant For You</u>! Every review helps us consider where to go next with this planned series and we want to hear from you whether it be passion or pain, that you'd like to read more books like this from us!

ACKNOWLEDGMENTS

First and foremost, the person who deserves the most credit for making this story work is Patrice. Your harsh words and red ink hit different at first, but without you *Meant For You* wouldn't have been possible. The Plot Genie was amazing at taking characters and plot points we wanted but turning it into more than something just in our notebook! To Steamy Book Designs, working with you for the covers for this series has been a delight and we can't wait to release the future books with your expertise! And to all buddies at our day job cheering us on from the time we went letter chasing for our USA Today bestselling title to constantly holding us accountable until we finished this book! None if it could've been done without y'all!

year ago, but being oceans apart forced their two-week long connection to come to an end. Or did it?

Damien Karagiannis couldn't believe his luck. Settling into a different country and a new practice left him less time to meet people, let alone date. Through a wicked twist of fate, he not only gets the chance to reconnect to his budding Dominant stranger through matchmaker Mistress Alice—she ends up being a part of his surgical team.

Leomie can't get the intimidatingly sexy surgeon out of her system. Damien craves that soft command he once explored. Their undeniable passion will have them breaking all their rules for each other.

Melt For You is a steamy May/December romance that features a gentle Domme with an appetite for masochism and an arrogant yet romantic male submissive who wants nothing but to make her wishes come true. It is BWWM with no cheating and a guaranteed HEA. If Dominance and submission aren't your style, sit this one out. If you like a little kink, let this Alpha submissive melt his way into your heart!

Pre-order now!

Luz De Los Santos thought her job was easy.

Being the Sex and Relationship Director of Modern Magazine, no one knew the art of dating and hookups like she did.

When the commitment-phobe Afro-Dominicana gets singled out by her editor to write a challenging column for the coveted, annual Valentine's issue, Luz is forced to confront her issues about relationships with her newly pitched project.

The Love Bet.

Is it possible to fall in love by the third screw? Maybe.

But she's not holding her breath once she recruits her blast from the past, Evan Cattaneo to help test her theory.

Evan regrets the way things ended between him and Luz.

The girl who charmed him all those years ago was now grown and sexy and has him more than ready to aid Luz in her little experiment. Only his plans won't stop at just f*cking her. Nope, he plans to make her fall in love all over again. Before they both know it, loving between the sheets turns into stealing kisses in the streets.

When emotions get wild and feelings grow deep, will the insecurities of Luz's past come back to haunt them?

Pre-order now!

PR firm in the country. Toya only had one task standing in her way of becoming a partner, but she was used to facing tough challenges.

Until that obstacle became a herculean, dimpled Boricua and his wacky ass family with a penchant for scandalous antics.

Kelly "K-Rod" Rodriguez has always had it all. Incredible talent, muscles worthy of a magazine spread and just enough book smarts to balance out his street. After suffering the loss of a World Series and gaining a life-altering injury, the aging Major League shortstop has two strikes against him. Now the only woman capable of spinning this disaster is the one who made it clear to him that their past hookup was just that—a hookup.

When the tabloids misconstrue the nature of their relationship over a heated viral dispute, there's only one way to find themselves out of it. To fake a relationship.

Kelly regrets the decision he made years ago choosing his career over a relationship with the bombshell publicist but now that they're thrown back into each other's arms, he'll do whatever it takes to hit a home run.

Pre-order now!

Book One
Same Page:

New to Providence, RI, **Naima Adewunmi** had every intention of fulfilling everything she left her New York borough for, finishing up her Bachelor's degree and finding a job while doing it.

She wasn't supposed to fall for **Timothy Ferreiro**, a smooth, slick talking, sexy specimen of a man, messy bedhead hair included, who also happens to be her new boss. From first wink she was under his spell, which wouldn't be a problem if there weren't one underlying issue: Tim's got a long distance girlfriend.

Drama unfolds in a tale of will they or won't they in this steamy office romance. Can two people in a messy game of attraction find themselves on the same page?

Available Now!

Book Two
Next Chapter:

Timothy risked everything he had last year on love. Had he meant to fall? No. But it hadn't stopped him from colliding into Naima. When it ended, nothing felt the same.

Until she came back...

After a Providence-free summer, Naima is just about ready for anything. Except resisting Timothy.

It's only a matter of time before their feelings for each other get the best of them, but will they be on the same page or completely different chapters?

Available Now!

MORE FROM G.L. TOMAS

FRIENDS THAT HAVE SEX SERIES

Available via Ebook, Paperback and Audiobook!

F*THS

If Teddy's dark secret is discovered, even her wealth and good looks won't save her.

When Asher Rose met Teddy King, he knew it'd be trouble, but it was just the kind of trouble he didn't mind falling in. What he hadn't planned on was falling hard for the girl no one could tame. Strap yourself in for a sexy ride fill of intensity and disaster that spirals all the way down.

Friends That Still

Teddy's back in Miami with her mind made up. Live like it's your last day. Love like it's your last day.
The moment those steel-blue eyes gazed back into hers, there was no question. Asher wasn't just the only one she wanted, but the only one she needed. This time around there would be no more room for regrets, but would they ever be more than friends that still...?

Friends That Collide

Teddy should be happy. She survived an eleven year battle with Hodgkin's Lymphoma, finished her B.A., and found the person of her dreams in a friend. From a distance she has everything, except the one thing she can't have.
Asher's supported Teddy from the moment they met, but even he can't ease her insecurity about her inability to conceive.
How We Start chronicles the emotional struggle over a three-day period of a couple's road to love, loss and life beyond a traditional route.

All Available Now!

Dying to know what the cover looks like? We know you are! Sign up for our <u>mailing list</u> and be exposed to all this melanin, as well as have access to perks like being offered to join our ARC team!

We promise you won't regret joining our 24/7 party!

9 781943 773497